Stirling Breed

Anne-Marie Price

This novel is entirely a work of fiction.
The names, characters and incidents portrayed in it
are the work of the Author's imagination.
Any resemblance to actual persons, living or dead,
events or localities is entirely coincidental

ISBN: 978-0-9942761-2-4

DEDICATION

To Shirley and Len Daley,
who encouraged me
to believe in my dreams.

The Stirling Breed Trilogy

2016
Stirling Breed
Stirling Masquerade
Stirling Conspiracy

ACKNOWLEDGMENTS

Stella Eversden
A gem of a Proof Reader.

Helen Iles
For convincing me to split
Stirling Breed into three novels.

Rebecca Schulz
For her invaluable information
in regards to beards

SATURDAY
The Cousins

Swirling Cognac around in his balloon glass, with his long legs stretched out in front of him, Lord Caleb Delacourt uttered a deep and melancholic sigh. Geoff Delacourt, sitting across the table from his cousin, looked up surprised. *The Inn we're currently staying at is clean, comfortable and well run. The Cognac Caleb is swirling in his glass is of extremely fine quality,* so Geoff was puzzled by the sigh.

'We've finally escaped from the barrage of female nagging Caleb, you should be happy.'

Another sigh emanated from the handsome young Lord. 'This is only a momentary escape Geoff, the nagging and the reason why our relatives are badgering will still be there when we return.'

'Well you know exactly what to do to stop the harassment!' Brushing a wayward lock of tawny brown hair from his forehead, Geoff suddenly sat upright.

'Yes I know.' Caleb nodded. 'That is why, in part, I came down to the village of Stirling in Sussex.'

'So you're not just here to purchase a horse?'

'No,' the monosyllable confirmed but did not offer any further information as Caleb sipped his liquor.

'I do so enjoy these close, intimate conversations that we have, cousin!' drawled Geoff as he leant back in his seat.

Uttering a slight chuckle, Caleb waved his hand around in an airy fashion, indicating the well populated tavern as his signet ring glinted slightly in the candle light. 'Hardly the locale for discussing private thoughts and plans,' his lips quirked in an attractive smile and his blue eyes twinkled.

'So you do have something planned then?' Geoff laid his glass down in fear of crushing the vessel between his trembling fingers.

In answer, his Lordship's smile widened. 'You're not going to start nagging me now are you cousin.'

Geoff gave a crow of laughter. 'Are you suggesting that I'm becoming an old woman?'

Half expecting an acid quip, Geoff was startled to observe the smile slide away from Caleb's face as his cousin's attention was captured by the arrival of three newcomers into the Stirling Arms Inn. Intrigued by this fascination, Geoff turned to cast a searching glance over the young men of quality, who were accompanied by a boy of about five years of age. The taller young man was good looking enough, but appeared serious with his horn-rimmed reading glasses and less attractive, especially when unfavourably compared with the extremely beautiful companions beside him.

Although Geoff supposed it, he found it hard to believe that the youth and the boy were related. *The young man is in his late teens, with chestnut red hair and a beauty that seems beyond belief. It is unusual these days for gentlemen to wear a sword but it seems to suit the older brother. The boy should look like a chubby happy cherub with his halo of blonde curly hair but there is no trace of baby fat on the boy's small frame.* Geoff wondered, *has the little chap been ill recently?* Unable to help himself, his eyes travelled back to rest upon the angelic features of the teenager.

'Upon my soul Caleb! You're a handsome devil, but if that young Adonis is also looking for a wife you haven't a chance in hell!' Geoff's words managed to penetrate the fog that had enveloped his cousin.

'Thank you! You are always such a comfort to me in my declining years!' drawled Caleb, his eyes not leaving his study of the new arrivals as the Innkeeper, Mick Cooper, came out from behind the bar to greet them warmly as he bowed.

The Brothers

'What a pleasure it is to see you my Lords. I knew that if my Ruth was to make her delicious apple pies you'd not be far away.' The big genial Innkeeper tousled the young boy's hair affectionately. 'How is your pupil doing Mr Duncan? Lord Aidan was always a handful for Nanny,' the Innkeeper asked the taller of the two gentlemen.

Duncan Gray smiled fondly down at the boy who was tugging impatiently at the hand of the beautiful Lord Tony. 'If we tackle some physical activity first thing in the morning, his Lordship is less fidgety during his lessons.'

Aidan looked up, aware that he was the subject of discussion. 'Tony is teaching me to ride,' he announced proudly to Mick.

A frown suddenly marred the brow of the beautiful young Lord. *I noticed at their arrival that Lord Tony seems distracted and worried,* mused the Innkeeper. 'You were roughly the same age when John Smythe threw you up onto your first horse my Lord,' Mick said.

A reminiscent smile swept away the anxious expression. 'Sorry Mick, I'm not worried about Aidan on a horse. It's Caviar, she's showing every sign that she's going into labour, but I'd swear that it is two weeks too early. I feel that I should be there in case there are any problems delivering the foal.'

'It's not the mare's first foal, and don't you dare tell me that you don't trust John Smythe to take good care of the expectant mother.' Duncan Gray shook his head indulgently.

Tony's smile was dazzling. 'Of course I trust him. I am a worrier, so sue me!'

'Come and have a seat and I'll let Ruth know to serve your supper.' Mick gestured towards the private parlour. 'I know my girls will be pleased to see you.'

Chuckling, Tony flicked a careless finger against his young brother's cheek. 'Hopefully we have time for a game, as Aidan is sick of me always winning.'

As they followed Mick out of the Public Bar, those left behind could hear the younger Lord protest in embarrassment.

'Tony!'

A Crisis Of Identity

With the departure of the new-comers, the spell cast by the young Lord's exceptional beauty seemed to break, for all except Caleb Delacourt. Slightly alarmed, Geoff noticed that his cousin had become quite ashen. Hesitating in raising his glass to his lips, Geoff exclaimed, 'Upon Rep, Caleb! You look like you've seen a ghost!'

'I'm having a crisis of identity.' Dragging is a shuddering breathe, Caleb struggled to breathe normally. 'I thought I knew my own desires, but that young man makes me doubt that I know myself at all!'

His cousin's eyebrows rose in surprise. 'Are you trying to tell me that you're that way inclined? Is that why you've always resisted the pressures to get married? Does that explain your failed attempts at courtship when you were a greenhorn?'

'Doth quote the greybeard?' drawled Caleb.

Geoff bridled in defence. 'I'm only six months older than you!' They were both only seven and twenty. Not able to help himself, Caleb grinned. *I never fail to get a rise out of my cousin on that topic.* At school they had often been mistaken for brothers instead of cousins and endured the resulting confusion as to why the younger was the heir. Most times Geoff had laughed it off; *I don't want to be in my cousin's shoes, but every so often it rankles.*

Although Geoff was as tall as his cousin and would be considered in any light to be a good looking young man, nevertheless he was in the shadow of his cousin in looks as well as title and income. Geoff often wondered, *if the women were interested in Caleb for his title, his money or his jet black hair, handsome features and muscular body?* Shaking his head, Geoff didn't want to follow that train of thought and tried to focus upon what his cousin was actually saying and not what he looked like.

'May I remind you,' Caleb said calmly. 'That neither Annette nor Constance were my idea. Annette would have married a hunchback if it gave her a title.'

'Who did you fob her off to in the end?' Deep in thought Geoff stroked his chin.

'Some Duke, who is now so infatuated with his beautiful wife that I don't think he cares that she spends money like there's no tomorrow.' Caleb gave a graceless shrug.

'At least Constance wouldn't have bankrupted you.'

'True, but Connie would have married anyone who could get her as far away as possible from that family of hers.'

Staring into his glass, Geoff studied the way the candlelight danced across the contents. 'Didn't you sort that out too?'

'All I did was set the Lawyers onto the problem.' Caleb waved an airy hand. 'Connie had every right to the money her mother had left her. Her father had no legal right to withhold it. She is now quite happily residing in Bath with an elderly cousin as chaperone, and can take her time deciding which eligible bachelor dancing attendance on her will suit her.'

'God's truth cousin! Are you sure you're not batting for the other side?'

'I just thought I had never found the right woman with whom I wanted to spend the rest of my life.' A frown descended upon Caleb's brow. 'But, having seen that young man… I don't know what to think anymore.' Finishing his cognac, Caleb rose to his feet. 'I'm going for a walk to try and clear my head.'

'Do you want company?' Geoff half rose out of his seat.

Patting his shoulder, Caleb pushed his cousin back into his chair. 'I just want to think things over.' Drawing his overcoat off the back of his seat, Caleb slipped into it before heading out into the twilight.

An Innocent Game

Over an hour later, when Lord Caleb Delacourt returned to the Stirling Arms Inn, his cousin was still sitting where he had left him. The only difference was Geoff now had a newspaper spread out in front of him, and was reading the latest news about Napoleon's downfall at Waterloo, and exile to the Island of Saint Helena.

As Caleb shrugged out of his overcoat and sat down beside Geoff, he noticed that the atmosphere within the tavern had altered slightly. The majority of the patrons were local men, enjoying a quiet beer, but there was one table of five strangers to the village. They had consumed a significant amount of alcohol and were becoming rowdy.

Caleb's eyebrows rose in surprise as a pretty blonde girl in her mid-teens dashed through the public area and hid herself behind the coats that hung on the wall beside the outer door. *Her attire suggests that this is one of the Innkeeper's daughters and not a girl of high rank.* His Lordship blinked twice as a younger carbon copy skipped into the room and hid behind the chair of a local farmer. Finally Caleb shot his cousin a questioning look as the five year old Lord Aidan raced into the room, giggling and wriggled his way between Caleb and Geoff. When Caleb cast an enquiring glance down at the boy, Aidan placed his finger against his lips.

'We're playing hide and seek,' the boy explained, and ducked his head down as his beautiful older brother came lightly down the stairs.

'Where, oh where can the children be?' Caleb was surprised by how musical was Lord Tony's voice as he began to search the room. 'Do they really think that they can hide from me?' Tony looked behind the bar, bobbed down to look under all the tables. As it looked like he was about to head towards the private parlour, the older girl betrayed her position by giggling.

Tony spun around and was upon the girl behind the coats before she could do more than squeal in disbelief. Capturing the girl about her waist, she was removed from her hiding place and swung around by Tony. He tickled the girl until she begged him to stop between tears of laughter. The locals smiled indulgently at the children's game as Tony released the Innkeeper's eldest daughter, Sarah.

'Now where may my next victim be hiding?' asked Tony and Aidan ducked his head down once more. Stalking through the tables Tony came across the younger sister, Hannah, and she too was swung around and tickled before being led to the stand with her sister by the bar. As Tony scanned the room once again, he absently pushed back a loose curl of chestnut red that had escaped during their game.

When do we get to play?

Although the locals were not put out by the children playing amongst them, the table of drunk strangers were becoming more vocal about their disapproval. Nigel Sutherland finally slammed down his tankard and pushed back his chair to address Tony, 'Enough of the childish games, me fine buck! When do the rest of us get a chance to share in the fun? I'm sure we can show the girls a much better time!' Nigel's friends laughed in agreement as the locals fell silent. Instinctively Tony drew the girls behind him; his hand rested lightly upon the hilt of his sword.

'I'm sorry if we have disturbed you sir, but it's a child's game only that we play. What you are suggesting is not for girls this young or innocent.' Tony spoke calmly and quietly. *My opponent is a huge brute of a walking mountain and although he's a wall of muscle now, it will soon be melting into fat if he continues drinking the way he has been.* Nigel towered over Tony as Goliath had once towered over David. Like the shepherd boy, Tony was not about to back down from an unequal opponent.

Snorting, Nigel asked, 'What makes ya so special that ya get to play and we can't?'

'The Innkeeper knows I mean no harm to his daughters. We grew up together playing these Innocent games.' Tony cast a sharp look around the room. 'Aidan, come to me now please!' There was an edge of nervousness in his voice that caused the five year old to immediately slip under Caleb's table and scramble to his feet so that he could run to join his brother. Leaning on the table, Nigel pushed himself up onto his feet and Tony's hand tightened upon his sword. Nigel's table stood between them and the safety of the doors that led to the back of the tavern.

'Sir, I must ask you to resume your seat! If you try to touch one of these girls I will cut you in half!' Slowly Tony's sword began to slide out of its scabbard.

Not For Sale

Looking at the slight, much shorter figure of the young Lord, Nigel burst out laughing. 'I'd love to see ya try little man!' He had not taken more than a drunken step towards Tony when Mick Cooper, the Innkeeper, came into the room. Casting a quick scrutinizing glance at the tense scene, Mick crossed the room to stand beside Lord Tony.

'What is it my Lord?' asked the Innkeeper.

'This Gentleman is under the misapprehension that our game is not so innocent.'

Uttering a harsh laugh, Nigel asked, 'How old are your girls, Keeper?'

'14 and 16 sir!' Mick stiffened in indignation.

'How much for either or both?' Tony's sword was completely withdrawn now, ready to protect the girls.

'They're not for sale sir!' Mick had his hand on Tony's shoulder.

'Everyone has their price!' Nigel laughed again, 'Or has this fine buck already secured the rights to their virginity?' Stiffening, Tony was finding it hard to keep rein over his roaring anger.

'My daughters are not for sale. To anyone!' Mick repeated firmly.

Let's Stay Calm

If Nigel and Tony clash in battle, Caleb mused, *I can see the attractive Lord coming off second best and getting hurt.* Something about seeing that flawless alabaster skin being blemished by bruises caused Caleb to slowly rises to his feet and approach the stand-off.

'Perhaps you should return your daughters to their mother. Now that you've made it perfectly clear that the girls are not available, the gentlemen may have another drink. On me.' Caleb's calming interference took the heat out of the volatile situation and Tony slowly lowered his sword. Mick took his daughters by the hand and led them safely away as Nigel fell backwards into his chair.

'Well me pretty buck, will ya join us for a drink?'

'Thank you, but no.' Shaking his head, Tony returned his sword to the scabbard on his hip. 'It's time I took my brother home.'

Nigel's anger flared up instantly and his hand flashed out to grasp Tony's lace covered wrist. 'Aren't we good enough to drink with, me pretty buck?' demanded Nigel.

Standing very still, Tony refused to show how painful was the hold on his arm. 'That isn't the case sir, it is just that I don't drink at all!'

'A prude, pretty boy?' laughed Nigel, his grip tightening. 'Or do ya need to run home to suckle upon y'r mother's tits?'

Tony's hands bunched into tight fists but he managed to keep a check on his temper. 'My mother died when I was ten! My abstinence is due to my grandfather dying of alcoholism, and my father's own battle against the bottle!'

Reason For Caleb's Visit

Looking sharply at Tony, Caleb dragged in a startled breath. 'So you're the Earl of Stirling's children!'

'At your service Sir!' Tony bowed, quite elegantly, considering his hand was still held in an iron grip by Nigel.

Stepping between Nigel and Tony, Caleb effortlessly broke the grip Nigel had on Tony's wrist. 'I'm actually here to see your father about a two year old colt he has for sale,' added Caleb, and without seeming to, he was putting some distance between the Stirling boys and Nigel Sutherland.

'I'm afraid Papa has gone up to London with my step-mother but you're more than welcome to come up to the Manor in the morning to look over the colt.' Tony refrained from massaging his maltreated wrist, *I don't want Nigel to know how much it hurts.*

'Thank you. I'm Caleb Delacourt and this in my cousin Geoffrey.' Caleb introduced his cousin over his shoulder.

Turning, Tony bowed elegantly to Geoff. 'Honoured Mr Delacourt.' He then inclined his head to Caleb, 'I look forward to seeing you tomorrow my Lord.'

Dignified Exit

Mick Cooper came back into the public bar, very quietly for a man of his large size. He quickly analysed the state of the situation before finally speaking, 'Your horses have been saddled Lord Tony, and Mr Duncan is just returning from visiting his father, Reverend Gray.'

Without looking around, Tony reached behind him to take his younger brother's hand. 'Thank you Mick. Let Ruth know that dinner was superb as always. Good night gentlemen,' he said, with a bow to the room.

The Innkeeper escorted the Stirling brothers to the door. 'I'll follow you out my Lords, Ruth has an apple pie for you to take home.' Mick cast a significant glance around the room before he went back into the kitchen as Tony led Aidan out of the Inn. Caleb waited until the Stirling brothers had shut the outer door behind them before he returned to his seat opposite his cousin. *I have prevented a bloodbath and actually discovered something important about myself. Right now though, I really want to try some of that legendary apple pie.*

Please Help

The Delacourt cousins had just settled down in the private parlour to await their dinner, when a rather agitated Mick came unceremoniously into the room.

'My apologies Lord Delacourt, but I didn't know what else to do. Nigel Sutherland has been mouthing off about revenge against Lord Tony. Just now Sutherland and a friend have stormed out of my Inn.'

Caleb leapt to his feet, 'Harness my horses to my phaeton,' he ordered.

'I've already issued the order. I hoped you would agree to rescue the young Lords.'

A bemused Geoff followed Caleb and Mick out of the Parlour. 'I don't understand the panic, two gentlemen against two gentlemen seems to be a fair fight, even with the presence of a young lad.'

'It's… It's… Just…' A muscle spasmed in the Innkeeper's cheek.

Pulling his overcoat off the hook by the door, Caleb said, 'Sutherland outweighs Lord Tony two to one.'

Accepting this explanation, Mick sighed in relief. 'Yes my Lord.' He anxiously followed the cousins out to their awaiting vehicle. Caleb threw himself into the phaeton and had barely allowed Geoff enough time to mount up beside him before he urged the horses into a gallop. Geoff held on tight as they raced after the men who were intent on revenge and humiliation.

Sutherland's Revenge

It was a clear summer's evening so it wasn't completely dark yet. It was therefore easy enough for the Delacourt cousins to see that Nigel Sutherland and his friend Peter Doyle had already caught up with the riders returning to Stirling Manor. The Delacourts were too far away to prevent Nigel from forcing Lord Tony off his horse. As Tony landed heavily upon the ground, his horse reared up on its back legs and galloped away in a blind panic.

Aidan had been sitting on the same horse in front of his brother, but managed to hold on as the horse reared up. He now screamed in terror as he desperately tried to stay on the fleeing animal as it bolted for home. Duncan was about to dismount to assist Tony but the Lord waved his hand for the Tutor to go after his brother.

'Rescue Aidan! I'll be all right,' Tony ordered, picking himself up as Duncan spurred his horse to chase after the frightened boy. Dusting himself down, Tony didn't see Nigel leap from his horse and draw his sword.

'Tony! Behind you!' yelled out Caleb as they were still too far away to assist the young Lord.

As Tony spun around, his hand had automatically drawn his sword so he was ready for Nigel's attack and there was a clang as their swords met. Tony was no match for Nigel's brute strength or the force of his blows against his sword but the young Lord had been taught by a master swordsman and was nimble and agile in his reflexes. In fact Tony was forcing Nigel back in defence and Geoff was starting to wonder, *what was the Innkeeper so panicked about?*

When the young Lord tripped over an unseen rock and fell to his knees, his sword went spinning out of his hand. Uttering a crow of laughter, Nigel used his sword to force Tony to raise his head as his other hand unbuttoned his own trousers flap. When Nigel pulled out his penis, Tony's eyes widened in horror and he tried to pull away but Nigel, throwing his sword to the ground, grabbed Tony by the hair to hold him in place.

'No!' Caleb roared, thrusting the horses' reins into his cousin's hands and vaulted out of the phaeton before they had even stopped. Rushing at Nigel, Caleb's hands were clenched into fists and before Nigel could humiliate Tony, Caleb decked the big man. Caught unawares, Nigel released Tony as he fell backwards to the ground. For a moment Caleb stood over Nigel, who raised his hands to cover his broken nose, as it spurted blood down his face. When Nigel struggled to sit up, Caleb calmly shook his head.

'Stay down or I will kill you!'

Nigel pulled his hands away from his face to look in disbelief at the blood. 'Who the devil are ya to interfere?'

'Your worst nightmare if you try to get to your feet!' Caleb bent down to pick up Tony's sword and pressed its point into

Nigel's throat. 'Give me one good reason I shouldn't slit your throat from ear to ear?'

Nigel turned pale and not just from blood loss. 'But… But that would be… would be murder.'

Regaining control of his temper, Caleb stepped back, allowing the sword to lower to his side as he bent down to assist Tony to his feet.

'I think it's called exterminating vermin.' Tony suggested, wincing as he tried to stand on both his feet. 'Damnation!' He was forced to lean on Caleb's arm as his right ankle refused to support his weight.

'Put your arm around my neck and I'll help you to the phaeton.' Caleb placed a supportive arm around Tony's waist and when the younger Lord obeyed, he helped him to hop towards the vehicle. Geoff held the horses steady with one hand and reached out with his other hand to offer it to Tony as Caleb gave him a boost up from the waist.

'I'm going to kill ya bloody toff!' Nigel screamed as he rose to his feet. Startled by the yell, Caleb abruptly released Tony to turn to confront the angry bully. That caused Tony to topple into the phaeton and into Geoff's arms.

The Highwayman

Steadying Tony, Geoff dragged in a sharp breath in disbelief and he quickly pulled his hands away from such an intimate hold.

'Please don't betray me,' Tony whispered. Swallowing hard, all Geoff could do was nod in agreement. Raising Tony's sword once again Caleb's attention was focussed upon Nigel who had bent to pick up his own sword.

'Don't do it Mr Sutherland. Cross swords with me and I will kill you!' warned Caleb.

Looking away from the stand-off between the two swordsmen, Geoff caught sight of another rider on horseback. When the Delacourts had arrived, Nigel's friend Peter had ridden after Duncan and Aidan so this new figure was a complete surprise, especially as he appeared to have his hat low over his eyes and a muffler around the lower half of his face. In both hands the rider held a pistol.

The life of a Highwayman was not romantic or glamorous, it was lonely and dangerous. Solitaire had given up his birth name to protect his identity and his family. Over 45 years ago Solitaire had started life on a farm not far from the Stirling village and an honest way of earning a living, but in desperate need to put food on the table of the family, Solitaire and his brother had taken to the road.

'Caleb,' Geoff tried to keep his voice from quavering at the sight of the silent Highwayman.

'What?' His cousin did not turn away from confronting Nigel.

'We have company,' Geoff added, a little puzzled as Solitaire, the Highwayman's pistols were aimed at Nigel and not the phaeton or his cousin.

Caleb glanced over his shoulder and his eyebrows rose in surprise, 'Hell and damnation!' *As if the situation isn't difficult enough, it now looks like we'll have to deal with being robbed as well,* thought Caleb.

Looking across at the silent figure on his horse, Tony gave a cry of recognition, 'Solitaire? Is that you?'

The Highwayman bobbed his head. 'Are you all right my Lord? I was about to come to your rescue when these gentlemen arrived. Are you safe with them?' Solitaire kept his weapon trained on Nigel.

'Yes, thank you.'

'All the same young master, I'll follow you home just to be sure. I've the blackguard covered if you wish to mount your vehicle Sir,' Solitaire added to Caleb. More than a little amused, Caleb bowed to the masked rider before throwing Tony's sword up for him to catch. It was a tight fit for three in the phaeton but they didn't have far to go.

Holding a handkerchief to his bleeding nose, Nigel shook an angry fist at the occupants of the phaeton. 'Ya haven't heard the last from me, pretty buck! I will have my revenge!'

'I've exterminated rats that were more pleasant than you!' Solitaire thumbed back the safety catch on one of his pistols.

Throwing up his hand in protest, Tony called out, 'Solitaire, please don't! You're not a killer!'

Slowly, very slowly, the Highwayman lowered his weapons before bowing to Tony. 'As you wish, my Lord.' His pistols disappeared into his overcoat as he addressed Nigel, 'Be warned Mister, lay one finger on Lord Stirling and you'll not live long enough to boast of the deed!'

Slightly un-nerved Nigel uttered an unrealistic laugh. 'I don't take threats from an outlaw seriously!' he blustered.

'That wasn't a threat Mister, that was a promise! If I don't get to you first, then the local people will have you strung up from a tree before you can cry "Mother".' With a nod of dismissal Solitaire spurred his horse forward, leaving Nigel swearing colourfully behind them.

An Unusual Convoy

The strange journey to Stirling Manor of phaeton and Highwayman was made in silence. This puzzled Caleb as he cast a searching glance, a couple of times, at his usually talkative cousin. Caleb wondered, *Is it a trick of the moonlight or does it look as though Geoff is extremely flushed and uncomfortable. In contrast, by the silver light, the young Lord's face appears very pale and even younger than I had originally thought. Is Tony 18 or 19? He seems no older than the girls he hadn't that long ago been playing an Innocent game with back at the Inn.*

Fighting against the pain so that he didn't throw up or pass out, Tony's eyes were closed and his head rested back against Caleb's shoulder. Carefully Caleb moved his arm between them to lay along the back of the seat to give Tony a little more room. His movement, though, caused Tony to sigh and open his eyes.

'Sorry, not far now. Take the next road to the left.' Tony didn't speak again until the phaeton had rounded a bend and Stirling Manor came into view. As they entered the stables, Tony uttered a sigh of relief at the sight of his younger brother, safe but hysterical as Duncan Gray tried to calm his pupil. 'Thank God, he's all right!' Tony whispered before turning to his rescuers, 'And thank you for your timely assistance gentlemen. I am in your debt.'

Caleb inclined his head, 'It might be wise to avoid Mr Sutherland until he manages to cool off.'

Safe Return

The stables were abuzz with activity. Several of the Grooms were already saddled up, about to ride out to rescue their young master. John Smythe, the Head Groom, was issuing his orders as other Grooms were looking after Duncan's and Tony's horses. A Footman, Charles, came running out of the house with a couple of blankets, one he handed to Duncan to wrap around Aidan.

When Caleb disembarked from the phaeton and held out his hands to assist Tony down, Aidan tore away from his Tutor and tearfully launched himself into his older brother's arms. Unable to remain on his feet, Tony was extremely grateful for Caleb's supportive arm as he tried to reassure the hysterical five year old.

'Calm down Little Bear. You're safe now. I'm safe now. The bully has been vanquished.' Tony managed to pull out a handkerchief to wipe Aidan's eyes and get him to blow his nose.

As the boy began to settle, Tony took an unaided step and stumbled. He would have fallen but Caleb's strong arms kept both Stirling boys upright. John Smythe and Duncan rushed forward, the Head Groom to relieve Tony of the boy while the Tutor supported Tony from his other side.

'How badly injured are you Tony?' asked Duncan.

'I don't know until I get these boots removed.' Tony tried to shrug. 'Probably only a sprain.'

Relinquishing his place to Charles, the Footman, Caleb added, 'You may have to cut the boot off if the foot is too swollen.'

'Damn it!' Tony groaned. 'I like these boots!'

May I Repay Your Kindness?

When Solitaire chuckled in amusement, Tony looked up in surprise that the Highwayman hadn't already vanished into the night. Reaching into the pocket of his breeches, Tony withdrew a bag of coins and tossed it up to the rider.

'I don't need payment my Lord.' Surprised, Solitaire blushed. 'These gentleman did all the hard work.'

'I don't want you to have to go out tonight Solitaire. If you run afoul of Sutherland and his friends, I would feel guilty for more bloodshed.'

The Highwayman nodded as he slipped the purse into his pocket, 'very well my Lord, although you know that I never hunt in your backyard anyway.' With a touch to his hat, Solitaire turned his horse and rode off into the night.

When John Smythe suggested that a cup of hot chocolate might be what both the young Lords needed, it reminded Tony that the Delacourt cousins may not have had their supper.

'Can I offer you something to eat or drink? Allow me to show you my gratitude,' suggested Tony.

'Thank you but no.' Shaking his head Caleb jumped back up into the phaeton beside his cousin. 'Mr Cooper will have our dinner waiting for us back at the Inn and he'll be anxious to hear that you're all safe.' Bowing, Caleb gestured to Geoff to set the horses in motion. On the short drive back to the Stirling Arms Inn both cousins were silent. Neither prepared to discuss what they had learnt that evening with the other in fear of betraying someone else's secret.

Lord Tony's True Identity

With the assistance of Duncan and Charles, the Footman, Lady Antonia (Tony) Stirling was assisted upstairs to her bedroom where her worried Maid, Mary was waiting to undress her Ladyship. Aidan had been carried up to his own room but insisted he be taken to his sister the moment he had changed into his night shirt.

As Duncan knelt before Tony as she sat on the edge of her bed, he removed the boot from her undamaged foot. Mary pulled out the plait that kept her Ladyship's waist-long chestnut red hair hidden under her jacket and assisted Tony out of her jacket and waistcoat. Charles had excused himself to get the medical supplies that would be needed. Tony manfully bore Duncan's examination of her damaged ankle still encased in its boot.

'How bad is it?' she finally asked. In answer the Tutor withdrew a knife from his trousers pocket and flicked it open.

'Do you want to look away while I destroy your favourite boots?'

Tony steeled herself for pain. 'Just do it Duncan!'

His blade was razor sharp and his hands steady but any pressure placed upon the ankle beneath the leather as Duncan sliced through it was excruciatingly painful. A gasp escaped from Mary as Tony passed out from the pain.

I'm not surprised, mused Duncan*, and I'm actually grateful because I know I will cause Tony even more pain as I peel the leather away from her damaged flesh.* When this was accomplished, Duncan rose to his feet.

'Get her Ladyship dressed for bed, I'll get rid of these boots and come back with what I need to tend to Tony's ankle.'

Mary bobbed a brief curtsey, 'Yes Mr Gray.'

Assessing The Damage

Regaining consciousness, Tony was aware of someone removing her breeches and she forced herself to sit up as she protested, 'No! Duncan you mustn't do that!'

Mary paused for a moment to reassure her mistress, 'It's all right, my Lady, Mr Gray will return to look at your ankle once I have redressed you.'

'Oh, I see.' Tony reached up to untie her cravat and slip out of her shirt. She permitted the Maid to ease a night gown over her head before having the courage to look down at her feet. One was definitely more swollen and a different colour to the other and an attempt to move the ankle brought a far from Ladylike oath to Tony's lips.

Having been Tony's Maid since she was a child, Mary was accustomed to her Ladyship's un-Lady like mannerisms but although she didn't reproach Tony, Mary did blush slightly.

'Try to stay still my Lady until Mr Gray has returned.' Mary picked up a brush and began to brush out Tony's waves of waist long curls. Tony endured this until there could not possibly be any knots or tangles and then reached out to lay her hand over her Maid's.

'Please Mary I know how much you love a hundred strokes but could you just plait it for me tonight?' At the obvious pain in Tony's voice, Mary laid down the brush without an argument.

'Of course my Lady.'

Hot Chocolate

With Tony sitting up in bed, banked up by pillows and decently covered in her night gown, Mary went to the door where Duncan and Aidan were waiting outside. Also dressed in his night shirt, Aidan slipped into the room around the Maid's skirts to launch himself onto his sister's bed. Duncan brought in a large basin of water as well as various medical supplies and Charles handed to Mary a tray of hot chocolate for both the Stirling siblings. Placing the basin on the floor Duncan had Tony swing her legs off the bed so that she could lower her swollen ankle into the basin. Involuntarily she gasped at the coldness of the water but managed to smile reassuringly at her worried attendees.

'It's all right, just the shock of the cold,' explained Tony. Her delicate eyebrows rose in question as she pointed to three cups on the tray as Mary poured out the hot chocolate.

Aidan giggled, 'That's for Duncan. His nerves are all churned up from having to decide between rescuing you or me.'

'With your father away, I'm charged with looking after both of you.' Blushing, Duncan coughed in embarrassment. Smiling, Tony reached out to take Duncan's hand.

'You did the right thing. Aidan is the heir and needed your protection more than I did. If I hadn't tripped over, I wouldn't have needed rescuing at all!'

I Need Answers

As the evening's events flashed past her eyes once more, Tony's brow was suddenly marred by a frown. 'Duncan I need to ask you about something that happened, or should I say didn't happen because Lord Delacourt arrived in time to prevent it. I just don't think it's something I can discuss in front of Aidan.'

Swallowing hard on the lump that suddenly formed in his throat, Duncan found his hands unconsciously tightening into angry fists. 'When you've both finished your drinks, Mary can take Aidan off to bed and you can then tell me as I wrap up your ankle.' He was surprised at how steady his voice sounded even though he felt like roaring in anger. *I can only imagine what an uncouth pig may have done to Tony.* Duncan took his hot chocolate to the window seat as Mary tidied up Tony's discarded clothes. The Tutor wrapped both his hands around his cup to disguise how much they were shaking. Covering his mouth as he yawned, Aidan handed Mary his empty cup to place on the tray before he gave his sister a rather chocolaty kiss goodnight.

'Sleep well Little Bear,' Tony wiped the chocolate from her lips. 'If you have any nightmares you can come and join me.'

Aidan smiled sleepily, 'thank you big bear.' He was very grateful for this lapse in the strict orders their parents had that Aidan should stay in his own room at night.

Typical Male Behaviour?

Duncan remained on the window seat until he had finished his drink before he finally moved to kneel once again in front of Tony. He gently raised her ankle out of the cold water and very carefully patted it dry. Once Duncan had wrapped a bandage around her ankle, he assisted Tony to swing her legs back onto her bed. He took her empty cup and placed it on the tray before sitting down on the bed beside her feet.

'What happened Tony?' Duncan tried to keep his voice calm and even in tone.

Tony had to take several deep breathes before she could recount the events after Duncan had raced off in pursuit of Aidan's frightened horse. He waited in silence until Tony came to the end and for her to ask the questions that were pertinent to that experience. *I don't want to think about what had almost taken place but fear that is what Tony has questions about.*

Moistening her lips, Tony took a deep breath before she could speak, 'There is no one I trust more than you, or feel that I can ask anyone else very intimate questions.' As Tony exhaled slowly, Duncan reached out to lay his hand over hers.

'Speak plainly Tony, I may not want to talk about what is troubling you but I will honestly answer your questions. Tell me what disturbs you about what happened.'

Slowly she nodded. 'When Sutherland pulled out his... his...'

'Do you want to use the proper words for the parts of the body or Aidan's childish metaphors?' Duncan's hand tightened over Tony's.

Exhaling deeply, Tony pulled herself together. 'Let's call a spade a spade.' Even so she found herself addressing the top button of Duncan's coat as she could not meet his gaze. 'When Sutherland pulled out his penis, I thought his intent was to... to urinate on me to humiliate me. But that doesn't explain why he forced me up onto my knees so that I was eye to eye with his... his penis. He could just as easily urinated on me where I had fallen on my hands and knees. So was that his actual intent? Or was he planning to do something else to me? Is that usual behaviour amongst men? Or had he penetrated my disguise and knew that I wasn't a man? If not, and he is interested in men, why offer to purchase the virginity of Mick Cooper's daughters?'

Honest Answers

Duncan held up both hands in surrender, 'Whoa! Slow down Tony. One question at a time. I doubt very much that he had penetrated your disguise and his plan to humiliate you had less to do with being a homosexual and more to do with proving he is the alpha male. That you're lower in the food chain than him. No its not normal behaviour amongst civilised gentlemen but I doubt very much that Nigel Sutherland is a gentleman; or even civilised for that matter.'

Pausing Duncan took several deep breathes before he continued, 'if he wasn't going to urinate over you then his plan was the ultimate humiliation… Sutherland would have made you suck his penis and then either ejaculate in your mouth or over you.'

Frowning, Tony managed to raise her eyes to rest upon Duncan's flushed countenance, 'Why? Oh I understand to humiliate me for standing up to him at the Inn but… Duncan, is it enjoyable?'

An involuntary groan escaped from the Tutor as he closed his eyes for a moment. 'Oh yes, very much so.'

'Is it always done to humiliate someone? Or can it be part of a normal sexual relationship?'

Opening his eyes, Duncan swallowed hard. 'It can be a part of a normal relationship. When… when you go up to London for your first season, you'll be able to observe how people of all walks of life use sex as a weapon. Some by offering it, others by refusing to engage. It doesn't have to be that way and perhaps it's time someone talked to you about what to expect so that you don't get hurt. Normally that should be your mother but I'm not certain that your step-mother, Lady Charlotte, is any role model for you.'

This Lie That I Live

A frown descended once more to disturb the symmetry of Lady Tony's beautiful face. 'It's my fault isn't it? I urged Papa to marry again. I knew I couldn't be the heir he truly needed and yet I'd been pretending to be a boy for so long that I didn't know how to change once Aidan was born. Now our female relatives are nagging and bullying Papa that I have to grow up, be a woman, seek out a mate and get married. But I can't face the life that Charlotte lives.'

'Do you mean how she never wants to be here but always in London or a fashionable resort?' Surprise was written clearly over Duncan's face.

'Yes in part.' She nodded. 'I know that they are fond of each other but I want more than that mild emotion with the man with whom I'm expecting to spend the rest of my life.'

Duncan chuckled, 'Have you been reading the Countess' romance novels again? Perhaps you're more of a girl than a boy than you are prepared to admit. Even to yourself.'

'Is it wrong to want more?' Blushing Tony looked away from his teasing eyes.

'You need to be careful that you don't make your dreams too unrealistic. I'd hate to see you disappointed if no man can fulfil an ideal that may be impossible to obtain.'

Duncan's Personal Pain

Sighing she laid her head back against her pillows, 'So do you have an impossible ideal mate?' She hadn't really expected him to answer so Tony was surprised to observe his colour deepen as he nodded. 'Who? No, let me guess... Penelope Stockton? She seems to have most of the eligible young bucks in the village mooning after her. Claire St James?'

A rueful smile appeared on Duncan's features. 'You really don't understand how attractive you are do you?'

'Me? But you've always acted like a brother towards me! You can't be interested in me!'

Raising one slightly unsteady hand, he caressed her cheek fondly. 'It wouldn't work between us. You should be striding in your male attire over your husband's estate, ruling him and his people with a firm but kind hand. I'm destined for London, maybe the continent in the world of politics and diplomacy. Upon coming down from Cambridge I was offered a position in the Foreign Office. With Mama so ill I wanted to stay close to home until she got better or... now that Mama has recovered, your father is already looking for another Tutor for Aidan. You'd be miserable in the world I'll be entering so I've kept my feelings to myself.'

Pity and regret were easily seen upon her face. 'Oh Duncan, I'm sorry if I've caused you any heartache. I'm fond of you but I want more than that mild emotion. I want…'

'Passion?' Duncan smiled sadly, 'Don't tell me you want a rake? Why do women always fall for womanisers? Do they really think that they can change them? Tame the wild beast where all other woman have failed?'

Laughing, Tony shook her head. 'Passion yes, but not a rake. I'd always be worried who he might be trying to seduce when I'm not there.'

'He'd probably end up with your sword against his throat.' He chuckled.

'More likely a different part of his anatomy!'

'Ouch!' Duncan winced at the thought. 'Remind me never to get you that angry.'

'I don't think you could.'

His eyebrows rose as he dragged in a shuddering breath. 'Oh? Not even if I do this?'

Taking A Liberty

Without giving Tony time to respond Duncan leant forward, one hand cupping her face as he kissed her lips. Tony's hands rose to push against his chest but there was no strength in the gesture. Drawing back slightly so that he could look deep into her eyes, Duncan read confusion, surprise as a delicate flush crossed her cheeks.

When Tony didn't say a word, Duncan kissed her again. A little firmer, a little more demanding, a little more passionate. This time, though, when she pushed against his chest, it was a little more insistent and Duncan immediately released her. Both were breathing a little faster and by the look of surprise on Tony's face, he knew that he had crossed the line.

'Oh Tony, I'm sorry. I shouldn't have done that! If you want me to leave the Manor tonight I'll understand.'

'No you don't have to leave.' Slowly Tony shook her head as she was still trying to process what exactly had just happened. 'It would mean having to make it known what has just occurred.' She spoke slowly as if carefully analysing the words before speaking.

'Did you... did you feel nothing at all?' He asked.

'It was nice but...' Tony sighed.

Holding up his hand Duncan did not let her finish. 'Not the passion you're looking for though?'

Sadly she shook her head. 'But at least it was nicer than when Patrick kissed me.'

Duncan's eyebrows rose almost all the way into his hairline. 'Patrick? As in your cousin Patrick? When was this?'

There was a delicate shrug of her shoulders. 'At the wedding of Papa and Charlotte. I was 11 or 12? He was aggrieved that I had orchestrated the marriage so that Papa could have a direct heir. Patrick droned on about what he planned for when he became Earl. Which included marrying me so that he could retain all un-entailed property that Papa might endow to me. When I headed up to bed, Patrick cornered me on the staircase and kissed me. Disgusted, I hit him.'

Duncan gave a crow of laughter. 'So that's how he broke his nose. I thought it a bit suspicious when he said he had walked into a door. Did you tell the Earl?'

Nodding, Tony sighed. 'Papa told Patrick if he ever touched me again he'd break all his fingers.'

Swallowing nervously Duncan asked, 'Will you tell your father that I kissed you?'

This time she shook her head. 'No, you did it out of affection and not possession. Otherwise you'd now be sporting a bloodied nose.' As he laughed, he rose off the bed and out of reach just in case Tony changed her mind about injuring him.

'Thank you for sparing me.' He bowed in mockery.

Tony's eyebrows rose. 'If I had disliked it then my response would have been immediate.'

'I see. Thank you for your restraint.' He was beginning to understand how painfully close he had come to paying for his indiscretion.

Tony laughed, 'I'm grateful that you kiss better than Patrick. I would've disliked having to hurt a friend.'

Duncan took another step backwards. 'By gad, Tony, when you talk like that I find it hard to believe that you're not a man! Am I lucky that you didn't have your sword on hand?'

A dazzling smile flittered across her face. 'No, you're lucky that you've had more practice at kissing than my clumsy cousin.'

'But if you were 11 how much older is Patrick?'

'Had you ever kissed anyone before you were 18?'

Deep in thought Duncan stroked his chin. 'Do you include kissing Nanny when I was three?'

'Yes all right.' Tony chuckled.

'Well then before I was 18 that would be 12.'

Sitting up straight, Tony looked startled. '12 girls? You heartbreaker!'

'So how many girls had Patrick kissed?'

'I was his first and he was 18?'

Duncan looked incredulous. 'First kiss at 18? What is wrong with him? Hang on, an 18 year old kissing an 11 year old? That is creepy!'

'More creepy than a 40 year old kissing a three year old?' one mobile eyebrow rose sardonically.

'That was different,' argued Duncan, 'it was the three year old who initiated the kiss and you're thinking of a later Nanny as mine was only in her 20's.'

Are We In Danger?

Slipping carefully off the bed, Tony threw back the bedding and rearranged the pillows. 'Do you think I stand in any danger of retaliation from Nigel Sutherland?' She asked as she settled back onto her bed.

'Well if Solitaire's threat doesn't deter him, then yes you'll be in danger. We'll just increase security until he finally decides to move on.'

Drawing her knees up against her chest, she suddenly looked very young. 'It's Aidan's safety that I'm worried about. I couldn't bear it if he was hurt because of me,' she admitted.

'We'll stay close to home for the next couple of days and if Sutherland continues to be a threat then we'll have to deal with him. You worry too much.' Duncan picked up the spare candle that Mary had left of him and lit it.

'I know, it's just that I don't like unpleasant surprises,' sighed Tony.

Standing with his hand on the door knob, Duncan said, 'You know the offer you made to Aidan if he had nightmares?'

'Yes, he can slip into my bed. What about it?'

Duncan grinned. 'Well I have the same offer for you!'

As she gasped, Tony's eyes widened in surprise. 'Duncan!' Laughing he slipped out of the room before she could throw anything at him. The offer had been made in jest to stop her worrying too much about Nigel Sutherland. Even so as he headed down the corridor to his own room, Duncan felt an ache for what could never be.

SUNDAY

Caviar's New Foal

When the Delacourt cousins drew up at Stirling Manor in the phaeton the next morning, the Footman awaiting them directed Caleb to drive straight round to the stables. There a Groom came forward to look after their horses as John Smythe emerged from the stables and bowed as Caleb and Geoff dismounted.

'My Lord, Mr Delacourt, if you'll follow me, we'll find Lord Tony with the new foal.' The Head Groom was a very small, elderly man who had once been a much sought after jockey. The cane John now needed to walk was not due to his age but a fall on the racetrack where his horse had landed on top of him. John Smythe ruled the Manor stables with an iron will but had a definite soft spot for the Stirling children, in particular Tony. Following the Head Groom into the stable, Caleb showed immediate interest.

'Was it as traumatic a birth as Lord Tony had feared?'

John Smythe chuckled. 'His Lordship has a tendency to worry about what might never happen! The mare is champion, my Lord. This is not the mother's first foal. The two year old colt you're interested in is also one of hers.' He opened a stall door to reveal a pure black mare, a pure black foal standing on shaky legs as he nursed with his mother and Lady Tony sat, in her male attire, upon a bale of straw as she wiped the embryotic fluid from the foal. As she looked up at their arrival, Geoff couldn't contain a gasp at the expression of radiating joy upon Tony's face as she smiled.

30

'Isn't he beautiful?' Tony's eyes shone with love and pride. The men could only agree as the foal was perfect. Yet they remained outside the stall knowing it could be dangerous for strangers to approach a mother and her new foal.

Caleb's Unexpected Behaviour

When Tony hauled herself to her feet, John brought to the doorway of the stall a set of crutches. He did not enter as the mare, Caviar, had taken objection to the wooden objects. So Tony used the side of the stall to limp towards the door but not heeding the danger to himself, Caleb stepped into the stall to place a supportive arm around her waist to assist Tony to hop out. John's bushy eyebrows rose in surprise but he remained silent as he held out the crutches for Tony once she was finally out of the stall.

'Can you ask one of the boys to bring Midnight out to the holding paddock so Lord Delacourt can look him over please John?' Tony led the two gentlemen out of the stables.

'Of course, my Lord,' John bowed, as he shut the door to the stall of the mother and her new born, and relayed his orders to a nearby Groom.

Geoff was puzzled by his cousin's behaviour and how even more quiet than usual Caleb had become. 'So Lord Stirling, apart from the ankle, how are you after last night's adventure?' Geoff asked as Tony led them through the gate into a fenced paddock. Pausing, she pushed back the lace from her wrist to show quite a bruise already forming.

'Next time he won't be so lucky!' Tony joked and turned as Simon brought out the two year old jet black colt.

Midnight had been broken in but was in a flighty, playful mood. He reared up on his back legs as his front ones tried to kick the Groom over. Reaching up her hand to caress Midnight's nose to calm him down, her crutches slipped on the damp grass.

As the horse came back down onto all four legs, he pushed Tony over before rearing back up to stand once again on his back legs.

The fall had knocked the wind out of Tony and as the Groom attempted to regain control over the colt, struggling for breath she used her arms to drag herself out of the way before the horse came down on top of her.

Ignoring the danger to himself, Caleb dashed forward to scoop Tony up into his arms and pulled her out from under Midnight's hooves. Carrying her over to the fence Caleb gently deposited her before going back to collect her crutches. These he thrust at his cousin before facing the highly excited colt.

Caleb didn't even hear his cousin's protest as he held out his hand towards the horse. With his gaze locked with the horse's eyes, Caleb began to speak in a language that Tony didn't know but she felt the power of his voice and his soothing tone. It had a similar effect upon the horse as he obediently dropped back onto all four hooves and lowered his head to Caleb's hand.

Not until the young horse was completely under the command of the Groom did Caleb finally turn around. Looking directly at Tony, Caleb unconsciously spoke to her in the same unknown language.

'An raibh Mheán Oíche Gortaítear tú?' When both Tony and Geoff looked at him puzzled, Caleb realised his error. Colour rushed across his cheeks as he laughed. 'Sorry once I start talking like that I find it hard to switch back. I asked if the horse had hurt you Tony.'

Shaking her head she said, 'Thanks to you, I'm fine. What language was that?' She felt quite breathless, flushed all over and a strange sensation in the pit of her stomach.

'It's Gaelic, I find it useful with animals especially frightened ones.' Caleb looked over his shoulder as the colt nudged him with his nose.

I'm Also Looking For A Mare

Walking around the horse, Caleb closely examined him. 'He's a very beautiful horse. There is great potential in him.'

'You've seen his mother, would you like to also see his father?' asked Tony.

Patting Midnight's rump, Caleb shook his head. 'No I'm quite happy with this young man's pedigree. I noticed a couple of young mares in the stable. Are any of them for sale? I'm looking for a nice, gentle horse for a Lady.'

'Georgiana?' queried Geoff.

'Yes,' Caleb nodded, 'she's been nagging me for a while to replace her poor old mare.'

Taking a deep breath, Tony fought to contain her disappointment as she presumed he was looking for a horse for his wife. *I'm surprised at how much that image hurts as I had begun to like Lord Delacourt. In fact I had begun to like him a lot!*

'Simon, bring out Missy and Silver Wings. They are half-sisters,' Tony explained to the Delacourts, 'Same father but different mothers and not related to Midnight if you wanted to breed them.'

The Groom took Midnight back to his stall and returned with the two mares. As Caleb inspected the horses, Tony pulled herself together.

'My apologies, my Lord, I should have asked if you want Midnight saddled up to see how he runs. That fall has knocked my brain askew.'

Caleb smiled, 'I trust the Earl to not sell me a horse that will be winded after a mile or pulls up lame. Even so, I would like to see him run, also these two ladies. Georgiana complains that she can't keep up with my hunters.'

Taking a deep breath, Tony managed to answer normally, 'Missy is placid and a walker, Silver Wings loves to run when she is given the opportunity but she's not a hunter. If you want a mare to keep up on the hunting field then you might want to look at Midnight's half-sister, Dusk.'

Bursting out in laughter, Geoff apologised at Tony's surprised look. 'Sorry but Georgiana has never been at a hunt in her life! If it's not her horse, she has to complain about, then it is something else! Georgiana is more than a little spoilt and although he won't admit it, the blame sits squarely upon Caleb's shoulders.'

While he examined the mares, Caleb hadn't been listening to his cousin. 'Which mare would you recommend for a woman who thinks she's a crack rider but is more likely to panic in a crisis?'

Thinking about it, Tony stroked her chin. 'Honestly?'

'Yes, of course.' Caleb glanced up at her in surprise.

'Then I recommend a barouche and a competent driver!'

'Gad Caleb now I know what to get Georgiana for her birthday!' Geoff collapsed against the fence as he laughed uncontrollably.

One of Caleb's eyebrows rose sardonically. 'Don't you think that is something her husband should purchase for her?' He drawled.

Tony hastened into speech to save Geoff from further retorts from his cousin. 'Missy would be better for a nervous or over confident rider. She's not timid so it would take something pretty dramatic to get her upset. Silver Wings will happily gallop the moment you ask her to or in fact the mood takes her.'

Caleb stroked the nose of Missy as she nudged him for a treat. 'I'd like to see Missy and Midnight saddled up.'

Nodding to Simon, the Groom, Tony asked, 'Would you like to ride yourself or are you happy to watch?' As Simon took both mares back to the stables Caleb joined Tony on the fence.

'I'll let your people handle the horses.'

Authority To Make A Deal

There was a moment of hesitation as Caleb sought to find a diplomatic way of raising his next question. 'I don't wish to insult you Lord Tony but are you Authorised to make a deal on behalf of your father?'

Tony chuckled, 'I'm 18, my Lord, but if you prefer to deal with Duncan Gray, he is currently standing in as guardian to Aidan and myself while Papa is away. In turn may I ask if you have proof that you have in fact been in correspondence with the Earl? As well as proof that you are in fact Lord Delacourt?'

'My word! You have an infernal cheek young man!' declared Geoff, deeply shocked. The gaze between Tony and Caleb met and held for a moment. When Tony raised one beautifully shaped eyebrow, Caleb's lips twitched and then he burst into unrestrained laughter.

'I would have been disappointed if you hadn't asked for proof of identity.' Caleb withdrew his pocket book from inside his jacket. From it he removed a calling card, a letter addressed to Caleb from the Earl of Stirling and a personal letter to him from his mother as well as his family crest on his signet ring. He handed them to Tony and after brief glance she handed the documents back again.

'How do I know that they weren't stolen or forged?'

'Upon my word! Impertinent lad!' Geoff exclaimed. Chuckling Caleb waved aside his cousin's protest.

'And how am I to know that you are in fact Lord Stirling?'

A sudden flush swept across Tony's cheeks and she gave a nervous laugh. 'Do you think that every member of Stirling Manor has also been duped by my impersonation? Or have we hidden the real servants in the cellars and all are a part of a criminal gang?'

Thoughtfully Caleb stroked his chin. 'Then your gang is very extensive as you'd have had to replace the Innkeeper, his family as well as all the locals having a drink at the Inn.'

'And a Highwayman?' Tony asked.

Caleb laughed, 'A hit! A very palpable hit! So my beautiful elfling, do we have a stale mate or is there some other way we can verify our identities?'

The Impasse

Feeling like he was intruding upon a private duel of words between the two handsome Lords, Geoff cleared his throat, 'If it's any help I can vouch for a birthmark in the shape of a star on Caleb's left outer thigh.' Both his companions looked at him in surprise.

'Well if you're part of his Lordship's gang, you might be privy to that information but it doesn't mean that it verifies that he is Lord Delacourt,' countered Tony.

'To hell with that, how the devil did you know about the birthmark?' Caleb demanded.

'And,' added Tony, 'did you expect Lord Delacourt to prove your claim by dropping his trousers?'

Holding up his hands in defeat, Geoff took a step backwards. 'Whoa there! Steady on! I was trying to lighten the mood. You two were the ones who were all serious and combative. As to how I know about the birthmark, have you forgotten how often we used to go swimming in the stream on your property?'

'The only way you could have seen that mark would be when we were skinny dipping?' Instinctively Caleb ran his hand against his left hip.

'Yes, so?' Geoff was puzzled.

'It raises the question why you were looking at me when I was naked?' A flush crept up Caleb's cheeks.

His cousin looked startled. 'I... I wasn't! I... Haven't you ever been curious to know how you compare to others?' Geoff blurted out. Tony moved slightly uncomfortably on the fence as Caleb stared incredulously at Geoff.

'No, not really!'

Much to the relief of all of them, John Smythe limped out to join them as two Grooms rode forward on Midnight and Missy.

'Oh John, Lord Delacourt and I have reached an impasse as to how to determine each other's true identity so that we may finalise a deal for the two horses.' Tony turned to face the Head Groom.

'Aye my Lord that is why I sent for Mr Gray who was with the Earl when he met Lord Delacourt the last time he was in London.' John ordered the Groom riding Midnight to take the horse to the track just outside the holding paddock. 'Show Lord Delacourt what Midnight can do Simon.'

Midnight's Run

The Groom had barely left the enclosure when he pulled up suddenly as Aidan came running down from the house, followed more sedately by his Tutor. Looking up Tony threw out her hand in warning.

'Stay!' Her order to her young brother was immediately obeyed and Aidan skidded to a halt. When Tony was satisfied that her brother was safe, she nodded to Simon to continue to ride Midnight towards the track.

Once the spirited colt was away from the paddock, Tony held out her hand to her brother. 'You know better than that Aidan! If Midnight can knock me over, I'm afraid of what he could do to you.' As she reached down to lift Aidan up onto the fence beside her, the young boy apologised.

'Sorry Tony but I wanted to see Midnight run.'

Affectionately Tony tousled his hair. 'All right just be more careful around the horses.' She made sure that Aidan was secure upon the fence before she signalled for Simon to start his run.

Silence fell amongst those gathered as Midnight showed off his high spirited manners but Simon was quite capable of controlling his mount's attempts to throw him off. Once in position, Simon spurred Midnight into a gallop and the colt eager to run, took off down the track. Actually the horse flew across the ground as if he had wings.

When the horse and rider reached the end of the track Simon slowed Midnight so that he could turn and they then raced back to the starting point. Clapping with joy, Aidan cheered as Simon brought Midnight back into the holding paddock. Caleb stepped forward to run his hand along the colt's flank. Midnight was breathing harder but he wasn't sweating.

'Beautiful! Superb condition!' Caleb lay his hand against the colt's chest to check his heart rate.

'Very impressive,' added Geoff, glancing across at Missy. 'So what can this little Lady do?'

Tony shook her head. 'Not until Simon has taken Midnight back to the stables. The mares can get a little silly around the young stallions.'

'Hey that's women of all species for you!' Laughing, Geoff slapped his cousin's shoulder.

'Really?' Both of Tony's eyebrows rose, 'Well once Midnight has gone we can continue.' Geoff blushed at his failed attempt at a joke.

Missy's Attributes

As Simon took Midnight back to the stables, Caleb looked over Missy who stood placidly under her rider.

'I know this is short notice but is there any way we can see how she handles with a woman?' Caleb asked, 'I'd like to see how Missy is controlled by a less confident rider.'

Caressing her finger tips across her lips Tony was thoughtful for a moment. 'I'll do you one better,' she finally said, 'Noah, dismount and throw Aidan up into the saddle.'

Duncan Gray was forced to break his usual taciturn nature. 'Tony that could be dangerous!'

She shook her head. 'Missy is gentle enough for Aidan to sit upon her back.' She glanced down at her brother, 'your choice Aidan, Noah will be right beside you the whole time.'

His eyes opened wide as he said, 'Me? On a real horse on my own? Yes please!' Having dismounted, Noah lifted the boy and placed him into the saddle.

Geoff was interested in Aidan's statement, 'If this is the young Lord's first time on a horse, what have you been training him on?'

'A pony of course but he'll soon be on his own horse. Aidan pick up the reins and see if she'll walk for you.'

'Giddy up!' Aidan pressed his knees together and urged the mare forward. Missy obeyed, walking around the paddock as Aidan giggled in delight.

As the rider's confidence grew, his nervousness lessened, even so Noah remained alongside Missy as Aidan walked her around the paddock.

'Gentlemen,' John Smythe said quietly, 'I'm about to make a sudden noise, so don't be alarmed.'

Tony reached down to place her hands upon the fence and braced herself. Even so when John yelled and banged his walking stick against the fence, she still jumped. Noah reached up to Missy's reins but the mare simply turned around to look at the Head Groom with her large calm eyes. When Aidan had recovered from his own shock and he urged Missy to walk again, she sedately continued to circle the paddock.

Seeing a possible flaw in a horse that was too placid, Geoff raised a question. 'Calm is one thing but is the mare a little too sedate for Georgiana?'

'What's she like if you want her to run?' Caleb turned to look up at Tony.

Gesturing to Aidan to bring Missy closer to the fence, Tony asked her younger brother, 'Do you want to stay on while Missy has a little run?'

Some of the doubt re-entered Aidan's face as memories of the mad dash on Tony's fleeing horse the previous night flashed before him. 'Is it all right if I say no?'

'Of course it is!' Tony smiled fondly at him, 'Last night was rather frightening wasn't it?' She held out her hands and Aidan allowed her to lift him off Missy and placed him back on top of the fence. Tony then surprised them all by mounting the mare instead of Noah.

'Tony!' protested Duncan, 'Your ankle's not up to riding astride.'

Laughing, she placed her left foot into the stirrup but angled her right leg across the saddle in front of her. There was no pummel as on a woman's saddle but Tony seemed more than comfortable being able to use only her left leg to control Missy. She moved away from the Groom and sent Missy dancing around the paddock.

The horse and rider were soon out of the enclosure and moving a little faster to the track that moments earlier had seen Midnight fly down its length. For a brief moment Tony leant forward, one hand caressing the mare's mane as she whispered words of encouragement. Duncan opened his mouth to protest but John Smythe dug him in the ribs with his walking stick.

'Leave be Mr Duncan! His Lordship won't heed your words in any case!' Rubbing his painful ribs, Duncan closed his mouth again and just nodded.

Showing Off

Whatever Tony had said to Missy, the mare shook her head and caused the rider to straighten up in the saddle. When Tony urged Missy down the track, the mare fell into a beautiful trot. It was like poetry in motion, again that dancing grace they had seen as Tony had ridden Missy around the paddock. When they reached the end of the track, Missy was definitely showing off as she turned a full circle and a half instead of just the half circle needed to face the men watching her.

Tossing her head back in delight, Missy gave in to Tony's request to run and broke into an elegant gallop, but slowed to a trot again as she drew closer to her audience. Missy knew she looked good as she danced down the track and had no desire to be fast like her half-sister Silver Wings, or the colt Midnight. Caressing her hand through Missy's mane, Tony brought her back into the paddock where the mare readily accepted the lump of sugar that Caleb held out to her.

A Deal Is Struck

'Sorry my Lord,' apologised Tony, 'I tried to talk Missy into showing that she can run but it looks like it's not just for the male horses she likes to show off.'

Chuckling, Caleb stroked Missy's nose. 'Not a problem, I think a horse that would rather be beautiful than a racer will suit Georgiana perfectly.' Tony was a little puzzled that he would talk that way about his wife but said nothing. Geoff wanted to know if this was a done deal.

'Well Caleb, are you satisfied with your choices?'

Stroking Missy's flank, Caleb finally nodded. 'So the question that remains is how much?'

'Two hundred pounds,' said Tony without any hesitation.

'Each?' asked Caleb a little surprised.

Tony shook her head, 'No, for the pair.'

John Smyth cleared his throat. 'Two hundred and fifty is the market price, Lord Tony, unless you're factoring in gratitude for Lord Delacourt rescuing you.'

Colour rushed across her cheeks. 'It would be different if Midnight was a known and successful race horse.'

Caleb glanced across to Duncan, 'And what do you think is appropriate Mr Gray?'

Duncan looked startled at being addressed, 'I have no idea, my Lord. I can't even fathom that amount of money!'

'Well Mr Gray, since you stand as loco parentis to the Stirling brothers, I'll agree upon two hundred and fifty with you.' Caleb held out his hand for the bemused Duncan to shake.

With a twinkle in his eyes, John said, 'Perhaps you should take his Lordship up to the house Mr Duncan. He can then write you a cheque for the two horses and you can write him a receipt.

'Of course.' Duncan bowed, gratefully accepting the Head Grooms advice.

'When would you like to collect the horses to take home with you Lord Delacourt?' Tony asked, accepting Noah's assistance down from the mare. Geoff held out the crutches for her.

'Actually I've been thinking about sticking around for a couple of days.' Caleb's statement caused Geoff's jaw to drop in surprise. *I'd been under the impression that we would be on our way once Caleb had purchased the horses he wanted.*

'Well you're welcome to inspect the horses any time you like,' Tony offered, 'I hope you don't find our sleepy little village too boring.' She gestured to Noah to lead Missy back to the stables.

'I'm sure I can find some way to amuse myself,' Caleb laughed and Tony, misinterpreting it, stiffened but she kept her disappointment out of her voice.

'Don't break too many hearts my Lord.'

Although he was puzzled by Tony's remark, Caleb turned to follow Duncan up to the house. *I want some time to think and further information before I can make any sense of the drama going on around us.*

Al Fresco Luncheon

The Delacourt cousins had completed their transaction and left Stirling Manor before Tony and Aidan entered the house. It wasn't a case of avoiding the cousins but Aidan had wanted to see the new foal. Alistair Preston, the Butler, bowed as the half-siblings came into the Manor.

'Mrs Preston thought that, since it is such a lovely day, you might like to have luncheon out on the patio.'

Aidan looked up eagerly at his sister, 'Oh Tony, may we?'

A tender smile answered him. 'Of course we can, so long as we're not creating too much work for you Preston.'

'No trouble at all my Lady,' inclining his head, the Butler departed to inform those under his command to make it so.

Duncan joined Tony and Aidan on the patio for luncheon. He felt a moment of embarrassment due to what had occurred between them the previous evening but most of the talking was done by Aidan. He was absolutely enchanted with the new foal and his first ride on a real horse. Tony allowed her brother to happily prattle on, only stopping him whenever he tried to talk with food in his mouth.

At the end of the meal, as Aidan dashed off through the rose bushes after a butterfly, Tony was fondly watching him, when Duncan tried to engage her in conversation.

'Tony, about last night…'

Her eyebrows rose as she transferred her gaze from the young Lord to his Tutor. 'Don't tell me you regret ever taking such a liberty?' she teased.

'Actually I don't regret it!' A delicate colour rushed across Duncan's features as he uttered a nervous laugh. 'I just want to know if it has created an awkwardness between us.'

Without needing to think about her answer, Tony shook her head. 'Now if you were to start making a habit of it then there could be a problem.'

A Masked Intruder

The smile that appeared in answer to Tony's wit suddenly vanished from Duncan's face as a masked and armed man ran out of the shrubbery and grabbed Aidan. Before Duncan could do more than half rise out of his chair and command Tony to get inside, the masked man was upon them.

Using the butt of his pistol, the intruder smashed it into the side of Duncan's head causing him to collapse to the ground unconscious. Tony rose to her feet, her hand instinctively reaching for her sword but the masked man placed his pistol against Aidan's temple.

'Don't do anything rash me pretty buck! Or I will kill the boy!' The familiar voice caused Tony to stiffen in indignation.

'Nigel Sutherland! Do you really think you can attack us on our own property?'

The intruder ripped down his muffler to show his grinning countenance. 'Y'r father will pay a pretty sum to have his sons returned safely. Now slowly remove y'r sword and pass it over to me.'

When Tony hesitated, Nigel tightened his grip upon Aidan. 'Don't make the little chap suffer for y'r disobedience me Lord.'

Reluctantly Tony withdrew her sword and watched in frustration as Nigel thrust it into his own belt before he jammed a piece of paper into her hand.

'Put that into his jacket and pick up y'r crutches, pretty boy. Attempt to use your crutches as a weapon and I will hurt y'r brother!' Nigel ordered.

Casting a desperate glance over Duncan's motionless body as she did as she was told, Tony wished desperately, *If only there was some way to get Aidan away from this brute before he hurts him.* As they made their way across the estate, she hoped and prayed *that someone, anyone would see us, would rescue us before we are forced to leave our home.* It was luncheon everywhere so there were no servants out attending to their duties. As Tony ascended into a nearby carriage, a little awkwardly due to her damaged ankle and crutches, she hoped, *that Duncan hasn't been seriously injured. That he'll soon be found and our plight made known.* A shiver of fear raced through Tony as Nigel thrust Aidan into her arms before he too climbed into the carriage, and she wondered, *how long can I keep my secret safe from our abductor?*

A Review Of Emotions

There was no opportunity during luncheon for Caleb to contemplate his turbulent emotions so once they had completed the meal that Ruth Cooper had presented, he went for a walk through the village, alone. After an hour and a half, Caleb turned around to stroll back to the Inn.

Deep in thought, he paused to admire the garden outside the Vicarage. Even though his eyes were feasting upon the pretty flowers, Caleb's thoughts were still dwelling upon the issues that had been plaguing him since he had first laid eyes on Tony the previous evening. That was how he missed noticing there was someone in the garden watching him. Amused, Reverend Matthew Gray dusted himself off as he rose from where he had been kneeling while he weeded.

'Good afternoon Lord Delacourt,' Matthew removed his hat to wipe a handkerchief across his forehead. Startled out of his contemplation, Caleb raised his eyes to meet the amused gaze of Duncan's father. Bowing, Caleb pulled himself together.

'My apologies Reverend. I was just admiring your beautiful garden.'

Removing his gardening gloves, Matthew stepped forward to open the picket gate. 'Thank you, my Lord but the gardens at the Manor are much more impressive.' He checked his fob watch before adding, 'it's a little early but how about a cup of tea?'

Hesitating for only a brief moment Caleb decided *that the Reverend could be exactly the answer to the questions that have been troubling me.* 'Yes, I'd like that.' He followed Matthew into the Vicarage.

Please Tell Me The Truth

Seated comfortably in the Vicar's parlour, with a steaming hot cup of tea in front of him, Caleb decided to be blunt about his queries. 'Tell me about Tony Stirling.'

The Reverend's smile slipped slightly, 'What would you like to know about his Lordship?'

'It's admirable how everyone in the village is protective of Tony, but it is her Ladyship isn't it?' Laughing, Caleb shook an unsteady finger at Matthew. 'Please put me out of my misery Reverend Gray. The moment I saw Tony enter the Inn last night I immediately and helplessly fell in love. If Tony isn't a woman then I've no idea who I am anymore!'

Seeing the desperation in Caleb's face, Matthew relented. 'You are correct, my Lord. Tony was the only child that Lady Grace, the first Lady Stirling, managed to keep alive. We lost count of the number of miscarriages, still births and deaths in infancy that the Earl and the Countess had to suffer before the final birth took both Grace and the baby. Tony felt that she had to be the heir that had never survived.'

'In a way it was how Tony and Julius, Lord Stirling, dealt with their grief until Tony realised that they couldn't keep pretending that she was a boy any more. Heather, my wife, thinks it was about the time that Tony acquired that monthly visitor women have to contend with.'

Caleb shifted slightly uncomfortably in his chair. 'Why the wholesale acceptance of the charade by everyone at the Manor and in the village? The more and longer Tony denies her true identity, the harder it will be for her to become female.'

Matthew managed to shrug his shoulders as he took a sip of his tea. 'It became a habit and habits are sometimes very hard to break. Why force the child to be something she didn't want to be? It is also beneficial to young Lord Aidan to have or seem to have an older brother. If any attempt were made on the Stirling heir then strangers would assume that Tony is the heir and not Aidan.'

'Putting her in serious danger!' Caleb felt his temper rising at the careless disregard for Tony's safety.

Matthew wasn't prepared to take the bait. 'My Lord, you have seen Lord Tony with a sword. If it had not been for a loose stone, she would have taken care of that bully, Nigel Sutherland.'

Swallowing down his rage, Caleb managed to regain his even tone. 'And have you considered the possibility that Aidan is her weakness? The bond between them is too strong.'

Matthew nodded, 'Yes, Lady Charlotte is concerned about that too. A little late to be considering her own relationship with her son as it was her indifference to Aidan that made Tony become more affectionate and protective of him. That is why Charlotte wants Tony married as soon as possible is to break that bond. When that happens, it will break Aidan's heart but the current situation can't continue. Tony is being urged to grow up and become the woman she is meant to be. That she has never been trained to be.'

'Who is going to teach her? From what I've heard her stepmother is hardly ever there.'

'There are plenty in the village to guide Tony. That isn't your concern, my Lord.' Matthew smiled serenely.

'That's the problem, Reverend Gray, it is my concern! I don't think I will ever feel for anyone else the way I feel about Tony!'

'What if she is unable to give up the masquerade?'

Caleb drew in a deep breath. 'Then I'll offer her marriage so that her relatives stop badgering her. Tony can continue to be whoever she is comfortable being.'

Matthew paused as he took another sip of tea. 'And what if she can never be a woman and give you the son and heir you need to silence your own relatives?'

'We'll deal with it, if or when, that situation arises. I'll love her regardless of whether she can change.'

Reaching out to lay his hand over Caleb's, Matthew reassured him. 'It may not come to that. Heather has, over the past couple of years, noticed certain feminine traits beginning to surface. It will take time, though, to un-learn a life time of behaviours.'

'But not impossible?' There was no hiding the eagerness in Caleb's voice.

Matthew smiled. 'My son, with God's help, many things are indeed possible!'

News Of The Abduction

An urgent knock on the parlour door was immediately followed by the Maid entering with one of the Grooms from the Stirling Manor.

'My apologies Reverend Gray but Simon has some urgent news.' Polly bobbed a curtsey to Matthew.

Simon dragged his cap off his head and held it nervously between his hands. 'I was sent to fetch the Doctor, Vicar. When Mr Preston went out to check on the Stirling Lords and Mr Gray at luncheon, he found Mr Gray knocked out cold.'

Caleb rose immediately to his feet. 'What about Tony and Aidan?' He demanded, his heart pounding painfully against his chest.

'There was no sign of them, my Lord,' Simon added, 'A gardener thought he heard a carriage. When Mr Gray came to briefly he said, "Sutherland."'

His hands tightening into fists, Caleb exploded, 'Son of a bitch!'

Matthew lay a calming hand onto Caleb's arm. 'Wait my son, get all the information before you go off half cocked.'

'Every minute we wait takes them further into danger!'

The Reverend patted his arm reassuringly, 'Simon was a ransom demand made?'

The Groom nodded. 'A note was left in Mr Gray's jacket. For a specified sum of money the Earl will get his sons back. A messenger has been sent up to London to alert his Lordship and Mr Preston is emptying the safe as well as any monies we can pull together to try and make up the ransom. His Lordship will never get here in time for the deadline.'

Gently Caleb detached the Reverend's hand and gestured to Simon to follow him. 'Come with me to the Stirling Arms, Simon, you can take any money and valuables I have with me to add to Mr Preston's ransom.'

'What are you going to do then, my Lord?' asked Matthew as he followed the men out the front door.

'Nigel Sutherland had several friends with him last night. If I can get my hands on any of them, I'll find out where to start looking for the Stirlings!'

Simon held up his hand, 'Two of them are in the Inn at the moment.'

'Then I'm going to introduce them to a world of pain until I find out where they've taken those children!'

'Wait a minute, my son.' Matthew threw out his hand to stop the two young men from stalking off to the Inn.

Caleb's eyebrows rose in surprise. 'Are you going to counsel us against violence?'

Smiling, Matthew shook his head, 'No but I do suggest you get a location before you beat his brains to a pulp.' Stunned, Simon followed Caleb along the road to the tavern.

Where Are They?

There were several people in the public bar when Caleb and Simon stormed into the Stirling Arm Inn. Mick looked up startled as Caleb pounced on Peter Doyle, dragged him out of his chair and pressed him hard up against the wall.

'Where has that fiend taken them?' Caleb demanded, his arm pressed against Peter's throat. Geoff Delacourt had leapt to his feet at Caleb's abrupt entrance and tried to ease his cousin's hold on his victim.

'Ease up Caleb, he can't speak if you crush his windpipe! What on earth has got you all steamed up?'

'The Stirling children have been abducted! Where did Sutherland take them?' The last question was aimed at Peter. In the meantime Simon had filled in Mick as to what had occurred at Stirling Manor.

'Ruth!' Mick called out to his wife, 'Get all the money out of the safe.'

Caleb added to Geoff, 'Go up to my room and get any money or valuables and give them to Simon to take to Mr Preston for the ransom demand.'

Peter managed to croak, 'You're gunna need all the ransom you can raise for I'll never tell you where they are!'

Geoff headed upstairs, as Ruth Cooper brought out a bag of money, Caleb glanced around to address her, 'Mrs Cooper, is your stove hot?'

A little startled, Ruth nodded, 'Aye, my Lord, are you still hungry?'

'No ma'am, but if beating him to a bloody pulp won't get any answers, then perhaps a hot Aga will be more persuasive!' Dragging Peter by the collar, Caleb signalled for Mick to grab Peter's mate Rhett to stop him running away.

Indicating for Caleb to follow her into the kitchen, Ruth showed no emotion but Mick was shocked.

'Isn't that a little drastic Lord Delacourt?'

Caleb pointed significantly to the Groom, Simon, 'What time do you think the Stirling children were taken?'

'Between 12.30 and one o'clock.' Simon scratched his head.

Caleb's hold tightened upon Peter's coat. 'Devil take it! It's after three now! We have to rescue them before Sutherland discovers Tony's secret!'

Missing a step on his way back down the staircase, Geoff grabbed hold of the railing to stop himself from falling flat on his face as Mick, glancing briefly at his wife, spoke the question they were all thinking.

'You know the truth then, my Lord?'

Caleb scowled as he felt that this was not important. 'Yes, that's why we must hurry!'

Seeing an opportunity for blackmail, Peter asked, 'Tell me the secret and maybe I'll tell you where they are?'

No one except the victim raised a protest as Caleb slammed Peter's head into a wall. 'That's none of your business! Where is Sutherland? Or you have a date with the Aga!'

As Rhett and Peter were dragged into the kitchen, only Rhett, held by Mick's firm grip, remained defiant.

'You're bluffing! You must be desperate to get your beautiful boyfriend back!' Rhett sneered.

Mick's large hand suddenly appeared around Rhett's throat. 'Shut your filthy mouth boy! Don't you dare speak disrespectfully of Lord Tony!'

Being thrown by Caleb against the Aga stove, Peter reached out to steady himself and swearing colourfully, quickly removed his hands from the hot metal. Caleb didn't allow him a chance to move too far away from the stove as he locked one of Peter's arms behind his back and forced Peter's face down towards the hot stove top.

'Steady on Caleb!' Geoff's protest went unheeded by his Lordship.

'Where has Sutherland taken the Stirling Lords?' As hot as the stove was, only inches from Peter's face, Caleb's voice was icy cold. Sweat beaded on Peter's brow as the heat from the Aga began to singe his whiskers and blister the top layer of his cheek. Struggling was useless against the iron grip that clamped on his neck and kept one of his arms pinned behind him.

When Peter refused to answer, Caleb pushed his face even closer to the hot, blistering stovetop. It didn't touch but the pain was too much for Peter and he screamed in agony.

'For fuck's sake! All right! Nigel will have gone to an Inn ten miles south of here, it's called 'On the Rocks.' It's the haunt of cut throats, thieves, pirates and murderers!'

Caleb didn't immediately release Peter as he looked up at Mick. 'Can you direct me to this place?'

'Aye, my Lord, but the truth is even if you manage to get inside, you'll have the devil of a job to get out alive!'

'I'll manage.' Caleb released Peter and threw him against Rhett. 'Keep these two here under guard; if I fail then you'll need them to deliver the ransom.'

Preparations

Caleb led the group back out to the main bar area. 'Do you have a local map to show me how to get this den of thieves?'

'Aye my Lord.' Mick threw Rhett and Peter into a corner of the room and from under the bar he pulled out a map and a shotgun. The first he spread open on the bar, the latter, he tossed to his good wife who immediately pointed it at Peter and

Rhett who looked as though they were about to try to escape. Glancing down briefly at the map, Caleb suddenly looked up again and across at Simon.

'Get the money to Mr Preston; if you need any more, try amongst the villagers. Keep track of how much is donated by each household as I'm sure the Earl will reimburse everyone when he does arrive. It's just that we may need the money before the Earl gets here.'

Simon hesitated, 'Is there any point taking what money has already been collected with you, my Lord? Or are you purely undertaking a rescue mission?'

Geoff looked up from the map. 'It is an idea Caleb.'

Pausing to consider it Caleb finally shook his head. 'No speed is of the essence here. If I fail to rescue them then we pay the money but I'll be damned if I hand over any money without a fight!'

Mick added, 'Ask the boys to ready Lord Delacourt's phaeton, Simon.' The Groom tugged his forelock and bowed to Caleb before he headed out to the stables.

Applying himself to the map as Mick outlined the route to the Inn, Caleb pointed out a wooded area just north of the On the Rocks Inn.

'Is this a good place for Geoff to hide the phaeton while I go on alone on foot?'

A little surprised, Mick looked up. 'Aye, my Lord, but should you perhaps take one of my boys to mind the horses as it will be a two man job to rescue the Stirlings.'

Caleb shook his head, 'If anything goes wrong I'd want Geoff to get back here in time to assist with the ransom.'

'And then rescue you?' Geoff drawled, 'Or do I have to raise a ransom for the release of your good self? What are you worth?'

Caleb grinned at his cousin. 'I'm hoping it doesn't come to that! Which reminds me, Geoff, upstairs you'll find a pair of pistols.'

His cousin trudged off muttering under his breath about having something else in mind for exercise that didn't include so many stairs. Caleb only laughed and shot his words after him. 'But surely this is healthier for you!'

In Pursuit

Ruth Cooper, puzzled, looked from her husband to his Lordship who had the grace to blush under her questioning look.

'My apologies, Mrs Cooper that was not meant for your ears.'

Colouring up, Ruth managed to laugh, 'Boys will be boys.'

'That doesn't excuse bad manners.' Caleb took his overcoat off the hook by the door and slipped it on. As the sun went down it would get cold very quickly and it would hide the holsters for his weapons when Geoff brought them down to him. Mick watched in silence for a moment as Caleb adjusted the gun holsters around his hips.

'Waiting with the phaeton will be a dangerous position if unarmed,' Mick said, trying to be tactful.

Caleb smiled. 'There's a shotgun behind the driver's seat so I'm not leaving Geoff defenceless except for his charming wit!'

Grimacing, Geoff pulled on his own overcoat. 'Have you thought to make your will, cousin?'

Not missing a beat, Caleb slapped Geoff on the back. 'Already taken care of, and you're not in it.'

Geoff burst out laughing. 'Good! I'd hate to be encumbered with a fortune and a title! Then the relatives would start nagging me to get married!'

'Oh yes, a perfectly good reason for not wanting to step into my shoes, cousin!' Caleb drawled. Watching the Delacourts head for the door Mick held his breath as he waited for Geoff's reply.

'Oh I've a better reason Caleb.'

Caleb's eyebrows rose in surprise, 'Oh? What is that?'

'My feet are bigger than yours!' Mick laughed out aloud and almost missed Caleb's quick come back.

'You know what they say about the size of man's hands and feet?'

'Yes?'

Caleb chuckled. 'It's a myth!'

'It is true!' Colour swept across Geoff's cheeks.

'Then why the insecurity of having to check out others?'

Geoff shot back, 'To see how you mere mortals fail in comparison!'

Mick ushered the cousins out of the tavern in case their argument became even more inappropriate for his good wife to overhear. Shaking his head, Mick thought, *I don't think I'll ever understand the gentry. By their conversation, anyone would assume they were off on a spree rather than a quest that could cost any one of them their life.*

Assessing Their Options

Everything Tony did, every movement, every word, every expression was in a calm and controlled manner. As Nigel forced Tony and Aidan into the carriage. As Nigel tied up her hands and then her feet. As Tony lifted her bound hands so that Aidan could wrap his arms around her and snuggle close in his fear. *By staying calm I hope to keep Aidan from freaking out and making the situation worse.* She spoke in a slow, soft tone, extolling the boy's bravery.

When Tony's soothing tone finally became too much for Nigel, compounded by the beauty of her face, he tied a gag around her mouth. He didn't separate the siblings as the last thing Nigel needed was a screaming child. The rest of the journey was undertaken in silence and Nigel stared out the window unable to stand the sight of the handsome pair.

Tony briefly and surreptitiously tried to undo the ties around her hands but Nigel had done a good job so Tony sat still when she realised that the rope wasn't going to ease without the use of a tool. *Nigel has taken my sword but the smaller version attached to Aidan's belt is still there but the way he is pressed up against me it's currently impossible for me to get to it without alerting our captor to my actions. I'll wait for a more opportune time, especially as I can't see throwing Aidan and myself out of moving carriage as a good escape plan.*

The Den Of Thieves

When they reached the On the Rocks Inn in Beachy Head on the coast of East Sussex, Nigel had already arranged for the driver to drop them off at the back entrance. The Inn stood precariously on the edge of the chalky sea cliffs near Eastbourne where the cliffs, the highest in England, rose 531 feet above sea level.

Refusing to remove the ties that bound her, Nigel ordered Aidan out of the carriage before he grabbed Tony and easily tossed her over his broad shoulder.

With the gag in her mouth, she couldn't scream; bound hand and feet, she couldn't run. Obediently Aidan, carrying Tony's crutches, followed Nigel into the Inn and up the back stairs and into one of the bedrooms. Nigel threw Tony onto the bed before he took the crutches from Aidan and laid them against the table along with his own collection of weapons.

Now that I finally have Lord Tony at my mercy, I don't know what to do with him. I can't even look at him. The perfect arch of his eyebrows, the way a lock of chestnut red hair falls against the fine porcelain cheekbone, the defiance in his deep blue eyes, pondered Nigel.

Tony managed to pull herself up into a sitting position and Aidan slipped under her bound hands to sit upon Tony's lap and hold on tightly to her. *We're in for a long wait and I pray that we get through this ordeal before Nigel discovers the truth that is sitting right under his broken nose.*

I Need To Pee

For a few hours Aidan slept in his sister's protective arms as she methodically considered and discarded possible scenarios that could assist their escape. *Interestingly it isn't the fact that I'm bound and gagged that I see as our biggest challenge but the fact that Aidan, being so young, is almost entirely reliant upon me for his fate. Also the state of my damaged ankle which means even if we escape the Inn, running is not much of an option. If this had been an ordinary Inn I could have hoped to find at least one decent patron to aid our plight but this is a renowned den of iniquities and exposing our presence to these people would only place us in even more danger.*

When Aidan finally stirred, Tony relaxed her arms as they held him close.

'Tony?'

She managed to raise her hands to draw the gag out of her mouth. 'Yes Little Bear, it's all right, I'm here.'

Scrubbing his hand across his eyes, Aidan yawned. 'I need to pee.'

That snapped Nigel out of his own thoughts and he pointed at the chamber pot under the bed.

'No, I want a proper loo!' Aidan was mulish.

Tony squirmed a little. 'Actually I'd like to go to the lavatory too,' she admitted.

Sighing deeply, Nigel rose out of his chair and picked up one of the pistols on the table. Sliding it into his belt, he approached Tony to untie her hands and feet.

'Not to be too critical of your organisational skills but you'd be better with a sword or knife because if you discharge that pistol we'll be quickly inundated by your friends downstairs.'

Standing over her as she massaged her wrists, Nigel glared down at her for a moment before deciding that he couldn't argue with her logic. With another sigh, Nigel turned and swapped his pistol for a blade.

'Come on, try anything and I'll cut ya both!' Nigel threw the crutches across at Tony.

Not waiting for the adults, Aidan ran down the passageway to the communal bathroom as he felt his need was greater than anyone else's. Tony was permitted to enter the room unaccompanied once Aidan came out again. Nigel knew *that Lord Tony will never attempt to escape without Aidan and besides which the window in the bathroom isn't large enough for even the five year old to climb through.*

When Tony emerged, Nigel was faced with a dilemma, he too wanted to use the bathroom but could not leave both Tony and Aidan in the passageway unguarded. So he took Aidan in with him and needlessly warned Tony against running or trying to ambush him.

Leaning back against the smoke-stained wall, Tony was contemplating more serious problems. *I felt a cool draft brush the wayward curl across my face and I know as night falls it will get very cool. Aidan is wearing only a thin jacket and as a baby he has been subject to bouts of, as the Doctor called it, bronchitis. A chill could be life threatening to my young brother.*

So when Nigel led them back to the bedroom, Tony politely asked their captor to wait a minute from tying her up again so she could remove her own jacket and wrap it around Aidan. Her hair lay hidden beneath her waistcoat. With that done, she calmly held out her hands to be bound again.

I'm Hungry

Clambering up onto the bed beside Tony, Aidan's next words were no surprise to her. 'I'm hungry.'

Sighing, Nigel drew out his battered old fob watch. 'I've arranged food to be brought up about five. It's almost that now. I'll untie y'r hands so that it's easier for ya to eat.'

Tony shook her head. 'I'm not hungry but I wouldn't mind something to drink.'

'Mrs Swan will bring up some ale.' Correctly interrupting Tony's silence, Nigel added, 'Of course ya don't drink do ya, me Lord? Would ya like some barley water or a pot of tea?' He sneered.

Immune to sarcasm, Aidan screwed up his nose. 'I don't like barley water. Can I have hot chocolate please?'

Seeing the look of frustration descend upon Nigel's face, Tony smiled sympathetically. 'It'll be better for you if you can organise chocolate for Aidan, he'll sleep after that and a little food. You really don't want to spend several hours with him whinging.'

Glancing from one adult to the other, Aidan realised that they were talking about him. He debated about whether he should be insulted but acknowledged that Tony only spoke the truth so he shelved any indignation.

Nigel wasn't completely convinced. 'I was hoping y'r father would've paid the ransom before we got to the whining stage.'

Smiling, Tony shook her head. 'That will depend upon how much you demanded for our return. You see Papa is currently in London. A messenger will have been sent to him but the banks will be closed now until morning and then there is his drive home again.'

'In the meantime the staff at the Manor will have drawn on every local available source to try and meet the ransom amount so that maybe we'll be home before Papa arrives. It depends upon how greedy you were in your demands.'

'It was more about humiliating ya than the money.'

One exquisite eyebrow rose in answer. 'How's that working out for you?' drawled Tony.

For a moment, Nigel stared blindly down at his hands and his face reflected the turmoil of his thoughts. Tony wondered, *have I got away with my insolence?* Nigel finally rose to his feet, his hands clenched into tight plate sized fists; she refused to flinch as Nigel loomed over her. At the last minute as his fist came down towards her face, his hands suddenly opened and Nigel slapped Tony hard.

As surprised as Tony felt, it was nothing to Nigel's own puzzlement. *I'd never slapped another man before. The only way I can explain it is that Lord Tony is still a child, not really a man... yet.* Before Nigel could really process that thought, they were interrupted by a knock at the door.

Trying to pull himself together, Nigel strode across the room to unlock and throw open the door. He stepped back to allow the Innkeeper's wife, Mrs Swan to enter with her loaded tray. Nigel cleared a spot on the table before he swallowed hard on the lump in his throat that was trying to choke him.

'Could we also have hot chocolate Mrs Swan?' Nigel forced himself to look at Tony as he asked, 'Do ya want tea?'

She nodded, 'Yes please.'

Following Nigel's gaze, Mrs Swan felt her chest tighten as she was robbed of breath at the sight of the beautiful young man tied up on the bed. A trickle of blood fell from the captor's desirable lips and a red hand print could still be seen on Tony's cheek. Even she was fooled by Tony's disguise but there was no hiding the effects of Tony's beauty. Mrs Swan dropped an instinctive curtsey before she hurried out of the room.

Distracted

As Nigel and Aidan sat down at the table to eat, Mrs Swan ran back down the stairs. She was rather flushed and felt quite giddy and absent minded as she made her way through the public bar towards the kitchen.

The sudden pushing back of a patron's chair tripped her up and she would have fallen onto her plump rosy face, if it had not been for a nearby patron catching her.

'Steady Mrs Swan, here have a seat for a moment,' said the patron, pulling out the chair beside him.

'Oh Gerry, thank you. I'm afraid I wasn't paying attention. It's not like me to be disconcerted by a handsome young man but I've just seen the most beautiful youth that must ever have walked this earth.' Mrs Swan raised a slightly shaking hand to tidy her hair.

Gerry's eyebrows rose in surprise. 'Surely not here, Mrs Swan! Why would God send a vision of heaven to this place?'

Pressing her hands against her flaming cheeks, Mrs Swan managed to laugh. 'You forget that Lucifer was said to be the most beautiful of all of God's angels and look where he ended up.'

Gerry bowed. 'Touché Madame!'

To steady her nerves, Mrs Swan took a sip from Gerry's glass. 'I must get on, the vision wants tea and a little boy wants hot chocolate.' She rose to her feet as Gerry stiffened suddenly. His hand reached out and firmly grasped her wrist.

'A child of about five years old?'

She looked down at his suddenly serious face in surprise. 'Aye, I shouldn't get involved with Nigel Sutherland if I was you, Gerry, he's a very volatile man.'

Gerry released Mrs Swan's wrist to pick up his glass. 'I don't want anything to do with Sutherland's schemes. You be careful of that man, he could easily destroy us all!' Draining his glass, Gerry donned his hat and overcoat and sauntered out of the Inn.

Full Disclosure

Throughout the entire drive, Caleb barely said a single word to his cousin. The jovial bantering that had existed as they left

Stirling Arms had quickly vanished as Caleb allowed the fresh horses to find their stride.

When Geoff tried to ask how long Caleb had known about Tony, his Lordship countered with his own question about why Geoff had left Caleb to sweat over his confession of his own sexuality. Trying to explain that Tony had sworn Geoff to secrecy seemed lame compared to his cousin's obvious anguish.

So the rest of the journey was made in silence. At the clearing just before the On the Rocks Inn, Caleb handed the reins across to his cousin before he checked the pistols in the holsters on his hips and jumped down from the phaeton.

'Caleb, Mr Cooper is right, this is a two man job,' Geoff pulled on his overcoat and checked the rifle behind his seat. Caleb checked over the horses to ensure they hadn't pushed them too hard getting there.

'I need you free to go for help if anything goes wrong. Even if I succeed we'll be on the run and when we get back to you, we'll need to be able to leave in an instant. There is no one I trust more than you to have at my back.'

Pressing his hand against his heart, Geoff was overcome with emotion. 'You unman me cousin!'

Laughing Caleb briefly reached up to grasp Geoff's hand. 'Just be alert for danger and ready to leave at a moment's notice. If we're not here in two hours, get yourself back to Stirling Manor.'

'I'm not leaving without you coz! I'll be here when you've rescued the Stirlings.' Tipping his hat further down his face Caleb disappeared into the woodlands.

Scouting For Entry

For a den of thieves, the security is absolutely shocking. Getting close to the Inn, let alone inside isn't a problem, as I walk around the outside of the On the Rocks unchallenged. Twice! The problem is I look too much like exactly what I am, an aristocrat. If we had more time, I could disguise myself and my breeding and just walk into the Inn unchallenged but there isn't time for that. I have to get Tony out immediately and surreptitiously. Caleb noted that there was one light shining upstairs and was the logical location to start his search.

He was debating the state of the rose trellis to get up to the first floor when a hand was placed upon his shoulder. Caleb grabbed the wrist and twisted as he spun around and drew out a pistol to press into the man's chest.

'Steady on Lord Delacourt, fire off your barker and we'll have more bandits upon us than either of us could handle.'

Releasing the man's wrist, Caleb peered closely at the stranger. 'Solitaire isn't it? Is this your local haunt?'

The Highwayman massaged his wrist. 'Nay, a friend of mine came to find me when he heard from the Innkeeper's wife of a most beautiful young man being held hostage and a small boy.'

'Tony and Aidan! So they are here!' Caleb uttered a sigh in relief. 'Do you want to tackle this from the inside? I can't enter without being noticed.'

Solitaire looked up at the rose trellis. 'No, I think the trellis is the best way for both of us to get inside. Anyone going upstairs from the inside would be suspicious and how would I explain myself to get into the room? The door will be locked. We need the element of surprise.'

Caleb glanced across to the first floor window. 'The window will be locked as well.'

Smiling, the Highwayman jangled a set of skeleton keys. 'I think I can help with that.'

Your Un-natural Bond

Once he'd enough to eat, Aidan picked up his mug of hot chocolate and climbed up onto the bed beside his sister. When Mrs Swan had brought in the tea and chocolate, she had poured the tea for Tony and placed the cup onto the bedside table close enough for her to reach it. As Tony wasn't eating, Nigel didn't untie her hands but she managed to drink her tea without spilling any of it.

In fact Nigel refused to look at her until he had finished his meal. Pushing his chair back from the table, Nigel ran a hand over his belly as he finally looked across at the siblings. Having finished his hot chocolate, Aidan had laid down with his head on Tony's lap and she tenderly stroked his hair. Letting out a huge belch, Nigel tossed down the remainder of his ale before he rose decisively to his feet.

Knowing full well that his eyes were greedily resting upon her, Tony refused to look up as she tenderly nursed her brother, not even when Nigel belched loudly once more.

'Ya avoiding looking at me, pretty buck?'

Finally looking up, Tony was frowning. 'If you're quiet, he'll sleep and soon you can be rid of us.'

Taking a step closer to the bed, Nigel loomed over the siblings. 'The bond between ya is devilishly un-natural.'

An exquisite eyebrow rose in surprise. 'I suppose the age difference makes me protective of my young brother or perhaps it is the lack of interest my step-mother has always shown to her own child. Unless you like incessant chatter or whining, please just let Aidan sleep.'

Nigel's lip curled in disgust. 'Incessant? What's that? Isn't that incest, ya know, funny business between family members?'

Tony tried very hard to not sigh. 'Incessant means non-stop, not indecent dealings between relations.' She also tried to not sound condescending but Nigel wasn't satisfied. He slapped her hard across the face. Aidan raised his head as his sister was rocked back against the pillows.

'Why do you keep hitting Tony?' asked the little boy.

'I find y'r brother insolent and disrespectful! It's time he was taught a lesson.'

Teach Ya A Lesson

For the first time, Tony displayed any hint of fear but she wasn't about to grovel to placate this bully. 'What do you want from me Sutherland? You've abducted me like a child, I'm trussed up like a chicken and there's nothing I can do to protect myself or my brother. Do you want me get on my knees and beg forgiveness for being born?'

A very wicked, diabolical smile appeared on Nigel's face. 'Oh I want ya on y'r knees all right pretty boy.' He took a step back to remove his jacket before pulling off his course shirt. 'I want y'r soft rose bud lips around me cock!'

Even though she had discussed this with Duncan, Tony still flushed in embarrassment. Swallowing hard, she tried to control her rising fear. 'Lips conceal teeth, aren't you afraid I'll bite your most intimate flesh?'

'Most intimate flesh?' Sitting down on the edge of the bed to pull off his boots, Nigel gave an ugly laugh. 'My God, ya really are a Nancy boy! Let me tell ya that if ya bite me cock, then I'll flip ya over and enter a hole that doesn't have any teeth!'

In shock, the colour drained from Tony's face. 'So you are a sodomite!'

'Not really but a hole is a hole!' Nigel threw his boots under the table.

As Tony moved uncomfortably on the bed, Aidan screwed up his nose and his hand slid towards the sword on his hip. 'You can't do that, nothing is supposed to be put up your bottom!' Frowning as he thought about it Aidan added, 'and you shouldn't put your pee pee in Tony's mouth. That is rude!'

Fighting against rising panic, Tony tried to keep her voice even. 'Aidan cut me free.'

'With that toy?' Nigel laughed, running his hand across his hairy belly. Afraid now are ya, pretty boy? Ya ever been with another man, me pretty buck?'

'Of course not!' Tony retorted as Aidan drew out his sword, which revealed to be not a toy at all but an ornate dagger. He sawed through the ropes around Tony's ankles as Nigel rose to his feet and drew off his trousers.

'Ya been with a woman yet, pretty boy?' Nigel threw his trousers and underwear over the nearest chair. Looking up at him, Tony's eyes widened in horror and she hurriedly averted her gaze from his overwhelming nakedness.

'Not that it's any of your business but no I haven't.' Tony swallowed hard in desperation as the dagger cut through the rope freeing her feet. *Nigel seems even larger and more menacing without his clothes, especially with a rampaging erection.*

As Aidan started to cut through the rope around Tony's wrists, Nigel stroked himself absently. 'What's wrong boy? Never seen one as impressive as this? Ya ever masturbated, pretty buck?'

You Deserve To Be Whipped!

Blushing, Tony refused to look up at him. 'No, I haven't.' she tried to move further away from Nigel without hampering her brother's efforts to free her. Nigel, though, wasn't about to let her get away from him and grabbed her by the ankle. Unfortunately it was her damaged ankle and as she cried out, Tony fought to retain consciousness.

'Get on y'r knees, me Lord, I'm going to further y'r education.'

Tony shuddered as Nigel ran his hand up her leg. 'Please Sutherland, don't do this.' Her tone was low and in control even though she wanted to scream. When Nigel's hand travelled up Tony's thigh, Aidan paused in sawing through the binds around Tony's wrists to threaten Nigel with the dagger.

'Remove your hand sir, or I'll cut it off.'

Staring down at the earnest five year old Nigel burst into laughter. 'Are ya challenging me to a duel, me Lord?'

Raising his chin, Aidan looked at Nigel in disgust. 'Duels are for men of honour, what you deserve is to be whipped!'

Nigel laughed. 'Big talk Lordling! But if anyone is going to do any whipping, it'll be me!' Knocking the dagger out of Aidan's hand, it fell just out of reach and Nigel smacked the boy across the face causing him to fall off the bed.

Tony screamed out her brother's name before turning her fury upon Nigel. 'If you've hurt Aidan I will kill you!' With her hands still tied, Tony attacked using her feet. She thrust her feet into his face, forcing Nigel to recoil away from her. Her next kick hit Nigel in the chest, which momentarily winded him and meant he was unprepared as Tony thrust her feet into his groin.

The language that exploded from Nigel was colourful and as he clutched his privates in agony, it gave Tony time to swing over the edge of the bed to look for her brother. Aidan popped his head up to show Tony that he was all right. Nigel was still swearing his head off.

'Jesus fucking Christ! Ya fight like a fucking girl!' Nigel's face was extremely red and he was sweating profusely.

Aidan couldn't take any more yelling and to Nigel's last accusation, he blurted out, 'That's because Tony is a girl!'

Nigel's Realisation

Silence reigned for several minutes as that information was processed. Aidan clamped his hand over his mouth but it was too late to retract his statement. With a violent punch to the temple, Nigel silenced the boy who slid unconscious to the floor. Tony's breathing quickened as she stared wide eyed at Nigel. He was becoming even redder in the face as realisation began to sink in.

'No, that's not possible! No woman could've matched me in a sword fight!' Taking a step backwards towards the table, Nigel turned to pick up the sharp blade before moving quickly forward again to grasp Tony by her shoulder making it impossible for her to escape.

He tore her waist coat open, popping the buttons. Nigel ripped away the cravat from Tony's throat before he raised a slightly unsteady hand to surround her neck as he ran his blade through her shirt and tore it apart. When Tony tried to struggle, Nigel tightened his fingers around her throat.

She swallowed with difficulty as Nigel laid bare her breasts. They were exquisite and her chest heaved as she tried to drag air into her lungs and her breathing quickened in fear. Nigel's hand slid from her throat to caress Tony's breasts, marvelling at how the tailoring of her clothes had concealed such perfect, full globes of flesh. Her hands still bound, tightened into fists as she fought against the need to vomit at Nigel's touch. Finally he raised his eyes, blazing in desire to her face.

'Y'r not a freak are ya? Ya not hiding a cock down here are ya?' Crudely Nigel slid his hand between Tony's thighs causing her to gasp in horror.

'No! I'm female, I assure you!' but her word was not enough for Nigel and as he began to salivate in excitement, he slit his knife down the front of Tony's breeches and underwear before tearing them off her completely. He dropped the shredded clothes onto the floor as he stared hungrily down at her.

'What else are ya hiding, me Lord?' Nigel's last words were said in mockery as he flipped Tony onto her stomach.

I Have Plans For You!

The blade tore through Tony's waistcoat to reveal the chestnut red plait that had laid hidden and Nigel bent over her to raise her hair to his nostrils.

'So ya have some female weaknesses,' his blade ran through the back of Tony's shirt and Nigel pushed the material out of the way so that he could caress his big meaty paw down her alabaster skin until he cupped her bare bottom. 'Nice, very nice!' Nigel knelt down to bite into the fleshy part of her backside causing tears of shame and disgust to form in Tony's eyes.

'Please don't sodomise me!' She begged as Nigel licked where his teeth had left a mark on her flesh. She felt a brief moment of relief as Nigel rose back to his feet and flipped her over again. Chuckling, he cut through the rope around her wrists and pulled off the shredded remains of her shirt and waist coat.

'I had planned to make a man out of ya, now I'm gunna have much more fun making ya a woman!' He kept Tony from kicking him by imprisoning her legs beneath his large hands as he loomed over her.

Perspiration beaded on Tony's skin in fear as she thought desperately, *If only I can get the knife away from Nigel.* Seeing her eyes resting briefly on the blade, Nigel threw it onto the pile of clothes accumulating on the floor and out of Tony's reach.

'I'm sure my father would pay you even more if I'm returned unmolested.' Her words came out of parched lips as Nigel began to lower his body down upon hers.

'There is no amount of money that ya could offer that would stop me from completely humiliating ya!' He forced her thighs apart, unmoved by Tony's fists thumping hard against his chest and arms.

The glint of Aidan's dagger on the end of the bed caught her eyes but to reach it she needed to be able to sit up and that meant distracting Nigel as he clumsily, roughly ran his hands all over her body.

'If you compromise me, my father...'

Nigel laughed as he paused and lifted his head from her breasts to look into her eyes. 'What? He'd force me to marry ya? Me and the daughter of an Earl? Like that would ever happen! I'll make a deal with ya... if ya beg...'

Tony saw a glimmer of hope. 'You won't rape me?'

His laugh was ugly. 'Nah, if ya beg, I'll make it slow and good. Fight me and it'll be hard and fast. Both are good for me!' Nigel moved one hand from holding Tony down to take his cock and slide it with purpose between her thighs. That allowed Tony enough movement to lurch forward and sideways as she desperately tried to reach Aidan's dagger.

When Nigel threw Tony once more onto her back, she had Aidan's dagger in her hand. He was too busy with one hand to hold Tony down on the bed and his other hand trying to ease his cock through her kicking legs to notice the blade in her hand. Crowing in victory, Nigel finally looked up as Tony thrust the dagger straight towards his heart. Nigel's crowing turned into a blood curdling scream.

Up The Rose Trellis

The trellis withstood the weight of the two men as Caleb led Solitaire up through the climbing roses and along the unstable ledge that allowed them to inch their way to the window. Caleb moved past the window to allow the Highwayman access with his lock picking tools. He had just removed his tool kit when abruptly the window opened from the inside.

Even as they had scaled the trellis they could hear Tony's pleas for Nigel to stop as he tore the clothes from her body. Aidan, unnoticed, had recovered consciousness and now his frightened little face appeared as he opened the window intending to scream for help but he gave a squeak of recognition when he saw Solitaire and Caleb waiting outside on the ledge.

As he climbed through the portal, Solitaire pressed his finger against his own lips and nodding, Aidan clamped a hand over his own mouth. Silently Solitaire pointed to Aidan and then under the table as he headed to the door to stop Nigel's escape or anyone entering from inside the Inn. Obediently the little boy hid under the table as Caleb also slipped silently into the room.

His Lordship's stomach tightened in horror as he watched as a naked Nigel threw a naked Tony back down on the bed and started to mount her.

Disabling A Rapist

When Tony thrust Aidan's dagger towards Nigel's heart, Caleb had silently come up behind him and putting Nigel in a headlock, dragged him backwards off Tony. The dagger missed Nigel, who passed out due to lack of oxygen from Caleb's choke hold. Caleb lowered Nigel to the floor and for a moment was unable to raise his eyes to Tony as she scrambled to her feet and hunted through the pile of her clothing for anything that was remotely wearable.

As Caleb had pulled Nigel off Tony, he had forced himself to observe carefully. He had to know if they had been too late, if Nigel had succeeded in penetrating Tony's virginity. What he saw, relieved him but it also took his breath away. *If I had found Tony's face completely captivating, then her naked body is exquisite!*

Managing to swallow down his lust, Caleb removed his overcoat and handed it to Tony as her own clothes were completely ruined. Blushing as she slipped into it and tied up the belt, she could not raise her eyes to meet his as she thanked him.

From the table Tony picked up her scabbard and sword and slipped it back on over her hips. Caleb pulled Aidan's dagger out of the bedding where it had ended up and as Aidan came out from under the table to hug Tony, Caleb slid the dagger back into the scabbard on the boy's hips.

Let's Go!

Solitaire glanced away from where he had his ear pressed against the door, 'We need to move, my Lords!'

71

Bending down to pick up Tony's cravat off the floor, Caleb swung Aidan up to stand on the bed. 'Climb onto my back, Aidan and Solitaire will tie you in place with Tony's cravat.'

They worked quickly until Aidan was securely attached to Caleb and Solitaire turned his attention to the weapons on the table. *I'm not technically stealing but disarming a dangerous man.* So he slipped the pistols into his own overcoat before using some of Nigel's own rope to tie him to the bed leg.

With the boy on his back, Caleb slipped out of the window and along the ledge. Tony limped after him and Solitaire hooked her crutches over his shoulder and followed them out of the Inn through the window. There wasn't a lot of time to make their escape as Caleb had only caused Nigel to black out and hadn't snapped his neck. *I had been tempted, having heard Tony begging for Nigel to not rape her but I know that when I finally get the opportunity to settle with Nigel, it will be face to face.*

Scaling down the trellis, Caleb reached up to assist Tony down. She was a little embarrassed by his attentiveness but they had more important issues to worry about. Solitaire had barely reached the ground and handed Tony her crutches when they heard Nigel roar in anger as he came to.

If We Can't Run... Then We Must Hide

Caleb had hoped that they would have more of a head start before Nigel alerted everyone in On the Rocks to their flight. Although Tony could move quite fast on her crutches, it could not in any way be considered as running.

'We're not going to make it to the phaeton before they start hunting us.' Caleb said quietly to Solitaire, who nodded.

'I've been thinking about that, my Lord. If we head west instead, there's an old barn you can hold up in while I double back and bring your cousin to you.'

'Won't that be one of the first places they will look?' asked Caleb as they heard the sound of pursuit behind them. Solitaire smiled, his teeth easily seen in the rising full moon.

'Maybe so, my Lord, but it is well protected.'

The Barn

More than that the Highwayman wasn't prepared to say until they finally approached the barn. Behind them, they could hear men on foot and horseback searching the countryside for the escapees. In front of them, they were met by a deep throaty growl that quickly became a vicious barking. A dog, the size of a small pony, stood in front of the barn and told them in no uncertain terms that they were not welcome.

That was until Solitaire began to whistle. It was a sweet tune that reminded Tony of one of their Irish Grooms. The dog immediately whimpered in pleasure and thumped his tail happily.

'Hello Benji, how are you old boy?' Solitaire removed a napkin from one of his pockets which held some of the scraps of food he had collected from the table at the Inn. 'I've got some friends I need you to protect for me.' Solitaire patted the hound as he fed him.

'What about the owner?' Caleb asked, allowing the dog to sniff his hand before he peered into the barn.

'An elderly couple, who are struggling to keep the farm going. Both are quite deaf but Benji and I are old friends.' Solitaire led them inside and Benji followed just in case there were any more handouts. As the Highwayman quietly searched the barn for any dangers, Tony untied Aidan from Caleb's back and checked her brother over for any injuries. When he whined, 'I'm all right!' she released him and Aidan ran after the two men to explore the barn.

There were no horses, the hens had ascended up into the rafters to roost but there was an assortment of other animals Aidan could see by the muted moonlight that streamed in through the open window in the loft. A cow, two pigs, a goat and half a dozen sheep that really needed shearing. The men were interested in making certain the barn was safe, Aidan was interested in making friends with the animals but Tony, slipping Aidan's dagger out of his scabbard, was interested in what she needed to do to protect her brother from the elements.

There was a mountain of bales of hay piled up along one wall of the barn and slicing through a bale, Tony spread it thickly in a pile across the floor. The men returned as Tony was valiantly hauling another bale to place it beside the spread hay.

'Are you thinking of a cocoon for Lord Aidan?' Solitaire asked, easily picking up another bale to place where Tony indicated as she was struggling on her damaged ankle.

'Yes, even though we may not be here long, I must keep him warm.'

Caleb glanced over his shoulder at the seemingly robust little boy who was happily feeding straw to the cow but assumed that Tony must know her brother best and began hauling bales of hay.

I'll Come Back For You

With the mountain of bales as one side of the square, the other three sides were made up of three bales each with the spread hay lining the middle of the square.

'I'll be as quick as I can, my Lord.' Solitaire wiped a handkerchief across his brow. 'If I fall into any trouble, I'll lead them away from here.'

Caleb nodded, *I'm not too worried about Solitaire as I assume the Highwayman can take care of himself in a sticky situation. I have left Geoff with only a shotgun to defend himself but I hope my cousin has enough common sense to get the hell out of there if he was in any danger.* 'Good luck.' Caleb held out his hand to Solitaire and the Highwayman was so surprised that he took it.

'I was born lucky, my Lord, take care of the Stirlings.' Solitaire signalled for Benji to follow him outside to stand guard over the barn until he returned.

The Straw Castle

Aidan came running across to Tony as she unbuckled her scabbard before untying the overcoat so that she could slip her belt on over her naked hips. She secured the coat shut again as Aidan wrapped his arms around her waist.

'Can I go out and play with Benji?'

Tony stroked her hand against his hair. 'Not right now, Little Bear. We're going to play a little game of hide and seek with this wonderful castle that his Lordship has created for us.' Tony lifted Aidan up and over the bales of hay.

'Are you coming in too Lord Caleb?' Aidan held out his hand to assist Tony over the bales to join him.

Caleb mounted the hill of bales of hay behind them. 'No, I'm going to stay on guard up here while you hide.' He drew out his pistols and laid them down on the bales on either side of him. Laying Aidan down on the bed of straw, Tony slipped her arms out of the sleeves of the overcoat. Caleb felt his breath catch in his chest when Tony knelt down beside her brother and undoing the overcoat, she spread it over both of them as she lay down and drew Aidan into her arms.

The brief glimpse of Tony's naked figure in the moonlight froze Caleb in his position. *I know that if I move I could end up doing something that would be very erotic but very inappropriate for the time and place.* Swallowing hard to control his rising desire, Caleb tried to focus his thoughts upon the danger they were currently facing. *It's going to be a long night. A very long and cold night!* With the delicious image of Tony's luscious, naked curves now etched permanently on his corneas, Caleb reminded himself, *I am a gentleman! I pray that Solitaire returns speedily before the cool night air, or lust gets the better of my resolve.*

75

Benji Does His Duty

When Benji began to bark sometime later, Caleb's head snapped up and his eyes opened. He hadn't been asleep but by closing his eyes he could focus all his attention on listening to the noises outside. It had also given him time to run through several alternatives for escape if Solitaire or Geoff didn't appear. As Benji's barking remained savage, Caleb silently slid his hands over each pistol and raised them to point at the barn door.

'Leave be Jacob before the mongrel decides to have a piece of ya! There's no way that dog would have let strangers get this close,' said one of the men outside.

Jacob hesitated, 'Do ya really wanna be the one to tell Sutherland that we left some place unsearched?'

'Why are ya so desperate to get bitten? Are ya so excited by how beautiful Nigel said the lass is that ya want first crack at her?' Caleb steadied the aim of his pistols as he heard Jacob thump his friend.

'Let's just try the side door and no more of y'r lip Samuel.' The two men rounded the barn but Benji wasn't tethered and placed himself between them and the door again. His barking became louder and more threatening. Neither of the men outside were prepared to get bitten or mauled over a woman they hadn't even seen yet.

'Come on Jacob, we're better off looking for a vehicle. They'd want to get as far away from here as possible.' Samuel tugged on his friend's sleeve and Benji continued to bark as they walked away, promising them more of the same if they ever returned.

Momentary Reprieve

Letting out a sigh of relief, Caleb hadn't even realised that he had been holding his breath. He lowered his weapons back onto the bales of hay beside him and silently promised, *I'm going to get Benji the biggest steak I can find once this is all over!* Caleb glanced down at the siblings huddled together under his overcoat as he heard a small voice say, 'Is Benji angry with us for being here?'

'No Little Bear. Solitaire asked him to protect us and he's just being a good watch dog.' Tony shifted slightly and managed to sit up without uncovering Aidan and yet still covered herself with the overcoat. From the front anyway. Caleb felt his breathing quicken at the sight of Tony's naked back in the pale moonlight.

'My Lord…' Tony started to say, causing a twisted smile to appear on Caleb's lips.

'I think in these circumstances it would be safer to dispense with titles,' he suggested.

There was a pause before Tony continued, 'I've been thinking about what we can do if Solitaire doesn't return.'

Caleb sighed, 'We can cross that bridge when we get to it.' *I'm a little surprised that her thoughts are on the future rather than the horror she had just escaped.* A beautiful, bewitching smile of understanding appeared on Tony's face.

'I'm a worrier, my Lord, about the unknown ahead rather than what has already come to pass and therefore cannot be changed. We'd be safe enough here with Benji to stand guard if you need to leave us. Whether to find suitable transportation or if it is necessary to rescue your cousin.'

When Caleb didn't immediately answer, Tony continued, 'You could leave me one of your guns, I'm not as good with pistols as I am with a sword but I'm sure I could wound anyone who tried to enter the barn.'

Unable to help himself, Caleb laughed. 'Remind me to announce myself if it turns out I do have to leave at any time.'

'That wouldn't be necessary,' his eyebrows rose in surprise at her words until she explained, 'Benji would tell us the difference.'

Solitaire's Return

As he chuckled, Caleb heard the sound of someone approaching outside. 'Lie down Tony or you'll get cold.' Although he picked up one of his pistols, Caleb was not too worried as he heard a familiar whistling and Benji whimpered in pleasure. Even so Caleb aimed the pistol at the barn door as it slowly opened.

'Please don't blow my head off, my Lord,' begged Solitaire as he stepped cautiously through the portal. At the sound of his voice, Tony sat up again.

'So now what do you suggest seeing you didn't find Geoff?' asked Caleb as Solitaire entered alone and removed his hat.

'I'll widen my search and explore the possibility that your cousin has been taken hostage by Nigel's friends. If I'm unable to locate or free your cousin, I'll return with a pair of horses. There's an old gig in the stables that'll get you back to Stirling Manor while I continue to look for your cousin.'

The Highwayman cleared his throat. 'You need to cover up, my Lady, before you're the one with pneumonia.' He suggested tactfully as all of her back was exposed to the moonlight and the overcoat had slipped to reveal one shapely calf. Following his gaze, Tony drew the coat over her bare legs before she raised blushing eyes up to meet Caleb's warm gaze. As her colour deepened, Caleb looked away from the delectable curve of her naked back and the effect she had upon his libido. *I had never been subject to rampaging lust but there is something so undeniable about the emotions that Tony stirs within me.*

Lowering her eyes, Tony sighed. 'Is that what those men were referring to? Do I truly inspire such carnal emotions in complete strangers?' She tried to cover up more of her sinful flesh without exposing her brother to the cool night air. When Caleb was unable to answer her, Solitaire shrugged expressively.

'Men are lust filled animals.'

Glancing from Solitaire to Caleb and back again, Tony asked, 'All of them?'

'Some are better trained than others,' the Highwayman admitted, shrugging at Caleb as he didn't know what or where Tony was taking the conversation.

'And Papa wants me to be exposed to that degradation by forcing me to wear female attire?'

'To be fair, my Lady,' said Solitaire, 'men are lusting after you because you're naked, not because you were dressed as a woman or a man.'

Tony's eyebrows rose. 'Does that make it any better?'

'No my Lady,' Solitaire shook his head, 'it means we need to get you somewhere safe... really fast!'

Climbing down from his perch on the mountain of hay bales, Caleb rubbed his chilled hands together. 'If we don't hear from you in two hours, I'll find another way to get the Stirlings home.'

Solitaire cast a swift scrutinising glance over Caleb, 'in the meantime, you need to keep warm my Lord. Being chilled to the bone won't make it easy for you to handle a horse or pull the trigger if necessary.' He glanced significantly at the hay castle and the siblings and Caleb followed his gaze.

'No, I won't compromise Tony!'

'Put the boy between you and think noble thoughts. You'll be no good to save anyone if you're frozen to the marrow.' Solitaire headed towards the barn door. Caleb wanted to yell after him that it was impossible but he could already feel the cold seeping into his flesh. The Highwayman vanished into the shadows and Caleb took a deep breath as he holstered both his pistols.

Shared Body Heat

'I promise I won't bite you if you don't bite me.' Tony's attempt at humour caused Caleb to groan.

'You shouldn't joke about your reputation Tony! Roaming around in male attire, everything that has happened tonight, it's all going to impact upon any chance you may have to take your rightful place in society.'

With her head tilted slightly on one side, Tony considered his words for a moment. 'I don't know if I want to be a part of a society that would lay the blame for our current predicament solely upon me because I dress like a man.' She extended one hand out to Caleb but he didn't need any assistance to scale the bales.

Sighing, Tony reached out to take his hand into hers anyway. 'My Lord, I need to know how cold you are. If I place Aidan between us and you're too cold, you pose a very real risk to dropping his core temperature.' She explained. 'As a baby we nearly lost him to a lung infection, that's why I'm so careful about keeping him warm.'

Sitting down beside her, Caleb already began to feel warmer but he thought, *I'm not certain if it is the protective walls of the hay bales that are responsible or being so close to Tony.* Especially when she slipped one hand into his jacket and against his shirt. Tony raised concerned eyes to meet his as his chest heaved in an attempt to drag in air for his tortured lungs.

'You're already cold, my Lord. Lie down behind me and I'll try to warm up your hands.' She lay down on her side, with Aidan curled up in front of her but Caleb hesitated.

'Tony, this is inappropriate.'

In response she sighed deeply. 'And is it appropriate for me to let my rescuer become so frozen that he's incapable of completing his rescue mission?'

'No, but…' The overcoat slipped slightly to reveal one of Tony's bare shoulders as she looked back at him.

'Are you a gentleman?' She demanded.

Caleb swallowed hard on the lump in his throat that was attempting to choke him. 'Yes!'

'Then as a gentleman, do you swear to not take advantage of the situation and compromise me?'

'Yes!' This time his voice was a little firmer and with his jaw clenched, Caleb lay down behind Tony and she threw some of the overcoat over him as well.

Lying there, pressed up against Tony's back, Caleb was as stiff as a board and not from being cold. He didn't know what to do with his hands but Tony had a more pressing problem to deal with first.

'Your pistol is sticking into the small of my back, can you please move it?' Apologising Caleb shifted slightly so that he could remove the offending weapon and laid it on the top of the straw bale behind him. 'Put your arms around me and I'll try to warm up your hands,' Tony added.

After a moment of hesitation, Caleb slid his arms around her waist and Tony laid her hands over his pressing them against her bare stomach so that he could draw on her body's heat. With her plaited hair caressing against his cheek, Caleb closed his eyes and took a deep breath as his body began to relax.

I know it is dangerous to accept her Innocent offer of warmth as I can already detect certain, not so Innocent parts of my body reacting to the allure and closeness of her naked figure. Oh, the intoxicating scent of her body, the hint of vanilla, almost undetectable at arm's length, but pressed hard up against her sensual body, the scent fills my senses. If it becomes too much for me to withstand, I resolve that I will turn away from Tony so that my rampaging desires are not evident to her. For now, though, I am content to let her warmth slowly chase the chill out of my body.

How I Envy Him

Stirring, half asleep, Aidan reached out to this sister. 'Tony?' His voice was a little muffled under the overcoat. She removed one hand from Caleb's to brush against her brother's hair.

'I'm here, Little Bear, go back to sleep.'

Mumbling inaudibly, Aidan reached out to lace his fingers through her shirt having forgotten that she wasn't wearing one and he brushed against her bare flesh. Not realising what he was doing, Aidan's mouth latched upon one of her breasts and Tony's body stiffened in surprise. Caleb raised his head, afraid that he had done something to upset her. *I hadn't realised until this moment my thumb had been caressing against her silken skin.*

'What is it Tony?'

She dragged in a shuddering breath. 'Aidan's suckling on my…my breast.'

'Does he suck his thumb?' Caleb slipped one of his hands from under Tony's to feel his way up to cup Tony's breast as his other hand covered Aidan's right hand.

'Yes he does.'

Caleb eased the boy's head back from Tony's nipple and placed Aidan's own thumb into his mouth. As Aidan curled up happily enough against his sister, Caleb removed his handkerchief from his jacket pocket and wiped Aidan's saliva from Tony's nipple.

Replacing his handkerchief back into his pocket, Caleb was privately pleased that his hands were not shaking. Tony's breathing wasn't quite so steady.

'Thank you.' As he hesitated about what to do with his hands, Tony secured them once more between her own. A deep sigh ran through Caleb's body as warmth spread throughout his veins.

'Oh how I envy young Aidan.' Caleb murmured against her hair. A shudder of pleasure increased Tony's heart rate at the sound of his rich, husky voice against her ear.

'Oh? His ability to sleep through all this drama?' She was surprised that her voice was barely more than a whisper.

Caleb chuckled. 'No, that's not what I meant!' As the implications of his words finally sunk in, Tony gasped in surprise and she was glad that Caleb couldn't see her properly as she was blushing all over at the very thought of Caleb's lips caressing her breasts.

You Need To Wake Up

A low sensual moan woke Tony. *What surprises me, though, is the fact that the moan had apparently emanated from me.* Blinking several times in the dim moonlight, she tried to focus upon what had woken her. *An erotic dream. Thoughts and feelings that I have never before imagined.* Dragging in a deep breath, her mind cleared enough for her to realise that the erotic thoughts and feelings weren't the result of a dream but in fact reality.

Caleb's hands were no longer secured beneath hers around her waist, but tenderly caressing her breasts. As he alternated kisses and words of love against her exposed neck and shoulders, Tony felt a strange sensation she had never felt before in the pit of her stomach... and lower. *His touch, his kisses, his words are reverent as Caleb promises what I had always thought impossible to obtain. True love! A perfect love! Devotion and worship! A need so great that it burns through to our very souls. It is intoxicating, bewitching and I could easily fall under its spell but somewhere in the back of my mind screams the nagging mantra that it is an impossible fantasy as I believe that Caleb is already married.*

Besides which, as the nagging mantra becomes louder, I am aware of something long and hard pressed into the small of my back again. 'Lord Delacourt, you have to wake up, your pistol is pressing into my back again.' She was taken by surprise when her hips jerked involuntarily as Caleb rolled her nipples between his forefingers and thumbs. His words of adoration and undying devotion as well as his soft lips against her shoulders continued unabated.

'My Lord please...' Tony felt herself weakening against the before unknown pleasures but Aidan had begun to stir at the sound of her voice.

'Say my name, Tony, please.' His hips rocked sensuously against her backside causing the long, hard object to press more insistently into her flesh.

'Caleb, your pistol…' Was all that she could get out as his fingers once again tweaked her nipples.

Realising that she wasn't getting through to him, Tony reached behind her to move his pistol herself. When her fingers fell upon the long hard object, her eyes widened and her breath caught in her throat as it wasn't metal and it was very much attached to Caleb. Surprising herself, Tony didn't immediately snatch her hand away but allowed her fingers to lightly explore the length of Caleb's erection. Although trapped beneath the confines of his trousers, it was still impressive as well as responsive to her gentle touch.

Caleb moaned against her shoulder blade. 'Oh God, yes Tony… see how much my body aches for you.' Slowly he caressed one hand down her stomach and hesitantly pressed his fingers through the curls at the apex of her thighs. 'Do you want me… as much as I want you?' One long sensual finger slid through the damp lips of her labia and circled her clitoris. Tony's hips jerked into his hand as she cried out in pleasure.

'Oh God! Oh Caleb! I don't want you to stop but please you mustn't touch me like that. Please Caleb, you're married!' His hands stilled and he raised his head but he didn't release Tony.

'I'm…I'm what? What made you think I was married?'

Tony sobbed. 'The mare you bought is for your wife isn't it?' *Every nerve ending is screaming for me to let Caleb continue pleasuring me but not if he is a married man. I must stick to what principles I do have.* Groaning in disbelief, Caleb said, 'Georgiana is my sister. Her husband Miles is a good man but he's no judge of horses.' *She is holding herself so still, I'm not certain that Tony is still breathing.*

'You're not married?' She didn't seem to understand that he had already answered that question.

84

'I'm not married Tony.' Chuckling as he placed a kiss against her bare shoulder Caleb added, 'Does that remove your objections for my actions?' Very tenderly he moved his finger against her clitoris. A whimper escaped from Tony but she reached down to lay her hand over his.

'Oh yes!' Tony swallowed hard. 'Please Caleb you must stop. For your sake!'

Please Let Me Explain

That captured his attention more than anything else had. 'My sake? Is it because of Sutherland?'

Tony shook her head. 'No please release me, I can't think straight when you touch me like this. I want to turn to face you to explain. Oh Caleb, that feels so good but I don't want Aidan to hear us. I've heard Charlotte when she and Papa were…'

Understanding what Tony meant, Caleb carefully removed his hands and drew back slightly. *The reason for being so careful is that any further stimulation could cause Tony to orgasm and that might not be quiet.* True to her word, Tony turned over to face Caleb but she surprised him by caressing her trembling hand down his cheek. Then stunned Caleb into silence by kissing him passionately on the lips. When he began to respond, Tony permitted it, enjoyed it and when he reached out to lace his fingers through hers, she felt her heart swell in love.

Sighing Tony finally broke off the kiss. 'Thank you Caleb, I thought I'd like kissing you and I was right.'

Surprise loosened Caleb's tongue. 'Like?' *I am a little hurt. For me, that kiss, had been the nectar of the Gods!*

Tony uttered a small sob, 'Please bear with me, you've scrambled my brains with your words and your touch, I can only talk in absolutes and not flowery descriptions. When this is over, when we're safe, I'll try and be better at explaining my feelings.'

Smiling Caleb raised her fingers laced through his, to his lips. 'Sorry if I've addled your wit.'

'You have not,' He was answered by a smile in return. 'I never thought I'd meet a man who truly made me feel like a woman. That actually made me glad that I am a woman, a first for me. The moment we met, I liked you. It hurt more than I was prepared for when I thought you were buying the mare for your wife. It was an irrational feeling for the role that I had been playing for so long.' Revealing her feelings was harder than she thought it would be and she had to pause to take several deep breaths.

Understanding her conflict, Caleb tenderly brushed his hand through her hair. 'Men can feel jealousy and disappointment too you know.'

'But I barely knew you! How could I be so possessive over a stranger? It isn't logical!'

Unable to help himself, Caleb smiled, 'Love isn't necessarily logical. The heart wants what the heart wants.'

'What exactly does that mean?' A frown marred Tony's brow. 'That the brain can be overruled by a whim of the heart?'

'I knew the moment I laid eyes on you when you entered the Stirling Arms that I was prepared to die for you, to kill for you!'

Tony's eyes widened in surprise at his declaration. 'Had you discovered my true identity even then?'

'No.'

'Then you thought you had fallen in love with a man?'

Caleb smiled. 'I admit you gave me several heart searching hours as I tried to work out if I had ever truly known myself at all. It was illogical that I would feel this way for a man when I have never been attracted to men before.'

'Ergo I couldn't be a man?'

'It wasn't that simple, especially when your servants and the villagers maintain a protective facade over your identity. There were small clues but it wasn't until I laid my heart bare to

Reverend Gray that he laid my fears to rest about your masquerade.'

'What clues?'

Caleb's eyebrows rose. 'I thought you were going to tell me how cooling my lust is for my sake and not yours?'

Tracing a finger along his arm, Tony said, 'Tell me what clues gave you doubts about me being a man and I'll explain why I wanted you to stop.'

'Blackmail my elfling?'

Blushing, Tony laughed. 'No, I just need time to cool down a little as you've left me fighting for control.'

'Really? I look forward to helping you lose control more often!' Her gasp of pleasure was all the answer he needed.

Pausing to collect his thoughts, Caleb instinctively drew Tony into his embrace and she willingly laid her head against his shoulder.

'There was too much tolerance from the Innkeeper and the villagers over your game with Cooper's daughters. When Sutherland raised an objection, Cooper should have perhaps told you that you were too old for such games to be seemly. How defensive you were in protecting the girls against Sutherland's sexual advances. If you were a man, Cooper wouldn't have asked for my cousin and I to rescue you when Sutherland followed you. The need inside me to protect you was overwhelming. The way you were completely comfortable sitting side saddle on the mare.'

A frown sat upon Tony's brow. 'That was Charlotte's insistence that I learn to ride like a Lady for when I'm presented in London when the season opens. At the Inn, though, something I said was an indication to you that we were the children of the Earl of Stirling. What was it?' She slid her hand inside his jacket to lay against his heart.

'When I met your father in London to discuss the colt and other matters; I had offered him a drink. The Earl refused and explained his reason for abstaining. You mentioned the same fact when refusing to drink with Sutherland.'

'What other things did you discuss?'

Caleb hesitated for a moment, *I'm not certain that this is the right time to reveal the Earl's master plan for his daughter's future.* 'By a chance remark of mine the Earl learnt that I was in the same position he is currently in, being pressured to find a wife…'

Raising her head, Tony felt her cheeks ablaze. 'So Papa was going to sell me just like the colt?'

'Not at all,' Caleb said calmly and quietly as Aidan stirred at the sound of indignation in his sister's voice. 'He simply suggested that I spend a day or two at the Manor to become reacquainted with his daughter and see if there was a chance of us being compatible. You should know Tony that your father would never do anything to hurt you.'

A sigh answered him. 'I also know that he cannot withstand the barrage of female relatives hounding him to see me married off. Including Charlotte.'

To Leave Here As A Free Man

For a moment they laid there in silence and Caleb watched as the moonlight reflected in Tony's eyes. She dragged in a deep breath before letting it out very slowly. 'I asked you to stop touching me so intimately because I want you to leave this barn a free man.' There was a knot building in her throat which she tried to swallow down before continuing, 'if… if you compromised my… purity, shall we call it, my father would force you to marry me. If it was only lust you felt for me and it was satisfied once you had taken me then you would be stuck with a wife you didn't love. This way, as a free man, once the scandal has passed, we can get to know each other without any expectations. If it proves to be more than just… just lust then perhaps there could be a future for us.'

Even in the dim light, Caleb knew that she was blushing and tenderly caressed her cheek. 'I admit I was caught up in the moment of passion but I don't think I would have allowed it to go that far. Your first time shouldn't be in a barn or with your baby brother present.'

Tony's breathing had quickened as she trailed her fingers down his body until they rested over his erection. Caleb's breath caught in a hitch and he tried valiantly to suppress the moan that rose to his lips.

'That suggested that the situation may have been beyond your control,' she added.

Dragging in a shuddering breath to steady himself, Caleb carefully drew her hand away from his erection. 'Please don't do that or I'll disgrace myself.' He tried to laugh but it came out more like a choke.

Tony's eyes widened in surprise. 'Just the touch of my hand excites you?'

This time Caleb managed to laugh properly. 'My beautiful elfling, just the mere thought of you excites me! I was… I was afraid that you wanted to stop because it reminded you too much of Sutherland.' *If we're going to lay our hearts bare, I want Tony to know my fears.*

'I didn't like him, didn't like what he was going to force me to endure. I like you, I liked the way you touched me, kissed me. I didn't feel in danger. The words you whispered seemed genuine when you spoke of love, devotion and pleasure, not punishment. You awoke within me a desire, a passion that I never thought I would ever find. But I didn't want you to be trapped if those feelings were only on my side.'

Caleb let out a sigh of relief. 'They're not one sided but you were right to stop us. You're in a vulnerable position and I shouldn't have given in to the temptation of your nakedness. I had given my word as a gentleman that I wouldn't compromise you and I should've fought harder to control myself.'

'You were asleep when you began to touch me, weren't you?' Cupping his face in one hand, Tony brushed her thumb along his five o'clock shadow.

'Yes but once I awoke, I should have immediately stopped. I knew it was wrong but you were so responsive and I thought it might be the only time I would ever have you in my arms.'

A light hearted laugh came from Tony. 'Oh I think there may be plenty of times in the future for that to occur.' She promised.

Are We Still In Trouble?

As Caleb's arms tightened instinctively around Tony, they both heard Aidan whimper. Caleb loosened his hold so that she could turn over to face her brother as he stirred.

'Tony?'

'I'm here Little Bear,' she drew the overcoat back from the boy's face so that he could see a little better with the aid of the moonlight.

'Oh I thought the barn had been a dream. Are we still in trouble?' Aidan rubbed the back of his hands across his eyes as he yawned.

'Just a little bit,' admitted Tony, her flippancy brought a reluctant smile to Caleb's lips.

'I need to pee,' stated Aidan, rising unsteadily to his feet. Negligently he threw the overcoat off and Tony had to quickly grab it to stop from being totally uncovered as well. Smothering a chuckle, Caleb more carefully rose from under the overcoat and lifted Aidan over the bales.

'I'll go out with Aidan and take care of my own need.' Caleb met the puzzled look on Tony's face with a raised eyebrow. Making certain that Aidan wasn't watching, Caleb patted the front of his trousers as he stepped over the bales.

'Oh!' Tony blushed but surprised Caleb by adding, 'I was going to ask you to show me how you deal with it.'

Caleb nearly came then and there. 'Maybe when we're not in so much danger.' He followed Aidan out through the side door where a discreet flick to the head of his penis took care of his erection.

With the boys out of the way, Tony allowed the overcoat to pool at her feet as she rose and stretched her aching muscles. Picking up the coat, she shook it free from straw before slipping it on. Tying up the belt, Tony struggled over the bales, balanced precariously on her damaged ankle, but she managed it without too much colourful language.

Caleb had left one of his pistols on a bale so Tony placed it into a pocket of her overcoat before collecting her crutches. She contained a scream as something hit the back of her knees. Turning sharply on the spot, Tony let out a sigh of relief as the goat nudged her legs once more.

'Hello there, you're not supposed to be out of your enclosure.' Using her crutches Tony limped over to the animals' pens where she discovered that the catch on the goat stall was faulty. Turning to shepherd the goat back into her night pen, Tony found that the nanny, was more interested in the straw bales Tony had erected for her brother.

Coming back to the goat, she pushed the front bales aside so that the goat could enter the small enclosure. Nibbling on the straw, the nanny goat wandered casually into the middle and Tony pushed the bales back into place trapping the goat. The nanny serenely blinked up at Tony who chuckled.

'That should keep you safe for tonight.' Tony told the goat. Bleating in disbelief at Tony at having been tricked, the nanny stared up at the young woman expecting immediate release.

'Goodbye nanny, be a good girl.' Tony limped off towards the side door by which the two Lords had left the barn.

The Arrival Of Trouble

Tony was half way across the barn when Benji began to bark viciously.

'Shut ya yap ya mongrel!' Tony froze at the sound of Nigel Sutherland's voice. Her heart began to pound in her ears as she fumbled for Caleb's pistol in her overcoat before attempting to limp as fast as possible to the side door. As Benji continued to bark, Nigel got nasty and put his boot into the dog's ribs. Benji yelped but he was under orders and attached his powerful jaws upon Nigel's leg. Colourful language lit up the night air as Nigel managed to shake Benji loose and he kicked the dog again.

This time there was only silence and when the main doors of the barn opened, Tony hadn't quite made it to the side door. She froze against the wall of the barn and raised Caleb's pistol as Nigel limped into the barn. He carried a lantern but the light it cast didn't penetrate the shadows where Tony stood petrified. Naturally Nigel's interest was captured by the bales of hay castle. With the lantern held high in one hand and a pistol in the other, he made his way slowly towards the hay bales.

Holding her breath, Tony waited as there would be only one chance for a single shot. Nigel edged towards the hay bales, being careful, so he thought, to stay behind the light cast by his lantern. He was almost on top of the straw castle when Nanny the goat suddenly raised her head and bleated. Swearing violently Nigel dropped the lantern, extinguishing it as he fell backwards in fright.

Tony almost laughed out aloud but used the moment of confusion to make her escape out through the side door of the barn before Nigel could realise that she was even there.

Stepping through the door, a hand descended over her mouth and Tony was pulled backwards against the outer wall of the barn. She tried to struggle but the arms that surrounded her were like steel.

'Stay still Tony, there's another of Nigel's men just beyond those trees. 'Caleb's voice spoke softly into Tony's ear causing her to stop resisting.

'Where's Aidan?' she whispered when Caleb removed his hand from her mouth. Taking the pistol out of her hand, Caleb eased Aidan from behind him so that Tony could run her hand through the boy's hair.

'Be brave now, Little Bear.' Tony whispered. Caleb picked up a plank of wood and quietly slid it over the side door making it impossible to open from the inside. As they sidled along the wall of the barn, trying to stay out of the light of the full moon, they could hear Nigel curse as he struggled to relight his lantern so he could continue his search of the barn.

The three fugitives cautiously made their way to the dilapidated stables that adjoined the barn. There were no horses there any more, not even a Clydesdale for the work on the farm. There was a gig, a little dusty from lack of attention but still in good condition. Leaning her crutches against the vehicle Tony and Aidan set about removing some of the dust and cobwebs on the vehicle as Caleb searched the stables for harnesses and reins in preparation for Solitaire's return with horses.

It isn't essential for our escape that the gig is clean, it is something to do to keep Aidan from realising how desperate our situation really is, thought Caleb. *I'm trying to not think about the possibility of the Highwayman not returning as our options for escape will then be very limited.*

Time To Flee

Caleb was just considering the need to double back to the On the Rocks Inn to steal a horse when a shadowy figure appeared in the stables doorway. Tony gasped in surprise but placed her hand over her brother's mouth to prevent him crying out. Although they could only see the man's silhouette, Tony recognised Solitaire by his old fashioned hat and the soft Irish tune that he whistled. Solitaire led two horses into the stable, not in the least put out by the fact that Caleb had both pistols levelled squarely at him.

'They're closer than I like, my Lord,' the Highwayman handed the reins of one horse to Tony while he assisted Caleb, who re-holstered his weapons to harness the other horse up to the gig. 'There's no sign of your cousin. Once you're safely away I'll try to find your relative.'

Tony stroked the nose of the horse she was holding. 'You've done so much for us already Solitaire. I fear that assisting us will cause a rift between you and your colleagues.'

Solitaire chuckled. 'Oh my Lady, I'd be content to be alienated from the whole of England if it meant your happiness!'

Aidan cast a searching glance between the adults. 'Are you in love with Tony as well?' The two men looked significantly at each other.

'As well as whom Little Bear?' asked Tony.

'Well Duncan is...' Aidan squirmed under all this attention. 'I heard Lord Caleb say that he is and... I love you Tony! I don't want Mama to force you to leave home!' As tears welled up in his eyes Aidan's face began to screw up as he struggled to keep from bawling. Tony bent down to pick Aidan up and held him tight.

'Shh! It's all right Little Bear. I'm not going anywhere just yet. You'll always be able to come and visit me. Hey maybe no one will want to marry me and you'll be stuck with me forever.'

'I don't ever want you to leave!' Snuffling as he laughed, Aidan clung to his sister.

She limped deeper into the stables in order to quieten Aidan's cries. 'Gentlemen I suggest you get the horses ready before we're found.' Tony ordered before focussing her attention on placating her brother as she limped away.

A Glimpse Of Our Future

When Caleb went to look for the Stirling siblings he paused, transfixed as Tony sat on a hay bale in one of the empty stalls with Aidan nursed upon her lap. She gently rocked him as she softly sang a lullaby and his thumb was in his mouth again. For a brief moment Caleb saw their own son on Tony's knee and the beautiful image literally took his breath away.

Glancing up, Tony smiled as she whispered, 'It's way past someone's bed time.' When Caleb didn't say anything, Tony struggled to rise to her feet with her burden. 'What is it? Has something happened?'

He pulled himself together and took Aidan out of her arms so that Tony could manage her crutches which Caleb had brought with him. 'Sorry, it's just that I saw you sitting there nursing our son. I so want that vision to become a reality.'

Tony stumbled slightly in surprise. 'Well then my Lord, you'd better take us home now.'

'Yes ma'am!'

God Speed You

Solitaire helped Tony into the gig before Caleb passed Aidan up into her arms. The Highwayman strapped the crutches to the back of the gig as Caleb took his place beside her. Leading his own horse to the doorway, Solitaire checked that the coast was clear before he signalled for Caleb to drive out. He then mounted his horse and followed them into the moonlight. *If we get away without detection, I'll follow them home before returning to find Mr Delacourt. If we're noticed then I'll try to lead the pursuit away from the gig.*

Luck wasn't going to be on their side this time. With the moon on the full and having risen to the highest point in the sky their escape attempt was immediately noticed by Nigel's posse. At the shout from one of his men, Nigel ran out of the barn and yelled after the escapees. Solitaire shot at the pursuers before spurring his mount in the opposite direction to the gig. When the chasers followed Solitaire, Nigel screamed after his colleagues.

'Not him! It's the gig we're after ya morons!' Nigel managed to fire both his pistols at the gig as it drove away. One shot hit a tree, the other caused Caleb to lurch forward in pain. Tony grabbed hold of the reins as she dragged her cravat from out of one of the overcoat pockets. She thrust this into her brother's hands as she forced him to wake up.

'Press the cravat against the wound Aidan! I need you to stop the bleeding.' Standing on Caleb's lap, Aidan held the folded cravat against Caleb's bleeding shoulder. 'Hold on to him Caleb. I need you both to work with me.' Tony drove the horse hard in the direction of home as Aidan valiantly tried to stem the blood spreading down Caleb's back.

I Need To Stop The Bleeding

After a couple of miles, when it became obvious that they were not being followed, Tony slowed the horse down to a walk. When she was absolutely certain that they were alone, she stopped the gig altogether. With difficulty Caleb managed to raise his head.

'Why are we stopping? Is something wrong?'

Tony handed the reins to Caleb as she took the dagger from Aidan's scabbard and the cravat from Caleb's wound.

'Can you take your jacket off? I'm going to bind your wound until we can get you to a Doctor.' With the dagger Tony cut through a section of the cravat to use as a pad and the rest as a bandage. Aidan assisted Caleb out of his jacket and held the pad in place as Tony tightly bound over it with the rest of the cravat. Caleb let out a sigh of relief as the boy helped him back into his coat.

'You handle a horse well Tony.' Caleb managed to say as she took the reins back into her own hands.

'Aren't you glad I'm not one of those hysterical women unable to do anything but swoon or cry?'

Caleb chuckled. 'I wouldn't change you for the world Lord Tony! Save us all!'

An Uneasy Journey

The most direct route would have been the obvious choice to take them home but fearing that Nigel or his friends could get ahead of them and ambush them at any moment made Tony decide to undertake a safer but longer journey. Caleb held onto Aidan and tried to stay awake but all he wanted to do was lay his head in Tony's lap.

For several miles, they had gained speed until they were on the out skirts of the Stirling village. At which point Tony slowed the gig once more. With super human effort Caleb opened his eyes.

'What is it? Where are we?'

Tony was carefully scanning the surrounding area as well as the road ahead. 'This is the perfect place for an ambush. How are you boys holding up?'

'I'm cold Tony.' Aidan snuggled in close to Caleb's chest.

'I don't think I can stay upright any longer.' Caleb admitted as he swayed slightly towards Tony's shoulder. Blood continued to seep through his makeshift bandages. She caught sight of a rope silhouetted in the moonlight suspended in the air between two trees across the road.

'Caleb lay your head in my lap; Aidan crouch down behind him.' Tony ordered the horse to pick up pace again as she slid as low as she could without crushing Caleb. He had toppled into her lap which suggested to Tony that he was close to passing out. She felt the rope brush across the top of her head and gave the horse free rein to break into a gallop once more.

Approaching the turn off to Stirling Manor, Tony wondered, *Would Nigel have the audacity to stage another ambush right on our own doorstep?* So instead of turning for home, Tony drove the gig towards the village.

'Aren't we going home Tony?' Aidan had popped his head up from behind Caleb's slumped body.

'We're going to see Doctor Masters first Little Bear. Then we'll go home, I promise.' Tony gritted her teeth, *I hope it is a promise that I'll be able to keep. Both my men need medical attention before we can consider ourselves safe again.* A flutter of excitement rose in her stomach at the thought that she considered Caleb to belong to her. *It could end up being far from the truth, though, as the resulting scandal from this night could destroy any chance we may have of being together. That is for the morrow and when we know we are safe once more.*

Doctor Stanley Masters

Pulling up outside the Doctor's house, Tony called out to the Doctor as she lowered Aidan to the ground so that he could pound on the door. Doctor Stanley Masters answered the door himself as Tony was assisting Caleb to sit upright. Casting a quick searching glance over the three of them, the Doctor called out to his Housekeeper, Mrs Clements and his valet Banes for assistance.

Daisy, the Doctor's Maid was a farmer's daughter and she ran forward to take the horse's reins so that Tony could assist Caleb out of the gig and into the men's waiting arms. Mrs Clements scooped Aidan up and hurried the boy inside to sit him in front of the fire in the parlour, find blankets for all of them and put the kettle on.

'The last we heard was that you and Aidan had been abducted, my Lord.' The Doctor addressed Tony as he and Banes eased Caleb into an arm chair close to the fireplace.

'It's all right Doc, Lord Delacourt knows the truth about me.' Tony could not stop herself from blushing as the Doctor cast a scrutinising look over her appearance. He refused to comment on her statement, simply ordering his servant to fetch his medical bag. Doctor Masters bent down to check over Aidan who was huddled in front of the fire, seated upon the floor.

Tony knelt in front of Caleb to help him remove his coat and cravat. As she undid her makeshift bandages, Tony was relieved that Caleb was showing signs of recovery.

'Are you able to lift your arms so that I can remove your shirt?'

Caleb tried to raise his left arm but the movement caused him to wince and sweat beaded his brow. Tony pulled Aidan's dagger out of her pocket and ran it through the front of Caleb's fine shirt. She ignored Mrs Clements protest at ruining a good garment as she eased Caleb out of it so that the Doctor could tend to his wounded shoulder.

The Housekeeper wrapped a blanket round Aidan as Banes returned with the medical bag. Tony removed Caleb's pistols from the holsters on his hips and placed them into the pockets of her overcoat. She sank to the floor at Caleb's feet. Her hand in his as the Doctor dug out the shrapnel from his shoulder.

I Must Protect Aidan

'Tony I'm hungry.' Aidan's statement was made as Doctor Masters had begun to bind Caleb's shoulder. Mrs Clement held out her hand to the young Lord.

'I'm sure we can find some biscuits in the kitchen Lord Aidan. Why don't you come and help me make the hot chocolate?'

Wrapping his blanket around him, Aidan trotted after the Housekeeper but couldn't help casting a concerned glance at his sister as he passed her. She was his rock but at the moment all she could do was smile reassuringly at him. Tony took the damp cloth Banes handed her and she tenderly mopped the sweat from Caleb's face. His fingers still clung tightly to hers as if afraid that releasing her hand he would lose her again. Once he had secured the bandage, Doctor Masters wrapped a blanket around Caleb and for the first time really seemed to look at Tony.

'Can I take your coat, my Lady?'

Blushing, Tony shook her head. 'No!' At the Doctor's startled expression, she apologised, 'Sorry Doctor Masters but it is all that is keeping me decent.'

'My dear child what on earth has happened?' The Doctor cast a significant glance at Caleb. 'Have you been violated?'

She couldn't meet his penetrating gaze. 'I… please I can't talk about it right now.' Tony dragged in a deep shuddering breath, shocked at how close she was to tears. 'Will Caleb… will Lord Delacourt be all right?'

'A couple of days in bed and he'll be as right as rain.'

Nodding, Tony glanced around the room, fear forming in her eyes. 'Aidan? Where is Aidan? I must protect him!'

Trying to place a blanket round Tony's shoulders, the Doctor comforted her. 'He's in the kitchen with Mrs Clement, Lady Tony. It's all right, you're all safe now.'

'No! Not safe! Please I want him with me!'

The Doctor's look of concern grew as Tony became more agitated and he wondered, *Am I going to have to sedate her?*

Caleb let out a deep sigh. 'Please Doctor, after all that they've been through tonight, Aidan must never be out of our sight.' A little bit of colour had reappeared in his ashen features as he seemed to be recovering from the Doctor's ministering.

Not Safe At All

Doctor Masters had taken only one step towards the door when it opened and Mrs Clement and Aidan came back into the room. But it was not a relief as Aidan was being carried by Nigel

Sutherland, who held a pistol against the frightened boy's head. Nigel had a marked limp from the damage Benji had inflicted upon him. An anguished cry came from Tony as she sprang to her feet, her hand reaching instinctively for the sword at her hip as the blanket fell to a heap at her feet.

'Don't do it, me Lady, or y'r pa will need to beget a new heir,' warned Nigel, thrusting Mrs Clement into a chair before moving away from the doorway so that one of his colleagues could drag into the room two more prisoners under gun point. 'I've two more patients for ya Doc.' Nigel said as Solitaire and Geoff Delacourt were thrust, their hands bound, onto a sofa. They had been beaten, were sporting cut lips, bleeding noses and bruises that would soon develop by morning.

Seeing the horror on Tony's face that they had been made to suffer for her sake, caused Nigel to laugh. 'I hope y'r good at mending toys Doc, I've broken these ones.' Nigel licked his lips as he stared hungrily at Tony. 'I'm gunna have fun playing with me new toy. There's nothing like a brand new toy that no one else has had the chance to play with! Maybe if she pleases me, I won't break her too!' Nigel handed Aidan to Mrs Clement before taking a deliberate step towards Tony.

No Longer In Mint Condition

Anger rising, her hands tightening into fists as she fought against the desire to vomit in disgust; Tony straightened up in indignation and cast Nigel a haughty look.

'I'm sorry to disappoint a filthy little boy but this toy is no longer mint in box!' She gleefully spat out the words at Nigel. As he stared at her in disbelief, Tony bent down to kiss Caleb's cheek and whispered a quick word in his ear.

'Oh Lady Tony! What have you done?' Doctor Masters looked at her in distress as Tony sat down upon Caleb's lap and leant her head back against his good shoulder.

'Ya and him? In the barn? I don't believe ya! He compromised ya?'

Tony laughed at Nigel's bewilderment as Caleb's bandaged arm possessively circled her waist and his right hand slid inside her overcoat to sensuously stroke against her breasts. A soft sigh of pleasure was extracted from Tony as the Doctor protested and Mrs Clement placed her hand over Aidan's eyes.

'My Lord! My Lady! This is totally inappropriate behaviour for your stations.' The Doctor's words were ignored as Tony kept her eyes focused upon Nigel's tormented features as he could not look away from the couple as Caleb pressed a tender kiss against her ear and then Tony's shoulder.

A strangled growl emanated from Nigel as his gun wavered in his hand, unable to take his eyes away from Caleb's hand as it slid slowly from her breasts and across her stomach. When his hand travelled lower, Doctor Masters opened his mouth to protest but his eyes met Caleb's and his gaze was drawn towards Caleb's other hand which had slipped into the pocket of Tony's overcoat. *Vaguely I remember that Lady Tony had placed Lord Caleb's pistol into the overcoat.* Doctor Masters closed his mouth again, not waiting to draw attention to Caleb's subversive actions.

Nigel's gaze never wavered from the way Caleb's hand untied the sash of the overcoat so that it seemed that he was about to trail his fingers even more intimately lower. Nigel was almost salivating.

'Doctor Masters! Are you going to permit this vulgar display?' protested Mrs Clement, struggling to keep her hand over Aidan's eyes as he wanted to know what was going on. The Doctor was more interested in watching Nigel as he lowered his weapon as the couple's intimacy tormented and frustrated him. *Is any of this real? Will Lord Delacourt really touch Lady Tony so intimately in front of all these witnesses?* The Doctor mused.

The moment Caleb wrapped his fingers around a pistol and began to withdraw it from Tony's pocket, his other hand veered away from her private area towards her hip and her sword. With a hand upon both weapons Caleb drew them out and Tony slid smoothly off his lap as he rose abruptly to his feet to challenge Nigel. He used the sword to knock the pistol out of Nigel's hand before raising his pistol towards Nigel's face.

'Tell your friend to drop his weapon before I decide to blow your head off!' ordered Caleb as Tony pulled her overcoat closed again and tied it tight as Nigel's colleague handed his pistol to Solitaire.

'Banes, go and fetch Squire Perkins, he's a Justice of the Peace,' ordered the Doctor, 'Mrs Clement find something to tie up these men.'

Once Mrs Clement had released Aidan, he ran across the room to wrap his arms around his sister. 'Can we go home now?' Aidan begged. Tony threw Aidan's dagger across to the Doctor so that he could cut the ropes binding Geoff and Solitaire's hands.

'Soon, Little Bear, very soon.'

Was Any Of That True?

Doctor Masters cleaned up Geoff and Solitaire as much as he was allowed without stripping them down for a proper examination. Neither man was prepared to leave the room as they didn't want to miss a thing. *If Tony's and Caleb's actions just now were any indication as to what had occurred between them in the barn, then I want to know the whole story,* mused Geoff as he took Nigel's weapon.

When Mrs Clement returned with twine to secure Nigel and his friend, Caleb sank back into his chair as the loss of blood had left him seriously weakened. Tony gently eased both the weapons out of Caleb's hands and returned them to her coat. With Aidan clinging to his sister, she bent over Caleb to mop a damp cloth across his forehead.

'You were magnificent Caleb!' She tenderly kissed his lips and brushed his hair back from his face.

'Are we safe yet?' He had grown ashen again and Tony was worried about the fresh spread of blood through his new bandages.

'Thanks to you, yes.' Tony glanced over at the two men now being made to sit down to await justice. 'Unless you have any other friends that may be about to burst in on us?'

Nigel shook his head. 'Was any of that true?'

A slow mischievous smile appeared upon Tony's face as she glanced back at Caleb. 'That's none of your business Sutherland!'

A Late Visitor

When the door opened to permit an unannounced visitor to enter the room, he was confronted by not only pistols raised by Solitaire and Geoff but also Tony as she stood protectively in front of Aidan's and Caleb. The intruder paused and glanced around the room with his eyebrows raised in mild surprise.

'I'm glad to see that you've been rescued Tony but do you think you can ask your friends to not shoot me?'

Immediately Tony lowered her pistol and the tension left her body. 'Papa!' As she launched herself into the arms of the Earl of Stirling, he removed the pistol from her hand and stroked his other hand down her hair. The Earl was a placid man, in his early forties and as fair as his son Aidan but the boy's curls had come from his mother, Charlotte.

'Hello baby girl.' Julius Stirling held Tony as she sobbed and struggled to keep back the tears. Over the top of her head, he glanced around the room. 'My compliments gentlemen. Thank you for your incredible efforts to safely return my children to me.' The Earl waved his hand for them to resume their seats as they had painfully attempted to rise.

Pulling herself together Tony accepted her father's handkerchief before she went back to sit on the floor at Caleb's feet and Aidan laid his head down in her lap.

'It is an honour to be of service to Lady Tony.' Caleb's words were soft and his ashen colour and perspiration worried Tony.

'Doctor Masters, I think the gentlemen could do with something to drink.'

Mrs Clement headed for the door. 'I'll make a pot of tea.'

Glancing hesitantly at the Earl, Tony added, 'If Papa can handle it, I think the three heroes could do with something stronger.'

The Earl smiled. 'Of course my dear.' He nodded to the Doctor who unlocked his liquor cabinet and poured out three glasses of brandy. Tony held the glass for Caleb but he managed to raise it to his lips before she placed it onto a small table within his reach.

Aidan had looked up as the liquor had passed over his head but didn't show any real interest until Mrs Clement came back into the room with the tea tray and more importantly hot chocolate for Aidan. He sat up to take his cup and permitted his father to raise his head to make sure he was all right but Aidan would not leave his sister's side.

Reviewing Their Adventure

It was to this genteel scene of tea that Banes returned with Squire Perkins. Doctor Masters tried to suggest that Geoff and Solitaire accompanied him to his surgery so that he could examine them properly but they refused. They wanted to hear the complete story. Tony took several sips of her tea before she began to explain from the moment she, Duncan and Aidan had entered the Stirling Arms the previous evening.

The Earl sat with his cup and saucer in his hands, Caleb's pistol sat negligently across his lap until Tony got to the point in her story where Nigel learnt that she was a woman and had shredded her clothes. Very carefully Earl Stirling placed the crockery back onto the tea tray and as a muscle spasmed in his cheek, his fingers moved instinctively to wrap around the pistol.

Nigel squirmed uncomfortably as Tony told of his attempt to rape and humiliate her. When the Earl raised his head to look directly at Nigel, the guilty man nearly wet himself as searing hot hatred blazed from the nobleman's eyes.

'You dared to lay a hand on my daughter? You're not even worthy enough to lick her boots!' The Earl raised the pistol in cold fury but Tony interjected.

'Papa, no! He's in the custody of the Squire now. Also he is unarmed.'

The pistol did not lower. 'You were unarmed when he tried to force himself on you!'

Having finished his hot chocolate, Aidan wanted to add to Tony's story. 'She was bound hands and feet Papa.' Frowning Aidan wiped his hand across his mouth. 'That man said he would do nasty things with his pee pee when he thought Tony was a boy but I didn't think what he was going to do when he found out she was a girl was any less nasty.' The tired little boy glanced wide eyed from his sister to his father as tears began to fall.

The Earl slowly lowered the weapon back into his lap. 'It's all my fault Papa! I didn't mean to tell that nasty man Tony was a girl, honest!' As Aidan began to cry in earnest, Tony put her cup down and bundled her brother up into her arms.

'It's not your fault, Little Bear, it's mine. Maybe all of this could have been avoided if I'd given up pretending to be something that I'm not! It's time I grew up baby boy!' Tony swallowed hard to try to stop her own tears but it had been a very emotional, exhausting adventure.

The Earl's Surprise

Caleb reached down to caress his hand against Tony's hair. 'Pass Aidan up to me with his blanket. You need to finish the rest of the story Tony.

Surprise was evident on not only the Earl's face but the Doctor's as well as Tony wiped away her tears and then her brother's before settling Aidan onto Caleb's lap. What surprised them even more was how readily the young Lord accepted being removed from his sister.

Tony wrapped the blanket securely over Aidan and settled back down on the floor. The Earl opened his mouth to reprimand his young son as Aidan closed his eyes and his thumb slid into his mouth, but Caleb caught the Earl's eyes and shook his head. *The boy doesn't need to be upset any further tonight,* thought Caleb.

As Tony continued to tell their story of Caleb's rescue and escape from the Inn, her hand had risen to caress along Aidan's back until Caleb reached out and brought her hand back to the arm of his chair. As she reached the scene in the barn, her fingers instinctively entwined through his.

Although Tony seemed unconscious of her actions as she tried to get through the story without being too graphic and yet not leaving any important details out; everyone else listening to her was aware of the connection of intimacy between them.

The Earl hadn't looked happy at the description of a naked Tony, Aidan bundled up in her jacket and Caleb huddled together under the overcoat in the hay castle *but I understand the necessity of shared body heat.*

There was absolute silence in the room as Tony chose her next words carefully. *When I imagined that I would have to recount what happened tonight, I hadn't thought there would be so many people present.* 'For a while we slept, when I awoke Caleb's... Lord Delacourt's hands were on my breasts. When I managed to wake Caleb... Lord Delacourt, he apologised and removed his hands.

That is all that occurred between us in the barn.' Tony broke off as Nigel screamed in disbelief.

'Y'r lying! We all saw how ya responded to his Lordship as he caressed ya! How could ya permit him to touch ya like that and not me?'

With a tired sigh, Tony shrugged her shoulders. 'I like him, I don't like you! I didn't stop Caleb touching me when we were in the barn because I didn't like it but because it was the wrong time and place.'

Groaning Doctor Masters buried his face into his hands. 'Oh Lord Stirling, what are we to do with the girl? She'll be ruined!'

Ignoring everyone else in the room the Earl sat forward, his eyes locked upon his daughter. 'Tell me,'

Tears sparkling in her eyes, Tony nodded. 'If Caleb asks me to marry him, I want it to be because he wants to marry me and not because he is forced to marry me. I wasn't compromised, Papa, although it was incredibly close before Caleb pulled that swine off me.'

She broke off as the memory of how close she came to being violated threatened to choke her. 'Doctor Masters can examine me to prove that my virtue is still intact. After tonight, though, I can't say the same for any reputation I may have had.' Tony raised her fingers to dash away the tears that began to fall as her father reached out to gently pat her shoulder.

'Finish your story and then the Doctor can examine you. This is as much my fault, Tony for not insisting you act like the girl you should be. I... I just wanted you to be happy.' The Earl's fingers brushed against Tony's cheek. *Her vulnerability reminds me so much of her dear mother,* he thought.

The gentlemen in the room allowed Tony the time she needed to calm herself so that she could conclude her story. Since all but her father and the Squire had been present when she had sat upon Caleb's lap and allowed him to touch her in order to gain access to the weapons to disarm Nigel; Tony didn't go into any details about what they did but simply explained why they did it.

When Tony had finished, she drank the remainder of her tea, putting her cup back onto the tea tray with slightly unsteady hands before rising to her feet. 'Doctor Masters, you've known me since the day I was born so I'm sure you'll understand when I ask that Mrs Clement is present when I'm examined.'

Nodding, the Doctor indicated for her to precede him out of the room. 'That was my intention my Lady.'

As Aidan stirred, Tony paused as he called out her name. 'Tony? Don't leave me!'

She reached out to take his hand. 'You're safe here with Caleb, I'll be all right with the Doc.' Settling back into Caleb's arms, Aidan accepted Tony's assurance and went back to sleep.

I Link Him To His Sister

When Tony had limped out of the room on her crutches with Doctor Masters, there was a moment of silence as the men left behind digested all the information. Thoughts of the scandal that was going to come crashing down around them were momentarily pushed aside for the Earl as he watched, perplexed, the strange bond that had formed between his son and a virtual stranger. Raising his glass of brandy to his lips, Caleb looked up and understood Lord Stirling's confusion. He smiled reassuringly.

'Tonight I'm a link to his sister and safety. Tomorrow he may hate me if he thinks I'm going to take his sister away from him.'

His eyes widening in surprise, the Earl's face drained of colour. 'Then something did happen in the barn!'

Caleb shook his head, 'No Lord Stirling, but in a day or two I would like to come and have a talk to you. In private.'

The Earl sighed. 'If only you or Tony had killed this swine when you had the chance, then you wouldn't have needed to hide out in that barn.'

Caleb shook his head. 'If Sutherland had succeeded in violating Tony, I would've snapped his neck, but I didn't want either of us to live with having murdered someone, even if he deserved it!'

Nigel opened his mouth to retort but catching sight of the murderous expression on Earl Stirling's face, he closed his mouth again.

The Highwayman Bows Out

Solitaire rose slowly to his feet and bowed respectfully to the Earl. 'I'll be off now, my Lord. I need to return the horses and gig we... we borrowed before day break.'

The Earl reached into his pocket and drew out a bag of coins which he pressed into the Highwayman's hand. 'There aren't enough words to express how grateful I am to you Solitaire.'

The Highwayman looked down at the purse for a moment before he finally handed it back. 'I think I'll be looking for a new line of work my Lord. I doubt my colleagues will be pleased with my actions this night.'

The Earl laughed. 'Come and see me tomorrow and we can discuss your new occupation.'

'Thank you my Lord.' Solitaire nodded towards Caleb before donning his hat and vanishing into the night.

The Squire looked up at the Earl, a little disconcerted. 'I'm not certain whether I should've arrested him or not.'

Caleb chuckled. 'Did you see him rob anyone? I distinctly witnessed Solitaire hand the Earl's purse back to him.'

Squire Perkins relaxed in relief. 'True, thank you my Lord. I was wondering how it would play out at Sutherland's trial.'

'There's no need to make reference to Solitaire's occupation and by the time this does reach the courts Solitaire will no longer exist,' explained the Earl.

'Can I take the prisoners away now my Lord?' asked the Squire.

Shaking his head, the Earl said, 'Just wait for the Doctor's assessment.'

'Yes my Lord.'

Keep A Civil Tongue In Your Head

The Earl dragged in a sharp breath as he tried to keep his voice calm. 'If there's so much as a tear to my daughter's hymen then you'll be taking away a corpse!'

Nigel began to panic. 'It's more likely that his Lordship dipped his wick when they were in the barn than me! I'm not taking the blame for his pleasure!'

'I didn't compromise Lady Tony!' Frowning, Caleb cast a quick look down at Aidan to make sure that the boy was asleep and couldn't hear the slander about his sister.

'Ya would say that!' Nigel retorted.

One of Caleb's eyebrows rose slowly. 'Are you calling me a liar? Believe me, I don't need much of an excuse to pound you into a paste, so watch your tongue.'

Nigel looked at Caleb's bandaged shoulder and ashen countenance from blood loss plus the five year old across his lap and started to laugh.

Caleb's other eyebrow rose as his lips thinned. He rose to his feet, lifting Aidan effortlessly to gently place the sleeping boy into his father's arms. Letting the blanket slip from around his shoulders, Caleb picked up Aidan's dagger and cut through Nigel's bound hands. Tossing the dagger back onto the sofa beside his cousin, Caleb then physically lifted Nigel to his feet. With a hand around Nigel's throat, Caleb thrust him up against the wall.

'Something amusing you Sutherland? Do you think this is all a joke? Say one disrespectful word about Lady Tony and I'll cut your tongue out!'

Nigel couldn't answer as he couldn't breathe. Not liking the look of pure hatred on Caleb's face, Geoff spoke carefully. 'Ease up Caleb, the man can't answer you if he can't breathe.'

Releasing Nigel's throat, Caleb took a step back as he dragged in a deep breath into his own lungs as he fought to regain control over his temper. For several seconds Nigel gasped for oxygen before launching himself at Caleb.

'Ya fucking toff! I'll kill ya and the whore!' He never laid a hand on Caleb as his Lordship easily blocked the blow and threw Nigel across his hip and onto his back on the floor. Caleb placed his boot onto Nigel's chest.

'Do you like pain?' as Nigel struggled, Caleb effortlessly kept him pinned to the floor.

Can't You Boys Play Nicely?

Re-entering the parlour ahead of Tony, Doctor Masters paused in the doorway and sighed as he looked around the room. 'Why can't you boys play nicely?'

Reluctantly Caleb removed his foot from Nigel's chest and staggered slightly as blood stained his bandages anew. The Doctor placed his hand beneath Caleb's elbow and assisted him back into his chair.

'For the record Lord Stirling, Lady Tony is still Virgo Intacta, there are bruises along her cheek, around her throat and upon her wrists, knees and ankles.' Doctor Masters dragged Nigel to his feet and Squire Perkins tied Nigel's hands again.

Laughing Nigel sneered. 'What's wrong, me Lord? Couldn't ya get it up?'

Bending down to check on Caleb's shoulders, Tony threw over her shoulder. 'It was more impressive than that sorry excuse for a weapon in your trousers!'

His jaw dropping to the floor, Nigel stuttered in disbelief. 'He… he exposed himself to ya?'

A seraphical smile appeared upon Tony's face. 'No he didn't! When we were forced to huddle together to keep warm, I thought it was his pistol against my back as he slept.' Her eyes opened wider in Innocence. 'You can't blame a man for what bodily responses occur in sleep.'

Caleb shifted uncomfortably only in part from the pressure Tony was placing over his bleeding wound. 'Tony, you don't have to explain anything to that man. Nor do you have to defend my… my proportions.' Caleb reached up to lay his hand over hers. 'It's time you took your brother home. I know the Earl isn't happy about Aidan leaving his room at bedtime but he might want to stay with you for several nights.' Tony wrapped a second bandage around Caleb's shoulder, adding extra pressure to stop the bleeding.

An ugly bark of a laugh erupted from Nigel. 'Hey if the boy doesn't want to take that offer, I'll take his place!'

'He's not worth another drop of your blood Caleb.' Tony's hand on Caleb's shoulder kept him from rising to his feet.

His jaw clenched. 'But it's worth a drop of his!'

Straightening up Tony bowed elegantly. 'As you wish, my Lord!' Limping, she took the several steps needed to face Nigel with a speed he hadn't expected. He was certainly unprepared as Tony's tightly closed fist slammed directly into his nose. There was a satisfying crunching sound and blood spurted forth even as Nigel screamed in pain.

'Well done my Lady! A nice flush hit!' Geoff forgot himself for a moment as he cheered.

Stay Away From My Children!

Nigel's voice came out muffled as he clasped a handkerchief to his bleeding nose. 'Son of a bitch! I'll get even with ya if it's the last thing I do!'

Rising to his feet, the Earl of Stirling did so carefully to not disturb his son in his arms. 'Mr Sutherland come anywhere near my family and I will shoot you like the rabid dog that you are!' He glanced at the cousins. 'Gentlemen, you're more than welcome to join us at the Manor but I know that Ruth Cooper has a hot meal and a warm bed waiting for you at the Arms.'

Caleb bowed. 'Thank you Lord Stirling.' Rising from his chair he nodded to Doctor Masters. 'Thank you for patching us up Doctor. Sorry for making a mess of your parlour.' Allowing the blanket to fall, Caleb managed to drag on his coat.

'Living with Lady Tony, my Lord, we get used to the unexpected.' Doctor Masters followed his visitors out into the darkness.

Tony took Aidan from her father so that he could climb into his awaiting carriage and then accepted his son back. 'I think I've been insulted.' She said to Caleb.

He chuckled. 'If the shoe fits my elfling!' Caleb assisted her up into the carriage.

'Would you like your overcoat back now my Lord?' Although Caleb laughed, the other men looked shocked.

'When I next see you will do.' Caleb surprised them all even more when he retained Tony's hand and raised it to his lips. Her colour heightened as a tingling feeling surged through her body from his touch. The Earl watched as his daughter was overcome by maidenly confusion. Being a true gentleman, he refrained from teasing her as the carriage took them home.

MONDAY

Reflection Over Breakfast

Normally the majority of the household, with the exception of Lady Charlotte, had breakfast early rather than the fashionable 11 o'clock of the gentry. The Earl, though, left orders to allow his children to sleep in. As expected Aidan had clung to Tony when they returned home from the Doctor's house the previous evening and his father had tried to put him into his own bed. The Earl relented and once they were both dressed in their nightwear, his Lordship raised no objection as Aidan slid into Tony's bed.

So the Earl wasn't surprised when Tony limped into the dining room on her crutches, that she still had her shadow. What did surprise him was the knowledge that his children had been awake since first light.

As Tony leant over to kiss her father on his forehead, she explained, 'He had such a goodnight's sleep that once Aidan was bouncing on the bed there were no more thoughts of sleeping.'

The Earl looked displeased as Aidan clambered up into his chair beside Duncan. 'Perhaps Duncan should have taken Aidan so that you could continue to sleep.'

Tony smiled reassuringly at Aidan who looked worried that he had angered his father. 'Duncan did try, Papa, but being forced to leave me only upset Aidan,' she explained. Observing her father's lips thin, she smiled. 'It's all right, really, it was better that we got up and were busy than lying there and thinking about how much disgrace I have brought to this family.'

The Earl's features immediately softened. 'Tony, this wasn't your fault. You and Aidan are safe. Whatever you had to do to survive I will support you all the way.'

For a moment Tony lay down her cutlery to place her hand over her father's. 'Thank you but others won't be so understanding, especially if the whole story becomes public knowledge.'

Duncan paused in raising his cup of coffee to his lips. 'A part from the kidnappers, only our own people know the full story or do you have doubts about Lord Delacourt and his cousin?'

The Earl shook his head. 'We have nothing to fear from the Delacourts.'

No Chance Of Keeping This A Secret

As everyone at the breakfast table looked at the Earl in surprise he smiled. 'My first task this morning was to return all the money that Preston had accumulated for your release. Although his Lordship was still in bed, I spoke briefly with Geoff Delacourt. He assured me of their total discretion.'

'They're not the one's I'm worried about,' admitted Tony as she buttered her toast.

'Then whom?' Duncan asked.

A secretive smile appeared on her face. 'Tell me Papa where in London did you leave Charlotte?'

'With her mother Mrs Henry.'

'And Charlotte knew I was abducted?'

'Of course,' replied his Lordship.'

'Then most of London probably know by now. Do you think you can keep the whole truth from Charlotte?' Tony correctly interpreted the look of regret on the Earl's face and added, 'You wrote to her first thing this morning didn't you?'

'Last night actually. I'm sorry.'

She smiled resignedly 'It's all right Papa, it would have become known sooner or later. We'll survive.'

Lady Charlotte And Party

The meal was over and Tony was about to rise from her chair when the Butler, Preston entered the room.

'You have visitors my Lord,' Preston bowed to the Earl but cast a quick glance in Tony's direction. 'Run!' The quietly added word from the Butler stunned her into immobility as she stared up at him.

'Who is it Preston?' asked the Earl, equally surprised by the uncharacteristic behaviour of his Butler.

'Lady Charlotte and party.'

Tony sprang to her feet and Duncan picked up Aidan but it was too late. Half a dozen people entered unceremoniously and all seemed to be talking at the same time. Actually it was one person doing most of the talking. Controlling the urge to sigh, the Earl of Stirling rose to his feet to greet his wife and entourage.

Preston issued an order to Charles, the Footman, to alert the kitchen to the arrival of visitors who would need refreshments. The Footman happily escaped on his errand but Preston remained loyally to assist his Lordship when the visitors eventually took their places at the table.

Right now though, they were all bombarding the Earl with questions and at the same time advice on how to deal with the crisis. Most of the noise came from Mrs Agnes Henry and her son Claude, mother and brother to Lady Charlotte, who looked as though it had been a trying journey from London with her family.

Tony received a heartfelt hug from the Dowager Countess, Lady Margarette Stirling, the Earl's mother, before she assisted her grandmother into a chair. Tony removed Aidan from the pinching of his cheeks by his uncle Claude to place him beside the Dowager Countess before turning to greet her other grandparents, the late Lady Grace's parents, the Honourable Mr and Mrs Frederick and Patience Sinclair.

Even when all the visitors were seated, Agnes Henry continued to dominate the whole conversation with her booming voice. Biting on her bottom lip to stop herself from uttering an annihilating remark, Tony whispered to the Dowager Countess, 'I bet you're glad you didn't travel with the Henry family!'

Frederick Sinclair, overhearing his granddaughter, had to turn his laugh into a cough but it meant that Agnes turned her barrage of words upon Tony.

'Do you think this is funny Tony? With your blatant disregard for your station in life you have brought shame and ruin to your family's name!'

Frederick, feeling responsible for this sudden attack, bridled up in defence of his granddaughter. 'That is ridiculous! Tony didn't set out to be kidnapped! She kept her head in a difficult situation and kept her brother safe.'

Tony laid her hand over her indignant grandfather's. 'It's all right, Mrs Henry's criticism is justified. I and I alone am responsible for the chain of events that unfolded. Therefore it is my name and my reputation that will suffer and no one else's.'

Agnes Henry snorted in derision. 'But you'll drag us all down with you! Dressing like a man! Your father is too weak to have broken you in!'

At this attack on the Earl, Tony's eyes blazed in anger. 'This is my father's house; you will speak of the Earl with respect or you can turn around and leave this instant!' She fought to keep control of her temper. Agnes' colour was rising alarmingly and she ignored her other daughter Lizzy's plea to calm down.

'How dare you speak to me like that! My daughter is mistress of this house, not you! For far too long you've had everything your own way! It's time you had a husband to master your reckless actions. That is why I bought Claude with us.'

One of Tony's exquisite eyebrows rose. 'Really? And here I thought it was for his sparkling conversation!' This was a low blow but fairly accurate as Claude Henry was as big a bore as his mother. Both Claude and Lizzy were dark haired like their father had been, whereas Charlotte was fair like her mother and Claude was a little man with a little man's problems.

'The announcement of your engagement to Claude will satisfy the gossip hungry Ton.' Agnes stated.

Tony shook her head. 'No it will make them think that there is something to cover up. I'd rather the world thought I was a ruined woman than a fool to become engaged to a man so dull and so repulsive that I'm likely to kill him before I allow him to touch me!'

Agnes turned on the Earl. 'Are you going to allow this baggage to talk to me like this? I am your mother-in-law!'

'Madam, I'm well aware of that fact as you never cease to remind me of it! If you want a husband to tame Tony. Then even you must realise that Claude isn't the man for the task. Although if you want Claude to amount to anything at all then someone like Tony could whip him into shape. Get him out from under your thumb and he might even make a reasonable human being but I doubt it!'

'Julius please.' Charlotte begged. 'Mother we agreed arguing about what has been done is pointless. We have to look to the future.'

Agnes' lips thinned. 'You agreed! Did you tell Jane to do as I asked?'

Charlotte buckled as she always did under the force of her mother's will. 'Jane is going to unpack first and then she'll do as you requested. Although why you need to criticise my choice of clothes.'

Agnes snorted again. 'You have no idea what so ever about colour and style! Half of the clothes in your wardrobe are more suited for a woman darker in colouring than you. They'll do well enough for Tony.'

The Dowager looked outraged. 'My granddaughter does not wear second hand dresses!'

Agnes waved away this objection. 'Jane has had the good sense to prevent Charlotte from wearing the more unsuitable attire. So most have never been worn.'

She Must Start Wearing Dresses

Tony rose to her feet as the Footmen began to bring in fresh trays of food. She signalled for Duncan to pick up Aidan. 'I'll have Mary take my measurements as I'm certain that adjustments will need to be made. That ridiculous diet regime that you inflict upon Charlotte means that she is little more than skin and bone.'

Agnes stiffened in indignation. 'It is to maintain her ethereal beauty!'

'If that means being tired all the time and unable to do anything practical but sit around and look pretty, then you have succeeded!'

'How dare you!' Agnes exploded.

'Mother please! Tony is correct, it is quite possible that the physical differences between us will mean that, even with alterations, the dresses may still not fit Tony.' Charlotte's defence of her stepdaughter, further angered her mother.

'So she not only has no feminine pride but she's fat as a cow!'

'How dare you!' Agnes had finally riled the Earl. 'You will speak respectfully of my daughter in this house or you will leave it! Tony has a normal appetite and since I married Charlotte I've been attempting to undo the harm that your years of abuse have inflicted on her!'

'I have done nothing to harm my children! How can you say I abused Charlotte? You, who has no control over how your own daughter appears in public, have no right to criticise my parenting skills!'

'Mother! Julius please! Tony if you could have Mary take your measurements and hand it over to my Maid, Jane. Duncan isn't it time Aidan was back at his studies?' Charlotte spoke calmly but her stomach was all a flutter with the conflict. *I can't face food but it is essential to eat especially right now.*

Fleeing The Battle Ground

Tony collected her crutches as Duncan hoisted Aidan up out of his chair. Tony hesitated over leaving the Earl with the wolves circling but he smiled and signalled for her to escape while she could.

'Don't forget the errand I want you to run Tony.' The Earl looked significantly at his daughter. 'Get your brother out into the fresh air.'

'Yes Papa.' Tony followed Duncan out of the room, grateful for the opportunity to escape. *But I know that I should stay and fight my own battles.* Once outside of the dining room, both Tony and Duncan breathed a sigh of relief.

'Make sure Aidan has a thick jacket to wear while I let Mary run a measuring tape over me for the in-laws. Then we'll go for a ride.'

Duncan hesitated. 'Is it a good idea to leave the house Tony?'

'Would you prefer I stay and murder one of my in-laws?'

Duncan blanched at the idea. 'We'll meet you down at the stables.' *The more I can keep Tony away from the destructive influences of Agnes Henry the better all our lives will be!*

Assessing The Damage

It was with extreme reluctance that Caleb finally opened his eyes. *It had been a pleasing dream. One where there was definitely no pain but the alluring aroma of a hot breakfast is beckoning me out of slumber.* The first thing that he did see wasn't the delicious tray of food but his cousin's battered face.

'Welcome back to the land of the living. How do you feel?' Geoff passed a cup of coffee under Caleb's nose.

'Like I've gone ten rounds with Gentleman Jackson,' groaned Caleb as he struggled to sit up. 'Do you feel as bad as you look?'

Geoff ran a light hand over his own bruises. 'It'll be a couple of weeks before I can break any hearts again.'

'The Lady was worth the pain cousin.'

'The trouble is, the Lady only has eyes for you.' A twinkle entered Geoff's eyes as he placed Caleb's breakfast tray onto his lap.

Caleb looked up startled. 'Do you really think so?'

'Yes you lucky man, now eat up, you need to build up your strength.'

Caleb ran a hand over his face. 'I need a shave.'

'And a bath!' Chuckling Geoff stole a piece of toast.

Reaching out to pick up the knife and fork, Caleb was surprised that his hand shook. 'Maybe I'll have to put off that shave for a day or two.' Rising to his feet, Geoff commandeered Caleb's coffee as well.

'If you don't trust me to shave you, we can always ask Mrs Cooper to do it.' Caleb managed to save his other piece of toast.

'It can wait a day or two. Do you think I can eat my own breakfast?'

Heading for the door, Geoff laughed. 'It's good to see you have an appetite, last night you barely touched your dinner. Tell me Caleb, what really happened in the barn between you and Lady Tony?'

As colour surged across Caleb's cheeks, he found himself lost for words as he flashed back to the barn. *Tony lying naked in my arms, my hands caressing her supple body until she sighed in pleasure. Her lips eager against mine and the way Tony had not been frightened by the physical evidence of my desire.* It took Geoff several attempts to regain Caleb's attention.

'My God! It was that good?' Opening his mouth, Caleb could not get the words out and Geoff laughed, 'Congratulations cousin, can I be your best man?'

'You're moving a little fast for me Geoff.'

'Eat up and I'll tell Mrs Cooper to draw you a bath.' Geoff felt so happy for his cousin. *Perhaps finally things are going right for Caleb?* Geoff thought.

You Can't Leave

There was a battle of wills going on at the Manor stables as Tony looked incredulous as a nervous Groom refused to saddle up a horse for her.

'I beg your pardon?' She said quietly.

Simon swallowed hard as he had never before said, "No" to Lady Tony. 'Lady Charlotte said… well actually Mrs Henry said you shouldn't leave the Manor today, my Lady… that it's not safe. The Countess agreed.'

'I see! Thank you Simon.' Tony spoke calmly and quietly which scared the Groom more than if she had screamed at him. Not that Tony was ever in the habit of screaming at the servants.

Turning her crutches, Tony contemplated creating a massive scene with her in laws as she headed back up to the house; when she finally decided that it was not worth it. *There is enough conflict and drama going on already at the Manor that I'm resolvedly not going to add to it over this matter.*

Catching up with Tony as she re-entered the Manor, Aidan was disappointed as he had wanted to see Caleb but so long as he could be with Tony, he didn't really mind. Duncan was rather alarmed by the calm acceptance from Tony as he had expected fireworks from the fiery heiress. That was exactly how the Earl felt when he looked up surprised as Tony limped into the study on her crutches.

'Oh sorry Papa, I was just after that book on Greek mythology that you used to read to me when I was younger.'

The Earl stretched back in his chair as he twirled his quill through his fingers. 'I thought you had taken Aidan over the Stirling Arms?'

Gracefully Tony shrugged her shoulders. 'Apparently we're forbidden from leaving the estate. Do you think Aidan is too young to learn chess? Duncan is tired of losing to you all the time.'

The quill fell from his Lordship's long fingers and splattered ink across the blotting paper on the desk. 'Who forbade you Tony? No, stupid question! That woman will be my early death. Are you very upset?'

Again the beautiful shoulders shrugged. 'It doesn't matter. Compared to the serious issues that we're going to have to deal with in the coming weeks, it is inconsequential. The scandal is going to be momentous and while Mrs Henry is here, it will be harder to get Charlotte to eat properly.'

You Can Talk To Me

A smug look appeared on the Earl's face. 'Actually I expect Agnes to encourage Charlotte to eat more right now.'

Glancing away from the shelves, Tony's eyebrows rose. 'Oh? Do we expect an announcement soon that Charlotte is expecting or will you wait until the scandal has abated?'

The Earl rose to his feet and stretched up for the book that was just out of Tony's reach. 'You don't have to bottle everything up inside baby girl. I'm always here if you want to talk. You don't have to be ashamed of what you're feeling or if you don't understand what these feelings really mean.' Tenderly he laid his hand over his daughter's. For a brief moment his Lordship was given a glimpse behind the facade that Tony had begun to erect around her.

'Have I made more out of it than what really happened? Will the scandal destroy any hope of his words becoming reality?'

Lord Stirling felt his chest tighten in fear. *I had realised that Tony had been brief about what had taken place in the barn but with Doctor Masters' examination any real fears had been laid to rest. Now doubts have arisen once more.* 'What did Lord Delacourt promise you?'

Tony dragged in a shuddering breath as she moved to stare out the French windows. 'He spoke of a pleasure that I'd never experienced before, a love so complete that I thought it would be impossible to obtain. When Caleb held me, kissed me, it was about devotion and worship. It wasn't forced or ugly. I wasn't repulsed by his touch like with Sutherland or Cousin Patrick.'

A groan escaped from the Earl and misunderstanding the reason behind it, Tony rushed into speech. 'I wasn't compromised Papa. When I asked Caleb to stop, he stopped.'

The Earl smiled sadly. 'I believe you baby girl. It's just when you mentioned pleasure and a complete love it reminded me of your mother and I.'

'Oh Papa, I'm sorry.'

He caressed his hand down Tony's cheek. 'Don't be, if you have found that then I'm happy for you.' Moved, the Earl drew his daughter into his embrace.

'But what if it was just… lust?' There was so much doubt in her voice.

'Take one day at a time Tony. Be friends first and get to know one another, if it is meant to be then the scandal won't keep you apart.'

Tony exhaled slowly to calm her nerves. 'I can handle this!' Outside they could hear Mrs Henry's voice ordering Charlotte around. 'I don't know if I can handle that!' Tony added.

The Earl sighed. 'Believe me, my dear, I know! Go and keep Aidan amused. I'm going for a drive.' He lightly patted Tony on the backside as he strolled out of the study.

The Earl's Invitation

Looking up from his newspaper, Geoff Delacourt was surprised when Earl of Stirling strolled into the Stirling Arms. The younger gentleman rose immediately to his feet and bowed.

'My Lord, a pleasure to see you again.' Geoff folded up his newspaper as he approached the nobleman.

'Is Caleb available for a visitor?'

Geoff nodded. 'Doctor Masters is with him at the moment. Would you like to come on up?' He gestured for the Earl to precede him up the stairs.

'Thank you,' as they ascended to the bedrooms, the Earl asked, 'How are you Geoff? Your bruises appear worse today.'

'I'll be interesting for a week or so.' Geoff grinned.

The Earl cast a quick scrutinising glance over the younger man. 'What an unusual way of looking at these events.'

'I'm an unusual kind of guy.' Geoff opened the door without knocking and gestured for the Earl to walk straight into Caleb's room.

Doctor Stanley Masters looked up from his task of rewrapping Caleb's shoulder. 'Good morning Lord Stirling, I've almost completed redressing Lord Delacourt's wound.'

Caleb sat on the edge of his bed, naked except for a pair of breeches. He attempted to rise to his feet but the Doctor pushed him back down again.

'A pleasure to see you again Lord Stirling but I had half expected to see Tony and Aidan this morning.' Caleb spoke with a light and easy tone but he was incredibly pale from the Doctor's administering.

The Earl nodded, 'It's about them that I want to talk to you and your cousin. My… my wife has forbidden my children from leaving the house.' He strolled across to the window as the Doctor assisted Caleb back into his shirt.

'Perhaps understandable sir, considering yesterday's events. How can we help you?' Caleb's voice had faltered slightly as he raised his arms to ease into his clothes.

'For several reasons I'd like you and Geoff to come and stay at the Manor for a couple of days.'

Doctor Masters glanced across at the Earl in surprise. 'Is that a good idea, Julius? I understand that you have a house full of guests.'

The Earl shook his head. 'Not guests, Stanley, family and that's one of the reasons I want the Delacourts at the Manor. Some of those family members are destined to annoy the life out of my baby girl and I really don't want Tony to end up having to kill someone. With you there, I hope to prevent this and at the same time protect my children from any future attempts upon their lives.'

'Don't you think the boys have been through enough Julius?' asked Doctor Masters.

''I trust them to do whatever they need to in keeping Tony and Aidan safe but more importantly Aidan trusts them.'

Doctor Masters still wasn't happy. 'Won't having the cousins at the house fuel the rumours that will escalate the scandal?'

A grimace appeared on the Earl's gentle features. 'Better that than Claude swanking around like he owns the place! Can you believe Agnes Henry had the gall to offer that dolt of a son as a suitable suitor for my daughter? Gad that woman infuriates me!'

Caleb bowed slightly. 'We're at you service Lord Stirling.'

A smile dispersed the Earl's look of disgust. 'Thank you. What are Doctor's orders for the wounded hero?'

Packing away his medical bag, Masters paused briefly. 'Bed rest for today. After that nothing too strenuous until that shoulder heals.'

'Good, we have an extensive library for you to peruse, Duncan needs a new chess opponent and it will give you time to become better acquainted with Tony away from public scrutiny,' concluded the Earl.

Geoff headed for the door and held it open for Lord Stirling and Doctor Masters. 'I'll just pack up my belongings and return to give you a hand Caleb.'

'I'll manage,' Caleb promised but his pallor and shortness of breath suggested differently.

The Doctor catching Geoff's look of disbelief, shook his head. 'Send up Ruth Cooper, she'll soon have you both sorted out.' Caleb didn't have the strength to argue and only managed to nod his head.

The Delacourts Take Up Residency

In a very short period of time, Caleb was seated beside Lord Stirling in his carriage as the Earl and Geoff thought hauling himself up into the phaeton would be too much for Caleb's shoulder. Geoff followed alone in the phaeton and was more than a little alarmed when Caleb didn't offer a protest as Geoff and William, one of the Footmen, assisted Caleb out of the carriage once they had drawn up at the front of the Manor. This lack of independence worried Geoff until he was rebuffed upon offering Caleb his arm to lean upon as they followed the Earl into the morning room.

With her legs curled up beneath her in a large easy chair, with Aidan on her lap and a book in her free hand, Tony looked up at their entrance. For a brief moment, fearing it was an intrusion of in-laws, her face reflected a haunted expression as she broke off the story she had been reading aloud.

The look of exasperation immediately vanished when Tony realised who had entered with her father and a delicate blush highlighted her porcelain skin. She didn't lower her eyes in maidenly modesty but an enchanting smile swept away her annoyance at being interrupted. Aidan immediately jumped down from Tony's lap and launched himself at Caleb who bent down and lifted the young Lord up with his good arm.

'Lord Caleb! Mr Geoff! Oh I am pleased to see you! Grandmother Henry said we can't leave the house.' Aidan wrapped his arms around Caleb's neck.

'So we understand, my Lord.' Geoff was pleased that he had been included in Aidan's warm greetings. 'So we've come to you instead. Your father thought we might be able to stand in as temporary playmates while her Ladyship's ankle heals.'

Unravelling herself from the chair, Tony rose to her feet and limping forward, took Aidan out of Caleb's arms and lifted him down. 'How kind of you to take on this role, although it doesn't look like Lord Delacourt will be able to play today.' Her eyes scanned his strained features as Caleb tried to hide his pain and fatigue.

The Earl nodded, 'I had left orders before I went to the Arms for a bed to be made ready for Caleb so I'll just see if everything has been prepared and then Aidan you can show our guests to their rooms.' The Earl left the room as Tony assisted Caleb into the chair she had just vacated.

'You shouldn't have left your bed today, my Lord.' Tony gestured for Geoff to also sit down. 'But I am so very glad to see you. Both of you,' she added.

Grinning, Geoff was amused by Tony's deliberate inclusion of him to her welcome. 'We do understand, Lady Tony, family can be very... trying shall we call it?'

Caleb looked up at his cousin suspiciously. 'Would that be a dig at me perhaps?'

Geoff laughed. 'Actually not this time, I was thinking of our own nagging female relatives which drove us away from home for respite.'

'Just as well,' Caleb sighed. 'Otherwise I'll ask her Ladyship to kick your backside.'

Aidan had been climbing up onto Caleb's lap but the boy started to giggle so much that he nearly toppled over the arm of the chair. Caleb reached out to grasp hold of Aidan so that he didn't fall on his head.

'Do you know what is really funny, Lord Caleb?' giggled Aidan.

'What Lord Aidan?'

'Tony wasn't only trained to fight with a sword but Papa has a little old oriental man to teach us hand to hand fighting. She really could kick his butt!'

Caleb's eyebrows rose. 'Really? I look forward to you showing me your moves.' Geoff broke out into peals of laughter as Tony blushed. Caleb cast him a pained look. 'Why do you have to make everything about sex Geoff?'

'I'm not the one who can't keep his hands to himself!'

'Gentlemen!' Tony calmly reclaimed their attention, 'please remember that there is a child present.'

Geoff shook his head. 'No, no, the saying is "please remember that there's a Lady present."'

'Funny man,' Tony lightly punched Geoff's arm, 'be careful what you say in front of Aidan, he is young, not stupid.'

'I'll keep that in mind, Lady Tony.' Geoff couldn't stop grinning.

Lady Margarette's Welcome

Both Delacourt cousins looked up defensively as the door opened. The sudden tension left their bodies as Duncan Gray entered with the Dowager Countess Lady Margarette leaning upon his arm.

'Please gentlemen, don't get up. My grandson looks very comfortable with you Lord Delacourt.' The Dowager waved them back into their chairs as they attempted to rise.

Caleb looked a little startled. 'How did you know which of us was which?'

A twinkle entered the older Lady's eyes. 'Julius said that Mr Delacourt was battered in the face and Lord Caleb had a bullet wound to the shoulder. Ergo I knew who you were.' The Dowager affectionately brushed her hand against her granddaughter's hair. 'Once Lord Caleb has been settled into his room and you have arranged something to amuse Mr Geoff, then, my darling girl, we have to meet Charlotte in her dressing room. To try on some dresses.' Although Tony sighed, she didn't argue but nodded in acceptance.

Geoff responded, 'You don't need to entertain me Lady Stirling. Caleb is going to be stuck in bed for today, so long as I have a rough idea of the layout of the house I can amuse myself. We're here to work as the Earl is worried about his children's continued safety.'

Duncan spoke for the first time. 'I'll show Mr Delacourt around. Maybe he plays chess?'

'I'm more of a card player,' Geoff admitted, 'Caleb is your chess player.'

Duncan shrugged. 'I'll take what I can get. Besides which my head still hurts too much for chess.'

Tenderly Tony brushed her hand against the bruise on Duncan's forehead from where Nigel Sutherland had knocked him out with the butt of his pistol. 'Well I suppose that rules out playing Snap then.'

Aidan's eyes lit up. 'Ooh! Ooh! Can I play?'

Duncan groaned as Geoff laughed. 'How about we find a more quiet game.' The Tutor suggested. 'One that won't cause my head to explode.'

Lady Margarette chuckled. 'Any game that includes Aidan can never be a quiet one.'

'Oh Grandmama!' Aidan giggled as the Dowager tickled him under the chin.

Charles, the Footman, quietly entered the parlour and bowed. 'Lord Delacourt's room is ready, Lady Tony.'

Turning, Tony picked up her crutches and reached out to draw Aidan off Caleb's lap and to his feet. 'Thank you Charles.' She turned to the boy, 'Aidan would you like to see Lord Delacourt comfortably settled into his room or do you want to come with me? Understand that will probably include Grandmother Henry.'

About to insist on going with Tony, Aidan hesitated as he thought about it. He glanced from Tony to Caleb. 'Will you read to me Lord Caleb? If you're not too tired?'

Caleb picked up Tony's discarded book on Greek mythology. 'You must really dislike spending time with Mrs Henry if you'd rather listen to me read.'

'If you please.' Aidan gave his big eyed puppy dog look. Caleb drew himself up onto his feet and held his hand out to Aidan. 'Well then, lead the way.'

When Caleb reeled unsteadily on his feet, the Dowager Countess reached out to support him.

'My apologies Lady Margarette.' Caleb was embarrassed as Geoff jumped out of his chair to offer his arm to his cousin.

'Don't be silly, Lord Caleb. You need to replace the fluid your body has lost in blood.' The Dowager released Caleb and transferred her gaze to the Footman. 'Charles ask Mrs Hill, the Cook for some lemonade or barley water for Lord Delacourt.'

'Yes my Lady.'

Tony added, 'or you could ask if there is any of Mr Preston's ginger ale.'

Charles bowed. 'Of course my Lady.' He held the door open as Lady Margarette led Tony out of the room. They headed with fatalistic dread towards Charlotte's dressing room while Duncan led the Delacourt cousins and Aidan to their rooms upstairs. *I'm surprised by the boy's ready acceptance of Lord Delacourt as a companion, especially as I had been unsuccessful in parting Aidan from Tony only this morning,* mused Duncan. *Considering the number of strong willed women who are going to be in a small enclosed area, there are bound to be arguments and I'm not surprised by Aidan's desire to be well away from the approaching storm.*

You Have No Power

Squaring her shoulders, Tony held her head up as she followed the Dowager Countess into the battlefield. Laid out over every available surface of the dressing room attached to Charlotte's bedroom was an array of dresses in a myriad of colours and styles. Long flowing dresses, high waisted, puffed short sleeves, some with long undersleeves. The neck lines were low, they were high, and there were adornments such as ribbons, embroidery, lace and buttons.

Grudgingly I have to admit to myself that Mrs Henry had been right about Charlotte's lack of an eye for colour, mused Lady Margarette. There was a deep crimson evening dress, an emerald green day dress, and a royal blue riding dress which caused the Dowager to frown as she had never seen Charlotte ride in her life.

Clearing a comfortable chair for her grandmother, Tony observed the frown and couldn't help smiling. *Even though*

Grandmama had never had to worry about where she would find the money for her next meal, when she had been mistress of Stirling Manor, she and not Grandpapa had been the firm hand that had stopped the family fortune from being drunk or gambled away. The obvious waste of money by the current Countess is probably only erased by the fact that if I am unable to use Charlotte's castoffs, then they would definitely fit Lizzy, Charlotte's younger and darker haired sister.

Gently easing Lady Margarette into the free chair, Tony kissed her on the forehead affectionately. 'What we can't cure, we will endure.'

'Saucy minx!' The Dowager's face relaxed into a smile as she chuckled.

Charlotte entered the dressing room from her bedroom, looking harassed and exhausted as Mrs Henry continued to criticize everything that her daughter did or said. So when Charlotte turned tear-filled eyes to Tony, she took pity on her young step-mother and turned to the Maid who followed demurely behind them.

'Jane, please take Lady Charlotte to my room to lie down. Perhaps a cold compress, a little peppermint tea or ginger ale and some sleep.' Tony took one of Charlotte's trembling hands into her own and affectionately kissed her cheek. 'Papa told me the good news that you're expecting again. Don't worry about us, have a rest and you'll feel more like having dinner tonight.' Signalling to Jane to take her mistress away, Tony observed the Maid refused to acknowledge Agnes Henry's protests but offered her arm to the faint Countess and led her out of the room.

'You overstep your Authority Tony!' Agnes' lips thinned into an ugly line.

Laying a gentle hand on the Dowager's shoulder, Tony's eyes blazed in restrained anger. 'I watched my mother miscarry more children than I care to remember! Laying all this stress on

Charlotte's shoulders will end the same way. So stop criticising Charlotte or you can pack your bags again!'

'You have no power to throw us out!' fumed Agnes.

Tony's eyebrows rose. 'Do you really want to test that theory?'

Gaping like a gummy fish, Agnes turned on Tony's Maid, Mary, as she was quietly turning a dress inside out. 'Stupid girl! What good is the dress inside out?'

In exasperation, Tony sighed, 'I am starting to lose patience with you, Madam. By turning the dresses inside out it will be easier for Mary to ease the darts and seams if they are going to fit me at all!'

Lady Margarette tapped her arthritic fingers against the arm of her chair. 'If you have finished with your interruptions Mrs Henry then perhaps we can begin?' Under the Dowager's glare, Agnes finally subsided and silently fumed as Tony began to strip down to her chemise and drawers. A gasp of horror was torn from Lady Margarette as the bruises around Tony's wrists, ankles and throat were revealed.

'Oh Tony, I… I have an ointment that will speed up the healing process.'

Tony felt self-conscious in her underwear. 'Thank you Grandmama.'

'You girl! Better start with something that has long sleeves and a high neck!' Agnes barked out the order to a startled Mary. Agnes wasn't even looking at the Maid as she was transfixed by the sight of Tony in her underwear. *All the hard work; planning, struggling and effort needed to get Charlotte and Lizzy even presentable, yet it is all perfectly natural for Tony!* Agnes fumed silently.

'Mary is her name and not "You Girl!" please remember that as she'll have very sharp scissors as she removes the darts of the dresses,' stated Tony.

'I promise not to stab Mrs Henry.' Mary blushed.

Tony shook her head. 'I'm more worried that you might accidentally stab me.'

The Maid smiled. 'I won't do that, my Lady.' Mary threw a dress over Tony's head and assisted her to adjust the clothes around her.

Transformation Begins

Struggling to breathe, Tony stood as still as possible as Mary picked up a pair of delicate little scissors and began to unpick darts around the bodice. The Maid looked directly at Tony as she apologised. 'If you'll excuse me, my Lady.' Mary reached into the bodice to adjust Tony's breasts so that they sat more naturally rather than being crushed beneath the material.

'Can you breathe Lady Tony?' The Maid removed her hands and stepped back as Tony took a deep breath.

'Just! How do I look?' She turned to glance into the full length mirror at the strange vision reflected back at her.

A strangled sound came from the Dowager and Tony turned, horrified by the look of pain on her grandmother's face. She immediately dropped to her knees to grasp Lady Margarette's hands between her own.

'What is it? Grandmama, are you ill?'

Patting her granddaughter's hands, the Dowager pulled herself together. 'Oh my dear child, for a moment you looked just like your dear mother. When you dress like a man it is so easy to forget that.' The older woman caressed her hand down Tony's cheek.

Agnes Henry tapped her foot impatiently. 'Do you think we can move onto the next dress? We have a lot of clothes to go through.'

A look of annoyance settled upon the Dowager's face as Tony rose to allow Mary to slip the dress over her head and start adjusting new one. 'If you have something more important you need to do Agnes, please don't let us keep you. Or are you waiting to see what dresses won't fit Tony so that you can take them for Lizzy?'

As Agnes' colour rose, Tony chuckled. 'How unfair you are Grandmama… Agnes has already taken the dresses she wants Lizzy to try on.'

'You shouldn't eavesdrop Tony, it isn't a becoming habit for a Lady!' Agnes' colour deepened.

Lady Margarette cast her a look of scorn. 'Even with my diminishing hearing I could have heard you arguing with Charlotte halfway down the hall!'

Stiffening in indignation, Agnes tried to defend herself. 'Why shouldn't my Lizzy receive cast offs from her sister? If I can't make her presentable I may never get her off my hands!'

The Battle Of The Matriarchs

Mary struggled to keep her hands steady as she undid a dart and bit down on her lip as her eyes met the mischievous laughter in Tony's. Both younger women remained silent as this was a battle between the matriarchs.

'So much for all your fine talk about doing everything possible to salvage Tony's reputation!' retorted the Dowager. 'You came down to Stirling to gloat and to see what you could get out of the situation! You don't give a fig about Tony's reputation or if she will ever manage to find a suitable husband now! In fact nothing would please you more than if Tony's reputation was ruined beyond repair!'

'How dare you! I care a great deal for Tony…' Agnes was cut off by Lady Margarette.

'Oh please! You don't care for anyone but yourself and perhaps that dolt you call a son! He is the one you need to worry about marrying off and not Lizzy. In fact what has suitors running shy isn't Lizzy's lack of dowry but being related to you and Claude!'

Agnes threw a couple of dresses across her arm and stormed towards the door. 'I don't have to stay and be insulted like this!'

The Dowager was just getting into her stride. 'Not in the least Agnes, where you are concerned, we will gladly deliver!'

The door slammed shut behind Agnes causing Lady Margarette to chuckle. Tony waited until Mary had removed her dress and eased her into another before she spoke, 'You enjoyed that too much Grandmama! I thought you said that it isn't dignified to lower yourself to that woman's level?'

The Dowager smirked. 'It needed to be said, Tony. That woman is insufferable! She really is taking pleasure in your misfortune.'

Tony winced as she shifted her weight off her damaged ankle and Mary continued to make the dresses fit. 'Maybe, but Charlotte will suffer for it. I was thinking of suggesting to Papa that Lizzy remains with us once Agnes and Claude can be encouraged to leave the Manor. Away from her mother's bullying, it may help Lizzy to come out of her shell a little.'

Lady Margarette nodded. 'Yes it would be good for Charlotte too. Mary let's try that blue riding dress next. I'd like to see if that will fit.'

'Yes my Lady.'

A Touching Scene

There was no more talk now with the exception of discussion about the clothes as they made their way through the dresses. Not all the clothes could be made to fit comfortably for Tony but Mary carried away at least a dozen dresses, whilst Jane took the rejected ones to Lizzy's room. Mary would finish the alterations downstairs and eventually place them in Tony's wardrobe once Charlotte had finished resting on Tony's bed.

There would, of course, be fall-out from the argument between Lady Margarette and Agnes but Tony tried to push worrying about that to the back of her mind as she went to check up on Caleb and Aidan. There was no answer when Tony quietly knocked on Caleb's bedroom door and as she slipped into the room, her expression softened. Caleb was banked up with pillows to sit upright, the book of Greek mythology lay open on his lap, but both males were fast asleep.

Aidan was curled up into Caleb's side, his arms around Caleb's waist as his head rested against the man's chest. They looked absolutely adorable but Tony needed to remove the pillows to lay Caleb down flat or he'd end up with a kink in his neck. Supporting one pillow beneath Caleb's head as Tony slid the other pillows out of the way, she eased him down onto the bed. He stirred as Tony mopped his brow with a damp cloth retrieved from a bowl beside the bed.

Instinctively, without opening his eyes, Caleb's hand reached out to ensure that Aidan was safe.

'Sorry,' whispered Tony as Caleb's eyes focussed to meet hers. She closed the book and moved it from Caleb's lap.

'How did you go with your step-mother's dresses?' Caleb stretched out his free hand to caress against Tony's cheek as she sat down on the edge of the bed beside him.

She grimaced, 'I look ugly!'

His body shook with silent laughter as Caleb tried to not disturb Aidan. 'That I don't believe. Do we get to see, at dinner, the new Tony or are there more adjustments needed?'

'I don't know if I have to wear them at home or do I have to start getting used to wearing dresses all the time? Anyway I don't know if you'll be allowed out of bed before tomorrow morning.'

A hurt look descended upon Caleb's features. 'I had thought you'd visit me before you go down to dinner. My own private fashion show.'

'Oh ho! Did you really? What makes my Lord so privileged?'

'Well it's not like I'm asking to see you naked.' He deliberately kept his tone light.

Tony blushed. 'You've already seen me naked.'

'Perhaps you would like to see me naked to even it out?' His fingers trailed tenderly along her jaw.

'Well I've seen you half naked.'

Caleb blinked twice. 'When? Oh yes you tore off my shirt last night didn't you? So that the Doctor could tend to my shoulder. Do you... do you want to see the whole package?'

Tony's breath caught in her throat. 'Actually yes, but...not just yet.' She swallowed hard. 'The sight of that hairy beast Sutherland naked made me feel sick, I just need to be certain that I can stand to see the naked body of any other man. In particular my future husband.'

Caleb's hand trailed lightly down the sleeve of her jacket until he reached her hand. Unconsciously Tony linked her fingers through his.

'So elfling, what will happen if you can't stand to look at even your husband naked?' His tone was light and encouraging, but the desperate need to know her answer made his chest ache.

'Well I suppose we'll just have to make love in the dark!'

Such Tender Loving Care

This time it was impossible for Caleb to contain the laughter that bubbled up in relief and Aidan stirred, drawing away a little from Caleb as he raised his head.

'Lord Caleb? Tony?' Yawning as he rubbed his eyes, Aidan sat up and looked around bewildered.

'Sorry Little Bear, I didn't intend to wake either of you. I only popped in to make sure you were both all right.' Gently Tony stroked her free hand through her brother's tousled hair.

'Can I have a drink please?' Aidan yawned again.

'Of course.' Tony glanced behind her and wasn't disappointed as there was a tray on the desk with a pitcher of ginger ale and a couple of small glasses. As he released Tony's hand so she could pour the drinks, Caleb pulled himself upright again.

'Yes please.' Caleb was surprised how thirsty he felt. Tony paused in pouring to rearrange the pillows behind Caleb so they supported him. Amused and touched by the care she was taking of him, Caleb raised his teasing gaze to meet Tony's.

'I should get shot more often,' drawled Caleb as he briefly raised one of Tony's hands to his lips. When she blushed, he let her hand slip out of his so that she could hand out some of Mr Preston's homemade ginger ale. Aidan hadn't understood the context of Caleb's statement and shook his head as he took a glass from Tony.

'Doesn't it hurt, Lord Caleb? You couldn't guarantee that the next bullet might kill you could you?'

Tony bit down upon her bottom lip to stop herself from laughing as Caleb meekly accepted the rebuke and took the glass Tony held out to him. 'You are of course correct, Aidan. I don't know what I could be thinking.' Caleb resolvedly did not look at Tony as he would start laughing.

Mary's Distress

A knock at the door caused Caleb's hand to twitch and automatically slide under his blanket. As Tony's Maid, Mary quietly entered, Caleb relaxed and allowed Tony to ease back the bed covers to reveal a pistol hidden. Tony's eyebrows rose in surprise as she smoothed the blanket back into place.

'You take your charge as protector very seriously.'

Caleb smiled. 'I won't let anyone hurt you or Aidan ever again.'

Feeling slightly breathless, Tony turned her attention to Mary and realised that the Maid was looking slightly agitated.

'Mary, what is it? Are you unwell?' Tony limped across the room to take Mary's hands and led her to one of the comfortable arm chairs in front of the empty fire place.

'Forgive my intrusion, my Lady. I should've composed myself before seeking you out.' Mary rose again from the arm chair but Tony refused to let her leave.

'Never mind that, you know you can tell me anything. My dear, you're trembling.' Tony drew Mary back into the chair and dropped to her knees beside her, tenderly rubbing Mary's hands between her own.

'I was down in the ironing room, Lady Tony, finishing the alternations to the dresses and hanging them before running an iron over the silk dress for you to wear tonight... he grabbed me from behind... he said it was my duty to... keep him amused.' Mary broke off on a sob and concern on Tony's face was replaced by anger.

Caleb understood the gist of her story but didn't know which "he" Mary was referring to. *Surely not Geoff or Duncan Gray? Was it then one of the servants? Had someone from outside gained entrance to the Manor?*

'He will be punished! Have you told Preston what happened?' Tony barely maintained her anger.

Through her tears, Mary nodded. 'He had me trapped against the table and he thrust up my skirts. As I hit and kicked at him, I must have been screaming because in raced William and Charles with Mr Preston and they pulled Mr Henry off me. Oh! They're not going to lose their positions because of me are they?'

'Why should they?' asked Tony.

'Well William hit Mr Henry in the face and broke his nose and Charles punched him in the stomach before Mr Preston told them to drag him outside.'

Tony shook her head. 'So long as Claude isn't actually dead, then no.' glancing up to see Caleb's confused expression she added, 'Claude Henry, my step-mother's brother.'

Sighing, Caleb said, 'I see! You must feel like you're surrounded by sex starved animals?'

'Not really, but Claude knows better than to try his antics in this house! What on earth is wrong with him?'

Mary drew out a handkerchief from the cuff of her dress and dried her eyes. 'Mrs Henry promised him that he would marry you, Lady Tony, to save your reputation. He was angry when you rejected him and… insulted him.'

A muscle spasmed along Tony's jaw as she clenched her teeth tightly together. 'That is no excuse for trying to rape you! That repulsive toad leaves this house right now!' Tony jumped to her feet but Mary restrained her. 'Come on Mary, we're going to Papa!'

'No, my Lady, it's not necessary.' Mary shook her head. Tony opened her mouth to explain why the hell it was necessary when the Maid interrupted, 'Mr Preston went directly to the Earl and told me to find you and make sure you didn't run into Mr Henry; as it's really you that he wants to punish.'

Her chest heaving in angry breaths, Tony's gaze rested briefly on the slight bulge beneath Caleb's blankets where a pistol lay hidden. Correctly interpreting her thoughts, Caleb shook his head. 'No Tony, let your father handle this! Pour Mary a drink and we'll keep her here safe with us.'

For a moment Tony just stared at him with so much hatred in her eyes that he was relieved that it wasn't aimed at him. Slowly the fire died and unable to trust herself to speak, Tony nodded and lowered her gaze to calm herself. The hand that reached out to pick up the pitcher was not exactly steady and Tony was forced to use both hands to pour a drink without spilling it. Mary rose to her feet to take the glass out of Tony's hand.

'Thank you, my Lady, perhaps you should sit down.'

A Chaperone Is Necessary

Taking a deep breath, Tony picked up the mythology book and limped around the bed to sit down on the bed beside Aidan. Mary sank back into her chair and sipped her drink. Aidan flipped through the book to the last story he remembered before falling asleep.

'This one Tony.' Aidan looked up from the book to find Mary watching the three of them on the bed with a curious expression on her face. 'Would you like to join us Mary? We can make room for you too.'

Touched by the young boy's words Mary smiled. 'No thank you Lord Aidan, I'll be able to hear from this chair.' As Tony shot a questioning look at her, Mary just shook her head. *I don't think that I can explain the emotion that stirred in my breast as I witnessed what a cosy picture they make. It is easy enough to imagine that this is doting parents with their own child and everything is at peace and right with the world.*

It was only an illusion and it was easily shattered. When Tony had barely begun to read, the door burst open without any warning. The Earl of Stirling pulled up short just inside the door as he realised that Caleb had his pistol trained upon him.

'My apologies Caleb, I forgot that I needed to announce myself. Preston had warned me.' The Earl didn't move a muscle until Caleb lowered his weapon.

'Understandable my Lord; you've had a trying afternoon. It's not easy throwing family out of the house.' Caleb slipped the pistol back into its hiding place. Tony cast her father a searching glance as he grimaced.

'Claude is leaving the Manor isn't he Papa?'

'Well, Doctor Masters has to see him first to let us know if he is able to travel. William and Charles really laid into Claude. Are you all right Mary? Did Claude hurt you?'

'I feel so embarrassed for making such a fuss.' Mary blushed under the Earl's concerned gaze. 'It's just that we've become accustomed to Mr Preston's strict guidelines about relations between the servants and the members of the household that I was unprepared for Mr Henry's attentions.'

The Earl shook his head. 'Not attentions Mary; assault! If he ever wants to step foot into this house again, Claude must never lay his hands on anyone else within these walls. You're not to blame yourself Mary.'

'Thank you my Lord. Are… are William and Charles in trouble?'

The Earl's eyebrows rose in surprise. 'Of course not. Although I was a little surprised by William, Preston and Charles had to pull him away from pounding Claude into paste.'

Blushing Mary admitted, 'That's probably because William and I are… walking out together.'

'Does Preston know?' asked Tony.

'Oh yes, before anything became serious we went to Mr Preston to get his blessing. So long as it doesn't affect our professionalism or we are not obvious in public,' explained Mary. Embarrassed by all the attention she rose to her feet. 'I'd better get on with my work.'

The Earl eased the Maid back into the chair. 'You are doing your work, Mary, you're acting as chaperone for Tony.' With a wave of his hand at the trio on the bed he added, 'to us this is Innocent but the outside world would not see it that way.'

Glancing across at Caleb, Tony felt guilty at not having considered the inappropriateness of their current position. *It had just seemed so natural to join Caleb and Aidan on the bed.* 'Should Aidan and I leave Lord Delacourt to rest?' Tony asked.

'Not until the Henrys have departed from the house. I have no doubt that Caleb is more than capable of dealing with Claude if he should be foolish enough to take his revenge on Mary or you, Tony.'

A frown descended on Caleb's brow. 'In how much danger does Tony stand from malicious gossip from the Henrys?'

A muscle in the Earl's cheek contracted and he looked quite formidable. 'One word leaked by either Agnes or Claude and they can wave goodbye to any allowance they get from me! Agnes has been upsetting Charlotte too. Firstly over taking dresses for Lizzy before you have even tried them, after that, her complaints about the lack of respect Agnes receives in this household.'

'Before she could have Charlotte in tears, Lizzy threw her out of the room and set about calming her sister down. I've asked Lizzy if she'd like to stay when her mother and brother leave. I thought it would be a nice break for her.'

Tony smiled enchantingly up at her father. 'That was very considerate of you Papa and it'll be good for Charlotte too. I'm not a very feminine companion.' There was no argument with that statement.

The Doctor's Assessment

When Preston knocked and quietly showed Doctor Masters into Caleb's room, the Earl of Stirling was sitting in the arm chair opposite Mary as they listened to Tony read aloud. They were so engrossed in the story and it was near the end of the story so the two men waited patiently for Tony to finish.

That wasn't to say that their entrance had not been noticed; both Mary and Caleb had looked up at the knock at the door but had immediately returned their attention to Tony's story once they realised that the intruders were harmless. The cosiness of the scene amused the Doctor's quirky sense of humour so he was less critical about being called out again for the family.

'Well Claude Henry will live. He'll be in pain for several days and probably should rest but I think he wants to get as far away from here as soon as possible,' reported Doctor Masters.

Seeing that the Earl was still lost in the world of ancient Greece, Tony addressed the Doctor, 'Are you sick of running around after us yet Doc?'

'I'm glad to see that you're not responsible for this latest violence.'

'Actually I think I am Doc.' Tony cast a guilty expression towards Mary. 'Claude was promised he could save me from ruin by marrying me and Papa immediately destroyed that illusion.'

Both the Doctor's eyebrows rose. 'That doesn't seem like a reasonable excuse for attacking your Maid. Mary do you need my services?'

'Thank you Doctor Masters but no, Mr Henry never managed to actually... do anything,' reassured Mary.

'In that case, I'll be waiting for the next exciting chapter.' The Doctor nodded to the occupants in the room before following Preston out again.

We'll Let You Sleep

'I'm not certain but I think I've just been insulted.' Tony cast a mischievous glance across at Caleb.

Placing his hand over his mouth as he yawned, Caleb replied, ' No I think the Doc knows you so well that he realises that there's more adventure to come.'

Reaching out to brush a lock of hair from Caleb's forehead, Tony asked, 'Have we tired you Lord Delacourt?' Closing the book on her lap, she slid off the bed and held out her arms to Aidan to lift him down. 'We'll let you get some sleep, then you might just be ready for that fashion show.' She removed the pillows from beneath Caleb's head so that he could lie down flat.

'Hum! You wouldn't tease a wounded man now would you?' He allowed Tony to take the empty glass out of his hand and place it back on the tray. Tony shook her father by the shoulder to try to bring him back to their century.

'No,' she sighed. 'If I have to learn to wear dresses, I might as well start now.'

'You never know you might end up liking it.'

'You are a dreamer aren't you?' Tony cast Caleb a saucy smile.

The smile he returned was just as enchanting. 'Regardless of what you wear, you'll still be the most beautiful woman in the room... or anywhere in fact.'

Pausing in the process of shaking the Earl's shoulder once more Tony looked back at Caleb in surprise. 'Flattery now, my Lord? You're not one of those smooth talking rakes my Papa warns me about?'

Caleb laughed. 'Only if my intentions are dishonourable my beautiful elfling.'

That seemed to bring the Earl of Stirling back to the present. 'Should I ask about your intentions, Caleb?' Slowly he rose to his feet.

'All in good time, Lord Stirling, but first you have some in-laws you need to throw out.'

Sighing, the Earl held out his hand to his daughter as she collected her crutches. 'Come on Tony, let's show the Henrys how little we need their presence to elevate this scandal!'

'Papa?' Aidan tugged at the hem of his father's jacket.

'Yes Aidan?' the Earl held out his hand to his son.

'Uncle Claude can't marry Tony because he would then be my uncle and my brother. That is just too weird.'

The Earl's lips thinned slightly. 'Claude isn't going to marry Tony. That was just Grandmother Henry's attempt to be...'

'Papa!' Tony interjected warningly.

'Helpful.' One sardonic eyebrow rose at his daughter for her approval. Her eyes twinkled in response.

'Good,' said Aidan, tugging on his father's hand to regain his attention. 'I want Caleb to be my brother.' His out spoken declaration brought about an embarrassed silence. 'I'm just saying, that's what I wish for, if anyone is interested.'

Caleb chuckled. 'Well it looks like Aidan has sorted it all out for us.'

Sighing the Earl permitted his son to drag him to the door, which Mary had already risen to open. 'We'll discuss this when Lord Delacourt is well again,' said the Earl.

Aidan glanced back over his shoulder as they went through the door. 'Bye Lord Caleb, thank you for letting me have a nap with you.'

Caleb was touched by his sincerity. 'You're welcome Lord Aidan. I hope we can both be more active tomorrow.'

Mary curtsied before quietly closing the door behind them. With a deep sigh, Caleb settled back into his pillows and for now allowed sleep to claim him.

Evicting The Henrys

Charlotte was grateful for Lizzy's arm through hers as they withstood the barrage of verbal and psychological abuse from their maternal relative as they gathered in the front driveway to see the departure of Claude and Agnes Henry. Stiff and very sore, and his eyes already turning black and blue, his nose packed with wadding to stop the bleeding; Claude was silent as he boarded the carriage that not that long ago had brought them down to Stirling Manor.

Agnes, though, was not prepared to leave until she had spoken her mind. The Earl looked bored as his mother-in-law picked apart each and every one of them. Tony played ball with Aidan as Geoff and Duncan kept an eye out for possible dangers.

Charlotte winced at her mother's grating voice and tried to stay focussed upon what she was being accused of, but Agnes flitted between each of them at random and Charlotte became confused.

'I'm sorry you feel that way mother.' Charlotte said yet again when Agnes paused long enough for anyone else to say anything at all.

'All I have ever done was to make it possible for my children to have the life that was denied me! Is it too much to expect a little respect in return? Your loyalty should be to me and not your step-daughter! Claude and I are your family!'

Lizzy struggled to not roll her eyes. 'We're not likely to ever forget that mother but to be fair Julius and Tony are Lotte's family too. Claude should've kept his hands to himself. We all knew how strict Preston is over the servants. You shouldn't have filled Claude's head full of delusions that he could possibly ever be Tony's knight in shining armour!'

Lizzy's Defiance

All of them looked at Lizzy, stunned into silence, including Agnes, as Lizzy had never spoken like that to anyone especially not her mother. All her life she had cowered beneath her mother's tyranny. Lizzy had never spoken back, or ever acted contrary to her mother's wishes or orders.

Whether it was Tony's independent and fiery spirit or the fact that Lizzy was going to spend some quality time away from her suffocating family, she was finally able to voice the frustration she had been bottling up for years.

'How dare you!' For once Agnes' indignation did not move her daughter. As Claude glanced out of the carriage, Lizzy pointed an accusing finger at her brother.

'Ask him why I dare say this to you? I've been blaming myself for it all these years but you should have protected me, mother! He had no right to do what he did but you never did anything to stop him!' The Stirlings continued to look stunned at Lizzy's revelations and Charlotte clung tighter to her sister.

'Oh Liz! Not you too!'

Pulling herself together, Tony cast a pleading glance across to Duncan Gray and placed her hands over Aidan's ears. 'Duncan please take Aidan inside.' She begged, *this is definitely not a conversation that a five year old should overhear.* The Tutor rushed forward to grasp Aidan's hand and suggested they went to the kitchen in search of biscuits. The look on the Earl's face as he turned to his wife was of pure disbelief.

'You were a virgin when we married.' Tony wasn't certain if that was a question or a statement but kept her mouth shut as this wasn't her concern. Charlotte held out a trembling hand to her husband, tears welling in her eyes.

'Yes of course I was! No matter what I had to do to him I never let him touch me there!'

Nodding in agreement, Lizzy added, 'It was all about Claude's satisfaction rather than anyone else's. Once you started supplementing his income, Claude could indulge some of his more freakish desires elsewhere and I haven't had to service him as often.'

'If you, either of you, had told me sooner, I would not have let this travesty continue for a minute longer.' The Earl took a hand of each of the sisters and pressed them against his heart.

Trembling all over now, Charlotte admitted, 'I was afraid that if you knew what we had to do, you would send me away or divorce me. That I'd be forced to go back to that life with them.'

His expression softened into affection as Charlotte raised her hand to her husband's cheek. 'Oh Lotte, I would never do that!' His Lordship looked up at the Coachman waiting patiently at the reins of his horse. 'Lewis isn't it?'

Surprise flittered across the Coachman's face that he had until that moment kept blank. 'Yes my Lord.' *I doubt that Mrs Henry or Mr Claude even know my name.*

'When you arrive back in London, ask the Housekeeper, Mrs Ashby, to pack up all Miss Lizzy's personal belongings and send them down here. She will no longer be residing with her mother.'

'Yes my Lord.' Lewis was even more impressed that the Earl knew the name of the Henry's Housekeeper.

While the girls had aired their dirty Henry family secrets, Agnes had fallen silent in shame but with the Earl of Stirling taking her daughters' side she achieved a comeback.

'I'll thank you to not issue orders to my staff, Julius. If Lizzy is going to remain with Charlotte I will arrange for her belongings to be sent to her!'

One slow sardonic eyebrow rose as the Earl turned to face his mother-in-law. 'In all future communications you will address me as "My Lord" or "Earl Stirling"! Both you and Claude are banned from Stirling Manor until I deem that you're acceptable to associate with your daughters or my children!'

'Spread one word of what you have forced upon your daughters and I will have you exiled from polite society. One word from either of you about Tony's abduction and I will bury you so deep that your remains could end up in China! Do you understand me?'

Although Agnes quaked at the fury in the Earl's words, she managed a 'How dare you?' before his Lordship completely annihilated her.

'One more word madam and you'll never see another penny from me!'

Frantically Claude reached out of the carriage to grasp his mother's arm. 'For goodness sake Mother let's get out of here before we're both murdered!'

'That's the most sensible thing to come out of your mouth Claude! Keep it up and you might even graduate to human being!'

Agnes opened her mouth to defend her son but one look at the fury on her son-in-law's face and she tightly pressed her lips together again.

'Good choice, now get off my property.' The Earl turned away from the Henrys in disgust and was surprised to find his mother as well as Grace's parents had joined him. The Dowager began to applaud and very soon the rest of the Earl's family joined in. Claude dragged his mother into the carriage as it was clear they had definitely worn out their welcome. Embarrassed by his family's accolades, the Earl blushed but didn't protest when Charlotte openly kissed his cheek.

The carriage drove away as the Earl led his family back into the house. He offered his arm to both sisters as Geoff escorted Lady Margarette back inside. Following her family through the front door struggling on her crutches, Tony couldn't help but smile. *There is still going to be some serious backlash to contend with over the abduction but I couldn't think of a group of people that I'd rather face it with.*

Yes Very Ugly!

When Caleb awoke, he felt refreshed and more energised than he had since waking the first time that day. Candles had been lit in the room and Mary brought in a tray for dinner. Although it smelt delicious, Caleb's attention was captured and held by the vision of beauty that limped self-consciously into his bedroom.

This reluctant angel was followed by her sibling, her shadow. Tony's hair had been swept up into a bun on top of her head, with random curls falling around her face. She wore her mother's pearl necklace and a low cut blue silk dress that echoed the fascinating colour of her eyes. Aidan slipped out from behind Tony's skirts and jumped up onto the bed beside Caleb.

'Oh yes elfling,' Caleb's words came out as barely a whisper. 'Definitely ugly!'

At Mary's shocked expression, Tony laughed. 'Private joke Mary.'

The Maid nodded. 'Do you want me to stay, my Lady?'

'Head on downstairs to your own dinner, I only came to fulfil a promise I made. His Lordship is in no condition to compromise me and Aidan is here to protect me.' Bobbing a curtsey, Mary let herself out of the room.

Assisting Caleb to sit up and banking up his pillows, Tony arranged the tray over his lap. Aidan picked up the napkin, shook it out and spread it across Caleb's chest.

'So I'm just an obligation my elfling?' Caleb gently laid his hand over hers. Smiling, Tony entwined her fingers through his.

'No, not at all, but just in case the emotions of last night were just full moon, midsummer madness, then I want to retain some dignity and not proclaim to the world my love for you just yet.' Her bravery in the face of overwhelming doubts, made Caleb want to sweep Tony into his arms and kiss away her fears.

'Are you trying to protect yourself from getting hurt or just offering me the opportunity to back out if I've changed my mind?'

Tony lifted her shoulders in a graceful shrug. 'A little of both actually,' she admitted. *I am valiantly trying to maintain a tight grasp over my emotions but something about being in a dress makes me feel more vulnerable.*

'How soon can we get married without it looking like we had to because of the abduction?' asked Caleb. A sigh escaped from Tony as colour rushed across her cheeks in relief. Chuckling, Caleb raised his free hand to caress her face. 'Doubting Thomas! Oh how I want to kiss you but I'm afraid I'll end up with my dinner in my lap.' He brushed his thumb lightly against her lips. Laughing Tony leant down to shyly kiss him. Releasing her hand, Caleb raised his to cup her face and take control of the kiss.

It was soft and gentle, Caleb holding his desires firmly in check for fear of frightening Tony with too much, too soon. His lips caressed tenderly, sensuously against hers, coaxing, encouraging with a hint, and a promise of the passion that would follow, when she was ready.

It must be her needs and desires that I serve and not my own which are screaming out for more. So much more! To throw the tray to the floor, to lay Tony across the bed and to cover her entire body with hot, searing, passionate kisses until she cries out in pleasure. To make her scream out my name and have her come back for more. That isn't going to happen, not yet anyway. Tony is too fragile, I don't have the strength to maintain my strict control and there is also the fact that Aidan is sitting on the bed beside us. So when Tony began to draw away, Caleb didn't force her to continue the intimacy. Although he was most satisfied with the far away gleam in her eyes.

'So, we don't have to hide our true feelings from each other?' Caleb picked up his cutlery as Tony brushed a wisp of hair out of her eyes.

'No, not at all. Aidan has already had his supper so may he stay with you for a little while?' Tony straightened up and readjusted her crutches.

'Of course, it means I'll get to see you again when you return to collect him.'

'Greedy baby!' Tony uttered a gurgle of laughter. 'Don't you think you'll get sick of the sight of me?'

'No never!'

Heading towards the door, Tony smiled. 'We'll see.'

Aidan made no protest as his sister left the room but put his effort into making certain that Caleb ate all his dinner. Even if that meant helping out; just a little. Especially with the dessert.

An Early Return

Once Caleb had finished eating and not expecting Tony to return for several hours, Aidan moved the tray to the desk and after they read another story, they occupied themselves with playing cards. The Dowager had indeed been correct, playing games with Aidan was not a quiet pursuit but as Caleb didn't have Duncan's tender head, he only smiled at the boy's noisy enthusiasm.

They looked up surprised when Tony returned much earlier than expected with Duncan and Mary following. As Aidan made room for his sister on the bed beside him, she smiled as she apologised and popped her crutches against the wall.

'Well my Lords, I must be uglier than I first thought. Grandmama Sinclair burst into tears every time she looked at me so as soon as dinner was over I offered to retire rather than join the ladies in the parlour.'

Caleb cast a quick glance from Tony to Duncan as there was an edge of pain to Tony's flippant tone. The Tutor shook his head.

'As the Dowager Countess had been with Tony when she had tried on the dresses, she had become accustomed to Tony's new appearance. It was therefore a shock to Mrs Sinclair as Tony now looks more like her mother, Lady Grace, than before.'

'I don't know why I should have that effect upon Charlotte as well, she never knew my mother.'

Chuckling, Duncan met Caleb's eyes as he explained, 'Your step-mother has grown accustomed to you as a beautiful young man, and she is finding it hard to cope with you as a stunningly beautiful young woman. Much more beautiful than she can ever aspire towards.'

Tony cast him a look of scorn. 'I'm sure you exaggerate Duncan. Apart from my clothes, I'm still the same person. Besides which I thought all the rage at the moment in London was for blondes?'

Mary had retired to the chair beside the fireplace with some embroidery. She laughed. 'In your rightful attire, my Lady, you accentuate your feminine charms that your male attire attempted to conceal.'

A Supervised Evening

Caleb glanced around at the group assembled in his bedroom. 'So have you all come to keep me company or is it time this young man was in bed?'

Duncan nodded as Aidan protested that he wasn't tired yet. 'Tony will take Aidan to change into his night wear while I offer you the opportunity to stretch your legs. Maybe take a walk up and down the corridor.' Duncan explained. Caleb nodded but Aidan was prepared to become mulish.

'Am I allowed to stay with Tony tonight?'

Duncan smiled. 'No need to raise your hackles Aidan, for tonight, your father said you may sleep in Tony's bed but tomorrow you must return to your own room.'

Aidan screwed his face up as he considered his options. 'But I don't want to go to bed yet! I'm not tired!!!'

Duncan was prepared to start an argument but Tony just shook her head. 'Don't do it Duncan. That was at least a two exclamation mark statement! Aidan, how about you get changed while Caleb stretches his legs and we return here so that you can play another couple of quiet games until you are ready to sleep? If you haven't overtired Lord Delacourt.'

Caleb threw up his hands in self-defence. 'Don't drag me into this argument!'

'Have I made you tired of me?' Aidan's bottom lip began to tremble as he raised big puppy eyes to Caleb's face.

Caleb bit down on his bottom lip to stop himself from smiling as the young boy's choice of words had a deliberate double meaning. 'I'm not ready to go to sleep either.' Tears were suddenly dried up as Aidan was immediately beaming from ear to ear. He jumped off the bed and dragged his sister out of the room. As the two men looked at each other in amazement, Mary chuckled as she rose to her feet and drew back the bed covers.

'Forgive me Lord Delacourt, but you'd better learn how to deal with manipulation or your babies are going to walk all over you!'

Swinging his legs over the edge of the bed, Caleb carefully moved the pistol hidden under the bedding. 'Do you really think that I'm easily fooled?' He allowed Duncan to assist him into a dressing gown as Mary straightened his bed.

'Time will tell, my Lord, but it does appear as if Lord Aidan has you wrapped around his little finger.'

Stretching, Caleb massaging his damaged shoulder. 'If it means being able to keep Tony by my side a little longer, I'm prepared to give the young Lord a little leeway.'

In stunned silence Duncan and Mary stared at Caleb in surprise. His charming smile appeared. 'Ah yes, Tony said she wanted to be more cautious about declaring her feelings in front of others but I see two people I believe I can trust. You both love Tony and understand my need to protect her.'

Another glance was exchanged between Mary and Duncan. 'Does she love you?' asked Mary.

'She says she does, but Tony is afraid.'

Mary nodded, offering her arm to Caleb as he staggered slightly towards the door. He politely refused the offer but not their company as he made his way down the hall.

'Understandable, my Lord,' said Mary softly, 'you only met again two days ago. What either of you are feeling may not be real.'

'The scandal, as well as the restrictions placed upon Tony will also grate upon her nerves.' Duncan added, his hand hovering beneath Caleb's elbow as he wasn't exactly steady on his feet. 'She won't be allowed to be alone and definitely not alone with you.'

Caleb agreed, 'If it's not enough that Aidan is constantly with us, then I ask that either or both of you chaperone us.

Especially while I need to remain in bed. I think too many other people hovering around will exacerbate the situation for Tony.'

Knowing Tony as well as they did, they already knew this was happening. 'Anything we can do to help Lord Delacourt,' stated Duncan and as they led Caleb down to the bathroom, the Tutor pointed out which bedrooms belonged to which family member.

Time To Retire

On his way to his own bed, Geoff dropped in to see if his cousin needed anything and pulled up short in the doorway at the sight before him. Mary sat in an arm chair beside the empty fireplace, her head lowered as she concentrated on the piece of work she was sewing. Duncan had drawn the other arm chair up beside the bed where Caleb sat banked up by pillows and a chessboard lay between them. Tony sat on the bed beside Caleb and Aidan had fallen asleep in her arms as the two men had patiently been trying to teach the boy how to play chess.

Geoff saw the momentarily glint of steel of Caleb's pistol upon his entrance. *So I know that Caleb's mind is not completely occupied by the game now being played against the Tutor.* Duncan was more than willing to concede defeat as he knew that there was no way he could win against Caleb even though he had been more interested in his Lordship's discussion with Tony. It had been an opportunity to get to know each other a little better. Each other's likes and dislikes, hopes and dreams, and plans for the future.

Although Duncan didn't participate in the conversation, he did listen with interest and the feeling grew that this was the perfect man for Tony. *Caleb can give Tony the life that suits her best. Having accepted that the world I'm about to enter into would make her miserable doesn't mean that I want Tony to settle with something less than she deserves.* Caleb's world was so perfect that at one point Duncan found himself blinking back tears of relief. *Caleb spends most of his days at his country estate, not many miles from Stirling Manor, with occasional visits to London or Bath, mainly to escort or at the insistence of his mother. He has travelled abroad, not the grand tour that our fathers and grandfathers used to talk about and which was fairly restricted of late due to war or conflict within one European country or another. He is well read, can speak several languages and shares Tony's interest in breeding horses.*

By the time Geoff interrupted their game, Duncan was satisfied to champion Caleb's cause. The Tutor picked up Aidan without waking the boy and Mary rose to her feet, collecting up her work before following Duncan out of the room. Tony cleared up the chess pieces and placed them and the board on the desk before collecting her crutches.

'Good night my Lord, thank you for a pleasant evening. I hope the Dowager didn't fleece you out of too much money Mr Delacourt, I should have warned you that Grandmama plays for high stakes.' Tony paused beside Geoff as he held the door open. Obeying the silent command from Caleb, Geoff offered to escort Tony to her room.

'I had the good fortune to be partnered with Lady Margarette and came away from the table considerably richer in the pocket.' Tony was forced to alter her usual manly stride as she was hampered by her dress and the crutches which seemed to work against each other.

'How was everyone once I left? I hoped that you understood that I wasn't abandoning you but I'm not used to so much feminine emotion.'

Looking down at her, Geoff laughed. 'The Dowager took the other women to task for forcing you to flee your own family, then she ignored them as the Earl organised a game of cards to keep his mother amused. Miss Henry took Lady Charlotte up to her room almost immediately but returned without her Ladyship.'

'That scene with their mother will be preying on Charlotte's mind. I'm sorry that you had to witness that melt down. I knew Claude had trouble keeping his hands to himself but I never realised the extent of his debauchery.'

Reaching Tony's room, Geoff paused, 'We all have relatives that we're embarrassed to own. Good night, my Lady.' The door was open and Geoff could see Mary easing back the bedding as Duncan gently laid the sleeping Aidan into Tony's bed. It was safe enough to leave Tony and return to his cousin.

I Can't Find The Right Words

Re-entering Caleb's bedroom, Geoff was surprised as he softly closed the door behind him. Caleb was no longer in bed but sitting at the desk, a quill in his hand but the paper in front of him was still blank.

'What on earth is so important that you have to write a letter now?' Geoff dropped gracelessly into an arm chair.

Looking round, Caleb exhaled slowly. 'I thought I should write to Mama before the rumours reach her ears. At least prepare her for the scandal.'

'So why the blank page then?'

'There is so much I want to say but I'm not certain that a letter is the best vessel for all that I think and feel.'

Examining one of his fingernails, Geoff stated calmly, 'Well don't eat me but I sent a brief note to your mother last night.' At the look of horror appearing on Caleb's face, Geoff hurried to add, 'not all the details, just the basics, the rescue, your wounding, staying a couple of days.'

Caleb groaned in disbelief. 'Well there's one thing I can guarantee you, tomorrow will see the arrival of Mama! You shouldn't have mentioned I was wounded. The fact that I haven't written to her, she's going to think I must be at death's door.'

Leaning back, Geoff stretched out his legs. 'If that was the case, her Ladyship would be here already. Anyway I did say it was a minor wound.'

'Minor?' Caleb ruefully massaged his shoulder.

'It's not easy to make you happy!' Rising to his feet, Geoff took the quill out of his cousin's hand before assisting him back to the bed. 'Does she make you happy cousin?'

'Who?' Caleb had still been thinking about his mother.

Geoff cast a speaking look. 'Caleb! Focus man! Does Lady Tony please you, my Lord?' As he rearranged his pillows so that he could lie down flat, Caleb silently cursed as he could not stop the colour rushing across his cheeks. His thoughts took him back to the sight of Tony in her silk dress, to her lips responsive against his and he willingly allowed himself to dwell upon the memory until Geoff managed to reclaim his attention.

'The silly expression on your face is answer enough coz, but you'll quickly become a bore if you're going to fall into a trance every time her Ladyship's name is mentioned!'

Straightening his bed covers, Caleb chuckled. 'Then stop mentioning it and go to bed. We're going to need all our strength tomorrow.'

'With Sutherland in custody, do you honestly think there is any serious danger to the Stirling children?'

Staring blindly up at his cousin, it was several minutes before Caleb finally answered, 'Call me paranoid but Tony is just so desirable that if she accepts my offer of marriage, I feel that it's going to put a few noses out of joint.'

Snuffing out all the candles except the one beside Caleb's bed, Geoff said, 'I think you may be right.' There was an odd note to his voice that his cousin immediately picked up on.

'Does that include you Geoff?'

His cousin laughed and patted him on his good shoulder, 'No coz, I'm not jealous but that independent streak in Lady Tony will make some men want to tame her, master her.' When

162

Caleb shot him a startled look, Geoff grinned. 'No, you don't have that desire, for you it will be a partnership, not about dominating Lady Tony. That's why I think it will work.'

Feeling guilty that his relief must be so obvious Caleb threw a pillow at Geoff. 'Go to bed.'

His incorrigible cousin grinned as he headed for the door. 'I won't say "sweet dreams" as I'm certain that if they're about Lady Tony they'll be very pleasant indeed!' Laughing, Geoff ducked out of the room before Caleb could find anything else to throw at him.

TUESDAY

Patrick Stirling

The next morning Caleb was permitted to leave his bed, although he was under orders from Doctor Masters to take things easy. Aidan still didn't want to be separated from Tony so, Duncan arranged for some short lessons that they could take outside where Tony and Caleb sat on the patio.

When it came time for Aidan to do his reading aloud, he climbed up onto the swing seat between Tony and Caleb so that they could share this with him. That was how Preston found them just before luncheon and he was moved by the touching scene.

'Lady Tony, you have a... a visitor,' announced the Butler.

'Is it my mother?' Caleb looked up from the book he was helping Aidan with his reading.

Preston's countenance was far from his usual stoic as he answered, 'No, my Lord, it is Mr Patrick.'

Tony groaned in disbelief as Patrick Stirling, her cousin, strolled out onto the patio. Caleb took one look at Patrick and knew immediately that he wasn't going to like him. *Patrick is a town dandy, his blonde hair beautifully groomed, his clothes fastidious and impeccable and his mannerisms are, to say the least, effeminate. He is tall and good looking but would always pale when compared to his beautiful cousin.*

'I was expecting to find my tom boy cousin Tony who dresses like a man, instead I find an elegant young lady. Let's have a look at you beautiful girl.' Patrick held his hands out as he drew Tony to her feet.

'Shelve the charm Patrick, I'm not buying it. This is Lord Delacourt,' introduced Tony as she pulled her hands out of her cousin's.

'Ah yes,' Patrick's voice became silken like a purr. 'Your knight in shining armour! Your hero in a barn!'

'Do you have a problem with that Mr Stirling?' Rising gracefully to his feet, one of Caleb's eyebrows also rose. 'Would you have preferred it if I had done nothing and that monster had raped your cousin? Or are you jealous because you weren't the one to rescue Tony and Aidan?'

For a brief moment Patrick's lips peeled back from his teeth in a snarl. Tony had never seen her cousin look so animalistic and she took a hasty step backwards towards Caleb's protective presence. The expression vanished so quickly to be replaced by Patrick's languid smile that Tony had doubts about what she had actually seen.

'Yes, no and yes.' Patrick's smile widened as Tony looked puzzled from him to Caleb.

'What is that supposed to mean Patrick?' she demanded.

Quickly scanning Patrick's smug countenance, Caleb said, 'Your cousin is answering my questions Tony. Yes, he has a problem with what happened in the barn, no, he didn't want Sutherland to rape you and yes, he is jealous that he wasn't the one to save you.'

Slowly Patrick clapped his hands. 'Well done, my Lord, but who wouldn't want to rescue a very beautiful naked young lady? Was that part of the story true, Tony? I do hope so as it adds a touch of spice to a fairly mundane adventure. Did either of these men dare to strip you of your clothes, of your station in life?'

Tony cast a quick pleading glance across to Duncan. 'Isn't it time for Aidan to wash up before luncheon?'

'Of course Tony.' Duncan held out his hand to the boy but Patrick laid his upon Aidan's shoulder to detain him.

'Are you ashamed of what you did, Tony? I thought baby brother was right there beside you? What could you possibly tell me that the Lordling doesn't already know?' mocked Patrick.

Tony placed her hand over Patrick's and raised it away from Aidan. 'My brother suffers enough from nightmares, he doesn't need to relive our abduction. If there are parts of it I was able to shield him from, he doesn't need to hear about them now! Duncan if you would be so kind, take Aidan inside!'

Aidan Becomes Defensive

Jumping up to stand on the chair, Aidan folded his arms across his chest. 'It isn't right that you talk that way about what Tony had to deal with to get us to safety. It was nice of Lord Caleb and Solitaire to come to our aid but Tony was about to deal with that pig man on her own.'

Patrick flicked his finger beneath Aidan's chin, 'Well Lordling, what about the barn?'

Aidan pushed Patrick's hand away. 'Tony built a hay castle and we all huddled inside it to keep warm. Lord Caleb didn't want to join us but Solitaire said we had to stop each other from freezing.'

'Why are you so interested in what happened to us in the barn?' Tony stiffened as she waited for her cousin's answer.

'Rumours abound over what really happened from Lord Delacourt taking advantage of your lack of clothes to the two of you making wild passionate love. I was hoping for your reputation that the rumours were untrue but his Lordship's presence at the Manor seems to indicate there was some truth in the speculation after all!'

A muscle jerked in Caleb's cheek as his lips thinned in displeasure but he remained silent. *It is up to Tony if or how much she tells her cousin.* Aidan glanced from Caleb to Tony before he spoke, 'Lord Caleb is a gentleman! He gave Tony his overcoat because her clothes were shredded. Nothing happened in the barn, Doctor Masters said so!'

Chuckling Patrick swept an unsubtle glance down Tony's dress covered figure. 'There are so many things that a couple may do without breaching a woman's... purity shall we call it for such a mixed audience?'

'Patrick! This isn't an appropriate discussion to have in front of Aidan!' protested Tony.

Her cousin laughed. 'And what took place in the barn was appropriate in front of a five year old?'

'Are you suggesting that I could act so inappropriately as to disgrace the family name?' Tony desperately tried to prevent her thoughts from drifting back to lying naked in Caleb's arms as her blushes would only add weight to Patrick's accusations. Her chin rose in defiance as a spark of anger entered her eyes.

Patrick's gaze transferred to Caleb. 'Maybe not willingly.'

A laugh escaped from Tony as she lightly punched Patrick's arm. 'Do you really think I'm incapable of dealing with unwanted advances?' Her words caught Patrick in the raw as he remembered Tony breaking his nose for kissing her.

He was quick to recover. 'So if there was any impropriety you were a willingly participant!'

Sorting The Facts From The Rumours

'Patrick!' Earl of Stirling's voice caused them all to jump startled. Not because the Earl had raised his voice, because he hadn't, but they had not heard his arrival. Patrick turned to bow to the Earl.

'Hello uncle, I've just been hearing all about my cousin's great escape.'

The Earl strolled forward and lightly placed his arm around Tony's waist. 'Oh? It sounded more like you were casting doubt upon my daughter's honour.'

'My dear uncle, much better I know all the facts so I can set the rumour mongers straight. To stop the idle chatter that can only bring further harm to Tony and her fragile standing in society.'

Sweeping into a deep curtsey, Tony laughed, 'How kind of you cousin, to be so concerned with how I am perceived by the Ton! Or are you scared that my fall from grace will ruin your position amongst your peers?' That low blow caused colour to streak across Patrick's cheeks.

'It saddens me, coz that you seem to hold such a low opinion of me. I defended you against those who criticised your choice to wear male attire. I tried to be understanding when you insisted Uncle Julius marry again to produce an heir aside from myself. Now I find you more than willing to welcome a stranger into your heart that I have long wished could be mine.'

Taken aback, Tony could only look at her cousin, rendered speechless. They were all surprised when it was Caleb who answered Patrick. 'I'm not a stranger to the Stirling family.'

Waving an airy hand, Patrick dismissed this solemn statement. 'I'm sure my uncle is very grateful for all you have done for his children in the past two days but that does not make you a lifelong friend!'

An enchanting smile answered him. 'My mother went to school with Lady Grace, I was present at both of the Earl's weddings as well as Lady Grace's funeral.' Momentarily taken aback Patrick made an immediate recovery.

'So you've been to a few official occasions.'

But Caleb hadn't finished, 'the Earl was my sponsor at White's club in London and introduced me to Gentleman Jackson when he learnt of my interest in boxing. Tony, do you remember the garden party your mother held? You would have been about seven or eight.'

Frowning as she cast her mind back to a favourite memory, Tony suddenly laughed. 'The one when it was supposed to be fine all day and we got wet by the only cloud in the sky? Were you the young man who threw his jacket over Mama's head and helped her inside out of the rain?'

Caleb nodded. 'That's right.'

A look of cunning entered Patrick's eyes. 'Then you must also remember meeting me that day?'

For a brief moment Caleb stroked his chin. 'Were you the insolent little toe rag pelting Tony with mud balls? If that was the case then I pushed you face first into a puddle.' Patrick's expression changed to annoyance as everyone laughed.

Interrogation Continues

A welcome interruption came as Preston cleared his throat, 'My Lord, luncheon has been served!'

The Earl tightening his hold around his daughter's waist turned gratefully to the Butler. 'Thank you Preston. Aidan, fetch your sister's crutches.'

The boy readily jumped off the chair he had been standing on to collect them from where they leant against the table. Patrick cast a quick searching glance over Tony.

'What is this? Apart from the bruises, are you injured?' He reached out to take Tony's hands but Aidan pushed Patrick aside so that he could hand over the crutches to his sister.

Smiling down a thank you to Aidan, Tony raised her eyebrows at Patrick. 'Surely the rumour mills have had much to say about my fall while duelling with Nigel Sutherland?'

'Was this when you were abducted?' demanded Patrick.

'No, the evening before when I had a confrontation with Sutherland at the Stirling Arms. Don't tell me the gossip hungry Ton missed that one?'

Following the Earl into the house, Patrick managed to remain by Tony's side. 'Well that explains how the abduction came about. You'll have to tell me all about it Tony, I've never known anyone to best you with a sword.'

'He didn't! I tripped over a rock otherwise he'd never have got the upper hand! I only went with Sutherland the next day because he held a gun to Aidan's head and had already knocked Duncan out.'

Patrick held the door open for them all to pass through, 'That explains the increase in security on the estate as I arrived. Well I have to admit Tony, life with you is never boring. It makes me wonder what you could possibly do to top this.'

Tony exchanged a speaking glance with Caleb. *I have a good idea what I'm going to do next but there is no way I am going to share that information with Patrick,* she thought.

Aidan's Chaperonage

If it had been Caleb's intention to achieve some alone time with Tony that was made impossible as Aidan refused to leave her side. So Patrick's hovering in assumed protection, Caleb found amusing and not annoying. Especially as every time Patrick attempted to get close to Tony, Aidan inserted himself between them. Watching this masterful performance, Duncan also wondered, *if it is the boy's need to be close to his sister or a deliberate act of sabotage?* When Aidan looked up and met his Tutor's puzzled gaze, he grinned wickedly leaving Duncan in no doubt as to the boy's motivation.

So it was a relief to everyone when Geoff Delacourt dragged Patrick down to the Stirling Arms for a drink after dinner to learn what the locals were saying about the abduction. The Earl didn't go so far as to call blessings down upon Geoff's head but he was able to relax and attend to the amusement of his in-laws.

Duncan took Geoff's place at the card table opposite the Dowager as Patience Sinclair sat beside Tony with her embroidery. Patience had now had enough time to become accustomed to Tony in a dress that it no longer upset her.

Aidan was permitted to remain downstairs in the parlour until Tony retired for the night and he lay on the sofa with his head in his sister's lap. Caleb managed to answer Mrs Sinclair's questions without missing a beat. Especially as Lady Margarette was lending half an ear to their conversation as most of the questions were to determine how suitable a suitor he made for their granddaughter.

When Tony called an end to the genteel interrogation by rising to her feet and lifting a sleepy Aidan up into her arms, Caleb was relieved that this signal for little boys to go to bed included him. Taking Aidan out of Tony's embrace so that she could utilise her crutches, Caleb willingly said, 'Goodnight,' and followed Tony out of the room.

Do You Need Help Undressing?

Upstairs, Caleb paused outside the bedroom he knew to be Tony's but she shook her head and led him to Aidan's room. There was a small tussle of wills as she helped Aidan to change into his nightgown but only a small one as he was already half asleep.

Caleb waited as Tony tucked Aidan into his own bed, found a bedraggled toy rabbit which had fallen under the bed and tucked it into the boy's arms. *I know that the Earl has insisted that Aidan at least starts off in his own bed at night but if it is a choice between having a stuffed toy or Tony in my arms, I know which one I personally prefer.* Caleb wondered if his thoughts could be read from his face because when Tony looked up at him, she suddenly blushed and with a hint of a smile, lowered her eyes again. Bending down to place a tender kiss upon Aidan's forehead, Tony then picked up the candle in the room and led Caleb out. He took the candle from her and paused outside his own bedroom.

'Do we have to re-join the others?' asked Caleb, with one hand on the door handle.

'You don't, I think you've been up long enough for today. Do you need any help getting out of your jacket?'

When Caleb raised his eyebrows, Tony added, 'I meant because of your injured shoulder.'

A smile, a cheeky smile answered her. 'Oh I thought you were going to take me up on my offer to see me unclothed.'

Her flush deepened. 'No, not yet! When that happens I want you a little fitter than you are at present.'

This time Caleb's eyebrows rose almost to his hair line. 'What on earth do you expect me to do while naked?' He said, amused as he opened his bedroom door and then stood back to allow Tony to enter before him. 'You're not thinking of doing anything inappropriate, my elfling?' He choked when Tony nodded and placed the candle down beside his bed.

'Well, only a little inappropriate perhaps. Mary would have to be present, of course, to chaperone.' Tony placed her crutches against the bed and raised, not quite steady hands to assist Caleb out of his jacket and waistcoat. *I can't believe how aroused I have become just by our conversation or is it because Tony is undressing me?*

'I see! Do you think it is safe for you to be alone with me right now elfling?' Although his tone was teasing, Caleb was half serious as she hung his clothes in the wardrobe.

'Safe? What a strange word to use. To protect me, I don't think I'd be safer with anyone else. If you mean safe for my reputation, Caleb, I think you'll find that we're not quite alone.' Tony gestured to the doorway and for the first time he noticed Mary's presence. 'Even so, I think you take the title of gentleman seriously and would do nothing to damage my already diminishing reputation,' she added as Mary came into the room to assist Caleb, with a little difficulty, out of his shirt.

Unintentionally that caught Caleb on the raw and he uttered a rueful laugh. 'I seemed to have forgotten that chivalry in the barn.'

Tony's breath caught in a gasp as heat washed over her entire body just thinking about the way Caleb had touched her, kissed her, his sultry tone as he had uttered tantalising words of love. She was startled to find the storm she felt was reflected in Caleb's eyes. Mary had knelt down to remove his shoes and stockings and looked up to chastise them like a pair of naughty children.

'Enough of that my Lord, my Lady! Neither of you are ready for where those thoughts may lead you!' A cheeky dimple suddenly appeared as Mary rose to her feet. 'Not yet anyway!' They laughed, a nervous sound as what the Maid had said in no way diminishing the sexual tension that had risen. Mary assisted Caleb into his night wear, taking extra care of his wounded shoulder. *I'm grateful that it is the Maid standing so close to me, especially when I sat down on the edge of the bed to draw off my trousers. If it had been Tony, I doubt I would have the strength to stop myself from reaching for her.* As Mary hung up his trousers in the wardrobe, Tony turned down the bed.

Very Adult Things

Slipping between the sheets, Caleb chuckled as he felt as if he was the small boy of five rather than Aidan. 'Do I get a bed time story as well ladies?' Exchanging a startled glance, the two women began to giggle.

'Sorry,' apologised Tony, 'it is perhaps easier in this situation for us to treat you like a child.'

Patting the bed, Caleb invited Tony to sit down beside him. 'Trouble is I'm not certain if I'm five or a hundred and five! Why is it easier? Does my attraction to you disturb you?' gently Caleb laid his hand over Tony's. She managed a nervous smile.

'Actually it's my attraction to you that disturbs me. I've never felt this way about any man… actually anyone, but to rush in to anything and end up getting hurt does worry me.' Tony willingly entwined her fingers through Caleb's.

An understanding smile answered her. 'You have all the time you need Tony, I will wait for you to be ready. But I can't deny that I want to do adult, very adult, things with you. When you are ready. Any advances on my part, though, seems to cause you to shy away in fear.'

A maidenly blush adorned Tony's cheeks. 'That's due to the fact that I want you to do those very adult things but I'm struggling to remember that I am a Lady and all the proprieties that my poor Governess tried to install in me. I may never have been the perfect woman but I've always upheld what was expected of me as a child of an Earl. Wearing male attire may be seen as eccentric but I have never brought the family name into disrepute.'

He raised her hand to press her fingers against his lips. 'I'm glad that it's not me that frightens you.'

Tony managed to smile as she rose to her feet. 'It's going to take a little time for me to get used to having to act like a female.' Leaning forward, Tony kissed Caleb lightly before straightening to settle upon her crutches. Mary moved across the room to open the door for Tony.

'Don't try to make too many changes,' Caleb said, 'I like you just the way you are.' There was relief written all over her face as Tony left the room and she said, 'Thank you!' Mary quietly shut the door behind them.

I Wouldn't Trust Patrick

When Geoff strolled into his cousin's room about an hour later, Caleb was still awake and reading. 'Some of us have it easy.' Geoff threw himself onto the bed beside his cousin. Putting in a book mark to keep his place, Caleb laid his book down on his bedside table.

'I presume my babysitting duties were much easier than yours?'

Drawing off his cravat, Geoff groaned, 'That's an understatement! Patrick Stirling will seriously not like your courtship of Lady Tony.'

'You didn't tell him that I'm in love with his cousin did you?'

Running a hand through his hair, Geoff chuckled. 'I only look like an idiot! But I don't think it will take him long to realise that we're not here purely on protection duty! Oh and I suggest we keep our eyes peeled for any little accidents that could befall Lord Aidan. Patrick really wants to be Earl.'

'Duly noted!' Caleb exhaled slowly. 'So what is the talk in the village?'

'Nothing about the abduction, not from the locals anyway. They're still ultra-protective of Lady Tony. In fact some stranger made a lewd remark and Mick Cooper literally picked him up and tossed him out of the pub. So whatever they may be saying in the privacy of their own homes, it isn't being discussed openly in any establishment loyal to the Stirlings.' Geoff covered his mouth as he yawned. 'Do you need anything before I head off to bed?'

Caleb shook his head. 'Do you think Aidan is safe enough from Patrick tonight?'

'Does he still share his sister's room?' Geoff slid off his cousin's bed.

'No.'

Geoff cast a quick glance back at Caleb, 'Don't worry, I'll take care of it.' With a wave of his hand he left the room abruptly.

Picking up the boy, Geoff made sure he tucked the battered toy rabbit under his arm but Aidan didn't stir until Geoff carried him, not to his sister's room but back to Caleb's. His cousin was a little surprised but Geoff whispered, 'There was no light on in Tony's room and I didn't want to scare her Ladyship by waking her.'

Accepting this, Caleb threw back the bedcovers beside him and Geoff laid Aidan down and tucked the bunny back into the boy's arms. This caused Aidan to stir but he barely opened both his eyes.

'Tony?'

Caleb gently pushed the boy's hair out of his eyes. 'No it's Caleb. We thought you'd be safer here tonight.'

The bunny's ear made its way into Aidan's mouth as he murmured, 'Oh all right.' He was already asleep again as Geoff pulled the bedcovers over the boy.

'You do know that he gets up at the crack of dawn?'

Caleb smiled. 'I'll manage. Goodnight Geoff.'

'Night coz. Good luck!' The soft chuckle as he left, Caleb could have done without, but that was Geoff.

WEDNESDAY
I Just Woke Up Here

At first Tony was relieved when she woke at a more reasonable hour the next morning. By the time she had managed to get through her early breakfast tray, wash and dress and still there was no sign of her brother, she began to worry a little. After checking Aidan's bedroom and finding it empty, Tony began to panic just a little more. Although Tony had allowed Mary to re-bandage her ankle, she had set aside her crutches. She picked up the skirt of her dress and tore down the corridor to Caleb's room.

Hearing the high pitched squeal of laughter before pulling up short outside Lord Delacourt's door, she was reassured. Remembering to knock before she unceremoniously entered, Tony managed to contain a very relieved sigh. A giggling but already dressed Aidan sat on the bed while William assisted Caleb into his jacket. *I am so relieved that I don't even feel any jealously that Aidan may have gone to Caleb and not me in the middle of the night.* Aidan, though, was quick to set his sister right in case he was in trouble.

'I don't remember leaving my bed Tony, I just woke up here.'

Turning away from the mirror as he had been adjusting his cravat, Caleb explained how Geoff had brought Aidan to him once he had returned from the Inn.

Bowing as he left the room, William's place was almost immediately taken by Charles.

'My apologises, my Lord, my Lady, but the Earl sent me to inform you of the arrival of a carriage.'

Tony acknowledged the message, 'Thank you Charles, we'll be down in a minute.' Charles bowed and left the room.

'It's probably my mother,' Caleb said calmly as a hunted look had suddenly appeared on Aidan's face.

'She's not like Grandmother Henry is she?' The boy was still dubious about the new arrival.

'No,' Caleb thought about his mother for a moment, 'I promise you'll like her Aidan, she's a lot of fun.'

The boy smiled. 'That's all right then.' He willingly jumped off the bed and led the way downstairs. Caleb gallantly offered Tony his arm, and when she realised it was gallantry rather than for her to lean upon, Tony shyly accepted. *It's going to take some time getting used to being treated as a woman.*

Lady Isabella Delacourt

Stepping into the parlour, Caleb was a little surprised that his mother didn't even look at him but her gaze was transfixed upon Tony.

'Oh my word! I assume that you're tired of hearing this but you so look like your mother.' The hand that Lady Isabella Delacourt raised to caress Tony's cheek wasn't quite steady. Tony rose from her curtsy and was embarrassed as Isabella drew her into her arms.

'Maybe that's why I chose to dress as a man to save Papa from that painful reminder each and every day,' explained Tony, submitting to the embrace.

'You should never be ashamed of the resemblance my dear child. Just looking at you takes me back to Grace and I in our first season! We were the toast of London,' reminisced Isabella as she released Tony. Not a trace of silver could be detected in Isabella's glossy jet back curls. *I don't have any clear recollections of Lord Andrew Delacourt, Caleb's father,* mused Tony, *but I can easily see that Caleb acquired his good looks from his mother. It isn't in the least hard to imagine Isabella and Grace as mischievous, giggling school girls, finally free from their over-watchful Governesses and ready to unleash their charms upon the unready and totally enchanted Ton in London.*

'That I can believe!' Tony looked down as Aidan tugged at the skirt of her dress and she reached down so that her brother could take her hand.

Accepting Caleb's kiss to both her cheeks, Isabella stood back to run a searching glance over her son. 'I was a little worried about Geoff's "minor injuries" but I couldn't come any sooner. Janet had come down with a cold and I've been unable to leave her side for more than five minutes.'

Caleb manfully managed to control his urge to grimace. 'I don't know why you felt it necessary to saddle yourself with an elderly cousin for a chaperone. That woman takes advantage of your kind heart.'

Smiling, Isabella patted her son's cheek. 'When your father died Caleb, it broke my heart. I needed time to heal and Janet made it easier to keep over-persistent suitors at bay. I needed to focus my attention on you and your sister.'

As Aidan peeked out from behind Tony's skirt, his worried gaze met Isabella's and she smiled warmly. 'Now who is this handsome young man? It can't be Aidan as the last time I saw him was when Reverend Gray was dunking him in the baptismal font. Such a happy baby! He thought all that water was jolly good fun.'

Aidan came a little further away from Tony's skirt but didn't relinquish her hand. 'I still love water,' he admitted and looked up at Caleb as he gently ran his hand over the boy's head.

'After our recent adventures, we're all a little nervous,' explained Caleb as the Earl gestured for them to be seated.

The Patterson's Farm

Aidan jumped slightly and moved closer to Tony when Preston quietly entered the parlour and gently cleared his throat.

'Mr… Solitaire to see your Lordship.' The Butler's hesitation was slight but caused Isabella to look up in interest.

'Oh, I've never met a Highwayman before!' Isabella looked around at the stunned expressions on the faces of those around her. 'Socially I mean.'

An adorable frown descended upon Aidan's brow. 'But he wouldn't be wearing a mask in a social setting so you wouldn't know that he is actually a Highwayman.' The young boy reasoned.

'Unless he was holding up the social gathering,' counter-argued his father.

A chuckle came from Solitaire as he stepped over the threshold. 'Then he would no longer be a Highwayman but an extortionist, a robber or a bandit.' He bowed to the room before raising Tony's hand to his lips. 'As handsome a young man you make, Lady Tony, you're even more beautiful as a young woman.'

As Tony blushed from the flattering attention, Aidan reached up to tug on Solitaire's jacket hem.

'What happened to Benji? Did that man badly hurt him for protecting us?'

Smiling reassuringly, Solitaire disengaged the boy's fingers. 'He was a little stiff and sore, my Lord, but nothing was broken so no permanent damage.'

Sighing, Caleb rubbed his fingertips against his temples. 'I promised myself that if we got out of there alive I'd take Benji the biggest steak I could find.'

The Highwayman chuckled. 'That's all right, Lord Delacourt. The hound has been regally rewarded for his bravery.'

'Which brings us to the farm,' the Earl rose to his feet, 'do you want to do this in private Solitaire?' He gestured towards the door but the Highwayman shook his head.

'Thank you, my Lord, but no, we're all friends here.'

The Earl gestured for Solitaire to take a seat opposite Caleb. *I know that Papa had a meeting with the Highwayman the day after our rescue but I don't know what they had discussed,* considered Tony.

'The Patterson's were overwhelmed by your Lordship's more than generous offer,' stated Solitaire, seemingly at ease surrounded by gentry. 'They also appreciate the time you offered so they can discuss your offer to purchase their farm and settle into one of the new cottages you have just built on your estate.'

The Earl smiled. 'You make it sound like I'm forcing them off their own land, Solitaire.'

'Sorry my Lord,' Solitaire cleared his throat. 'They've been thinking for some time that the farm had become more than they can manage any more. Even with your offer to restore the farm to an operational estate, they feel that maybe it is time to retire and not have to worry about where their next meal is coming from.'

Leaning back in his chair, the Earl steepled his fingers together. 'So are the Pattersons interested in accepting my offer?'

'Yes my Lord.'

'And are you interested in accepting my offer to you?'

Solitaire took a deep breath. 'Yes my Lord.'

A wry smile twisted upon the Earl's lips. 'You don't feel like I'm purchasing your inheritance from under you and selling it back at an inflated price?'

Tony gasped as she realised Solitaire's relationship to the farmers and why Benji had been pleased to see him. Solitaire chuckled. 'Not at all, Lord Stirling. You're giving my parents the life I'd love to give them but never could achieve. It also means that my brothers and I can return to the occupation we were born into but had to find other means to put food on the family's table.' A tired smile adorned the Highwayman's face. 'To be honest, my Lord, I'm getting too old for my current profession. It also meant that I couldn't settle down. I had nothing but worry to offer a wife.'

The Earl shook his head, 'Old friend, you knew that I would have found honest work for you.'

'I'm a proud man, my Lord, I don't want something for nothing. At first I thought the service I rendered to your daughter didn't warrant such a generous reward that your Lordship has offered. But it isn't just myself to consider, as the security for my parents and a life away from crime for the rest of my family is a dream we thought impossible.'

Solitaire's Doubts

Even though my acquaintance with Solitaire is not as lengthy as the Stirlings, I have the impression the Highwayman is holding something back, thought Caleb. 'Something other than thoughts for your family's future is worrying you isn't it?' he asked.

Solitaire cast a quick glance at Tony before moistening his dry lips. 'I hadn't really thought that what I did to rescue Lady Tony was of any value. You're probably not aware of it, as here you're protected from the talk. Your people on the estate and the local villagers will do everything they can to protect her Ladyship's reputation. But this isn't the case beyond the village. Some of the stories circulating are wildly defamatory. Some of them have no resemblance to the truth whatsoever. It made me realise exactly what Lord Delacourt and I saved Lady Tony from.'

'What if she had missed with that dagger and Sutherland had raped her? What if she had managed to stab him and had to live with the guilt of killing a man for the rest of her life? Either of those scenarios would lay a heavy burden of guilt upon her Ladyship's shoulders. I'm not certain though that these wild stories and rumours aren't going to do more harm to your good name.' Flushed, the Highwayman wrung his hands together. *I've never spoken so much at one time in my whole life.*

Tony had become quite pale. 'We know some if not the whole story is circulating London already as my cousin Patrick came down to see if there was any truth in what he had heard.'

Glancing from Caleb to the Earl, Isabella was startled. 'But it is only the scandal we have to stand against together isn't it? These darling children aren't still in danger are they?'

Caleb laid his hand over his mother's. 'That's why Geoff and I are staying at the Manor, Mama, to prevent a repeat attempt. Even so we must deal with the lies that are circulating before they take on a life of their own.'

The Earl nodded. 'My mother and Grace's parents will be returning to London soon and they will make short work of the rumours.'

Brushing her hand against Aidan's hair, Tony asked, 'You don't think these rumours have come from the Henrys?'

'Not if they know what is good for them!' The Earl's handsome countenance hardened.

Not liking the angry colour on her father's face, Tony rose smoothly to her feet and crossing the room to sit on the arm of the Earl's chair, she leant forward to place a gentle kiss against his brow. 'Please don't make London too hot for them to remain there.' She begged, her eyes dancing with laughter.

'Why's that, baby girl?' The Earl looking up into her face, patted her knee.

Her smile now reached her lips. 'It might force them to make an extensive stay in the country and I don't think dear Charlotte can handle them on our doorstep again so soon.'

'True.' Laughing, the Earl reached up to stroke his hand against his daughter's cheek. 'Now then, why don't you show Isabella to her room and I'll take Solitaire to my study to complete our business.' Earl Stirling glanced back at the Highwayman, 'I think that now you're going to make an honest man of yourself, you'll have to drop your highway name.'

'It was so much easier to hide behind the name as to hide behind a mask.' Solitaire nodded as he rose to his feet. 'It'll be nice to be just Albert Patterson once more.'

The Earl rose out of his chair and headed towards the door. 'Well Mr Patterson, would you like to follow me?'

Flushed in pleasure, Solitaire nodded. 'Yes my Lord.'

In The Rose Garden

After showing Isabella to her room, allowing her opportunity to take off her hat and tidy her hair, Tony then led them outside. Tony sat beside Aidan as Duncan tried to settle his pupil to a little school work as Caleb took a stroll with his mother into the rose garden. They walked together in peace, Isabella's arm through his as they didn't need words to fill the silence. *It won't last, I know that Mama must be bursting to ask all sorts of questions.*

'Well Caleb?' Isabella finally broke the silence as Caleb plucked a particularly beautiful rose for her.

His lips twitched. 'For a couple of days, my shoulder injury will limit how much I can use my arm but otherwise I am quite well.'

'Do you really want to play that game Caleb?'

Caleb thanked the gardener who came across to hand him a pair of secateurs and a basket to cut more roses. Isabella took the basket and placed her rose into it.

'I didn't recognise Tony at first in her male attire. I suppose she wore dresses whenever I remember seeing her as a child.' Caleb continued to snip off rose blooms as they wandered through the floral display. 'I had been wondering if I would ever find the perfect woman. I didn't realise that I already knew her; that I'd just been waiting for her to grow up.'

A small crooning noise rose from the back of Isabella's throat. 'Oh Caleb! I prayed that you could find true love but I didn't dare dream that it could be my best friend's daughter!' Isabella's hand shook as she took another blossom from her son and placed it into the basket she carried. 'Does Tony feel the same way?' A shiver of doubt ran through Lady Delacourt as her son hesitated in answering the question.

'There's attraction but the sight of that hairy naked brute looming over her has made her a little nervous. I promised Tony all the time she needs to be comfortable with my suit but this scandal may be a major hindrance.'

Raising the pink rose Caleb handed her, Isabella breathed in its delicate perfume as she considered his words.

'Do you think that Tony would refuse an offer from you to protect your name from being dragged into the scandal?'

Caleb shrugged as he cut another bud. 'We're already in it up to our necks! An offer from me so soon after the abduction would lead the Ton to believe that it was made as an necessity because of what did or did not happen in the barn.'

An enchanting smile swept away Isabella's frown as she reassuringly patted Caleb's arm. 'Due to the long-standing friendship of our two families, no one would be really surprised by a marriage between the two houses. It could be made known that the official announcement of your engagement had been interrupted by the abduction.'

Pausing in the process of snipping another rose, Caleb stared at the bloom intently but didn't really see it. 'Then why was the announcement not made the moment Earl Stirling returned home?'

'To allow the dust to settle from the scandal, and the chance for either of you to back out before anything was placed in the papers. Once the notice is printed, Tony will be the only one who can break the contract. Julius didn't want you to feel trapped if you had made a mistake.'

Finally cutting through the flower stem, Caleb glanced down at his mother. 'Do you think it is a mistake?'

Isabella caressed her hand against her son's forearm. 'Up until now you have always seemed a little lost. Now you appear to be filled with a fire and a real purpose. I also like the natural paternal instinct I've seen arise from your dealings with Aidan. I think you'll make a wonderful husband and father.'

Leaning down to kiss his mother's cheek, Caleb chuckled, 'You wouldn't be biased now would you?'

'It's my right!' Isabella's dimples appeared. 'There has to be some privileges to being a mother.'

'That doesn't surprise me! Do me a favour Mama, don't tell Tony that, as her maternal instincts are already quite strong.'

Her eyes lit up in delight. 'Does that mean you're both looking at starting a family straight away?'

'When nature permits Mama! You won't be able to miss Tony's maternal instincts when she is with Aidan. It makes me wonder how Charlotte is going to handle the new baby on her own this time.'

'Charlotte is pregnant again?' Halting in her tracks, Isabella's eyes opened wide.

Caleb immediately realised his mistake. 'Oh! I'm not certain that is public knowledge yet. So keep that under your hat.'

A look of scorn was cast up at her son. 'I'm not Agnes Henry!' An ironic bow was given in way of an apology. 'Well perhaps Charlotte will show more interest in this one,' added Isabella. 'Didn't you say that her sister Lizzy is currently staying here?'

'Yes but I think it's only a temporary measure as Tony suggested last night that Charlotte should take her sister to visit the local gentry in the area or spend a week or two in Bath. I got a little lost at this point of the conversation but something about drinking the waters was beneficial last time that Charlotte was pregnant.' Cutting off another rose, Caleb glanced at the basket that was now overflowing with so many different colours of roses.

'Morning sickness I expect.'

Isabella glanced deep in thought up at her son's face. 'Is there anything I can do to help? With Tony I mean, not Charlotte. If you need a discreet chaperone.' Colour rushed up Caleb's cheeks. *I can't believe I am having this conversation with my mother.*

'Mary, Tony's Maid, has agreed to keep us in line which isn't that hard considering Aidan hardly ever leaves his sister's side.'

Her Ladyship's dimples appeared again. 'That didn't seem to hamper too heavily upon your actions in the barn, if the rumours are true.' That was a low blow which caused Caleb's colour to deepen.

Even more so as his thoughts swept him back to the barn. *Tony's warm, supple, naked body pressed back into my arms. The shiver of delight and the soft moans that fell from her lips as my fingers had teased and moulded her breasts as my lips had pressed tender, gentle kisses against Tony's shoulders and neck.* Feeling an awakening response to these memories in the lower half of his body, Caleb dragged his mind back to the present. An irrepressible twinkle entered Isabella's eyes.

'A word of warning my son, no one is going to believe that nothing happened in the barn if you go misty eyed every time you dwell on the memory.'

Caleb couldn't hide his guilty grin. 'Sorry, but just thinking about Tony causes my heart to race.'

'I'm glad it seems that you've finally got it all.' Isabella patted his hand. 'I hope you're going to be very happy.'

Taking the basket from Isabella, Caleb guided their footsteps back towards the house. 'Well I don't have it all yet so let's not jinx my future. Shall we take these flowers to Tony before we denude all the rose bushes?'

Isabella giggled. 'You said nude!'

'Oh Mother!'

Floral Tribute

While Aidan worked manfully on his mathematics at the table, Tony sat curled up on the swing seat with a book in her hands. She looked up a little puzzled when Caleb presented her the basket laden with roses as Isabella sat down beside Tony. Accepting his floral offering, Tony's eyes began to dance with wicked laughter.

'Papa warned me about Casanovas who overwhelm a lady with presents and flowers but isn't it a little cheap if they come from my own garden?'

Caleb grinned. 'Actually it's worse than that as we were so deep in conversation that I wasn't really aware of what we were doing. Should I offer them to Lady Charlotte in apology for stripping bare her rose bushes?'

Raising one rose to breathe in its delicate perfume, Tony shook her head. 'No, I'll take these to Mrs Preston. If she has enough flowers for the house then these will be perfect for brewing. Our cook, Mrs Hill has her own recipe for making soaps and bath oils as well as rose water for cooking.' Uncoiling herself, Tony automatically took the hand Caleb held out to assist her to her feet. 'Next time you feel like pruning, I'll point you in the direction of the herb garden. Lavender goes really well with roses.'

Caleb bowed mockingly over Tony's hand as he raised it lightly to his lips. 'As it pleases my elfling!' A tingling ran through Tony at the touch of his lips to her skin and the thought of him kissing other parts of her flesh caused a delicate hue to spread across her flawless skin. As their eyes met, it was as if Caleb could read what she was thinking and a satisfied smile appeared as he slowly released her hand.

Premature Declarations

'Aunt Bella!' Geoff's exclamation, as he strode across the lawn from the stables, broke the intimate mood between the courting pair. Geoff swept his aunt up into a bear hug. 'Have you come to see what trouble your son has led us into this time?'

One of Caleb's eyebrows rose sardonically as he turned to look at his cousin. 'Into trouble cousin? I thought that was Tony.' He received a punch on his good arm for his teasing from Tony.

'I have come to see how much damage you boys have done to yourselves and offer support to my future daughter-in-law.' Isabella gave a gurgle of laughter as Caleb uttered an exasperated sigh and Tony looked surprised.

'Oh? So has that become official then?' Geoff asked, 'or is that just wishful thinking Bella?'

'Nothing is official yet!' In displeasure Caleb's lips had thinned. 'No pressuring Tony, there is no need to rush into anything yet.'

Geoff took Tony's place on the swing seat beside his aunt. 'I don't know coz, you're not getting any younger.' A cheeky grin swept across his face. Although Caleb opened his mouth to retort, it was Isabella who spoke.

'You mustn't remind Caleb how old he is, Geoff.'

Glancing fondly down at his aunt, Geoff took one of her hands between his. 'Why is that?'

Isabella's dimples appeared. 'Because it reminds me how old I really am!' They all laughed until Aidan glared them into silence as he was trying to concentrate. Leaving his mother in his cousin's capable hands, Caleb followed Tony into the house with the basket of roses. *Declarations may be premature but I still take seriously the task to protect Tony and Aidan. If it also means a snatched moment alone with my heart's desire then even better.*

Serious Chaperonage

Not that fate was going to allow Caleb time alone with Tony. When they had given Mrs Preston the basket of roses, they were heading upstairs to the morning room when Patrick waylaid them. He tried to drag Tony off to join him on the piano. Patience Sinclair foiled that plan by deciding that this was a good time for a piano lesson for Aidan. That drove most of the household as far away from that room as possible, and although Duncan bravely stayed close at hand to protect the young Lord; he didn't refuse Preston's offer of ear plugs.

Earl Stirling collared Caleb and took him down to the stables. A gleam entered Patrick's eyes as he offered to escort Tony on a walk, alone. His plan was sabotaged by the Dowager Countess who wanted Tony to try on some more dresses. To which Patrick was definitely not invited to join them.

The family's protective attitude and their need to provide Tony with continuous chaperonage did not annoy Caleb. *In fact I am gaining a great deal of amusement at how much it is annoying Patrick that he can never be alone with his cousin. I realise that Tony and I have the rest of our lives to be alone together.* So he enjoyed interacting with the rest of his future in-laws.

He discussed horse breeding with the Earl, in particular his own hopes for his new purchases. Caleb managed to manfully hold his own in a philosophical debate with Frederick Sinclair, and the current state of international affairs with the exile of Napoleon on the island of St Helena with the Dowager Countess. Lady Margarette had fond memories of Paris before the revolution in 1790 as her mother was French, but wasn't certain that she could return there again now.

Caleb even managed to keep up with Charlotte's and Lizzy's discussion on their planned trip to Bath. Lizzy had never been before and wanted to know what else Bath had to offer apart from the waters. When the attractions had been discussed and the ladies had swept Caleb into a sea of shopping, clothes and such feminine pursuits, Isabella rescued him and sent him off to assist Duncan who was again trying to teach Aidan how to play chess.

Secret Liaison

By the time he retired for the night, Caleb had barely managed more than a couple of words in private with Tony but he was actually glad about that. *It is becoming a greater struggle to remember that I am a gentleman and that I have to keep my hands and lips to myself. For now anyway.* So Caleb was surprised when he entered his bedroom and found a folded note on his bedside table.

'Please wait up for me, Tony.'

His chest constricted around his lungs making it painful to breathe and the muscles on his stomach tightened into a knot. Trying to drag in deep breathes, Caleb fought to control his thoughts racing ahead to impossible erotic scenarios. *I don't think Tony is ready for that level of intimacy just yet.* There had to be another reason and as he raised a hand to untie his cravat, his shoulder twinged in pain. Caleb exhaled slowly. *Of course, that is probably it,* he thought. He managed to suppress the regret and the arousing thoughts that had threatened to consume him as he continued to undress.

Sitting down on the edge of the bed to remove his shoes and stockings, Caleb was mildly pleased that he had managed to slip out of his shirt without too much pain or difficulty. *My shoulder aches now more than the stabbing pain of a couple of days before.* Standing up he absently massaged his bandaged shoulder as he strode across to open the window. A light breeze swept through the room and Caleb breathed in deeply to allow it to cool his body, flushed by his earlier speculations.

So far away were his thoughts that Caleb was barely aware of the knock at the door before it opened. He didn't realise what an arousing, gothic, and tragic figure he portrayed standing in only his trousers, his muscular well-toned back to the door as he seemed to stare broodily out into the night.

A gasp of surprise from Tony caused Caleb to glance around and quickly returned to the present. She was dressed in a nightgown with a shawl around her shoulders, her waist long hair was hanging loose down her back and the breeze from the open window made it dance lightly around her. Mary quietly shut the door behind them, locking it and laid medical supplies out on the bed.

Glancing from the bandages to Tony, in a nightgown that when the candles were behind her seemed to make it transparent, Caleb was getting mixed signals. *Is Tony here to change my dressings or something more intimate?* He was further confused as Tony ran into his embrace, wrapped her arms around his neck and kissed him passionately. Caleb didn't question what was happening as he took control of the kiss and threaded his fingers through Tony's hair.

Still in some doubt, Caleb maintained a tight rein upon his desires, keeping his hands still and not caressing her all over as he wished to. Giving as much of him as she wanted but still able to let go if she drew away from him. When her hands travelled down his neck to caress his shoulders and bare chest, Caleb managed to release her lips and draw back so that he could look deep into her eyes.

They were both breathing a little faster and a becoming flush to Tony's cheeks added to the sparkle in her eyes.

'I need a little context here, my elfling.' Caleb brushed his thumb against Tony's cheek as her hands rested lightly upon his bare chest.

'I... I need to change your dressing and check your wound. If...' Tony's blush had deepened. 'If you're up to it, I'd then like to take you up on your offer... to see you naked.'

'We don't have to rush into this Tony.' Caleb placed both his hands over hers as they trembled slightly. 'I'm prepared to wait for you to be ready.'

Doubt suddenly entered Tony's eyes. 'Have you changed your mind? Do you no longer want me?'

Cupping her face between both his hands, Caleb drew her into another kiss, this time he allowed his control to slip a little so that Tony was aware of just how much he wanted to be with her. As his mouth parted hers so that the kiss deepened in intensity, Tony placed her hands over Caleb's and drew them down to cup her breasts through the thin material of her nightgown.

The shawl had fallen from her shoulders as his passion was all the heat she needed. Obediently Caleb caressed and fondled Tony's breasts as they continued to kiss, her nipples hardening, not from cold but from the warmth of his touch.

Tony's low sigh of desire almost snapped clean through Caleb's control. *I want to sweep her up into my arms, lay her down upon the bed, tearing off her nightgown and cover her entire body with my lips.* When Caleb released Tony's mouth, swollen now with kisses, he lowered his head to lick one of her nipples through the thin material of her nightgown. As she gasped in pleasure, Mary came forward to place her hand on Caleb's shoulder.

Medical Aid First

'My Lord, we do need to change your dressing first.' Her calm insistence took some but not all of the heat out of the lovers. Reluctantly Caleb released Tony as he uttered a shaky laugh.

'Thank you Mary.' He exhaled slowly as he struggled to regain control and allowed the two women to sit him down on the edge of the bed. As Tony began to unravel Caleb's bandages, her hands were not exactly steady especially as his slightly faster breaths blew lightly against her breasts.

Mary shut the window before assisting Tony as she laid bare the bullet wound. It was healing nicely and once Tony had cleaned and sterilised the area, she redressed and bandaged his shoulder with fresh bandages.

Mary cleaned away the soiled dressings as well as the unused medical supplies as Caleb gently placed his hands around Tony's waist and looked up into her eyes. 'Well Doc? Will the patient live?' His flippancy was rewarded by a gurgle of a laugh as Tony lowered her mouth to claim his in a passionate kiss. Before Caleb could really begin to enjoy it Tony took a step back from him and drew him to his feet again. From the other side of the bed, Mary threw back the bedding.

'Will you... do you need any help undressing?' Tony moistened her lips as they had suddenly become very dry. Caleb took one of her hands into his.

'Are you sure you want to do this?' Her hands, in fact her whole body, was trembling but the eyes that stared into Caleb's were filled with desire.

'Please.' Tony lowered her head to shyly press her lips against one of his nipples. His body jerked in pleasure as the tip of her tongue darted out to lick his nipple just like he had to her only moments earlier. 'May I also touch you?' Caleb moaned as he nearly fainted in desire.

What Do You Think?

With his control fragmenting around him, Caleb drew Tony away from him and turning her around, sat her down on the edge of his bed. His hands shook as Caleb undid his trousers and slid them and his underwear off. Taking a deep breath, he stepped out of his clothes and raised his eyes to rest upon Tony's face.

There was surprise, awe and even pleasure reflected back at him as she slowly scanned Caleb down from his head to his feet.

His body was muscular, his stomach taut but Caleb thought, *that might just be the knot of apprehension building inside*. His penis wasn't completely erect but was still an impressive sight. *It is agony to wait in silence as Tony studies every inch of me but I'm not going to be the one to speak first.* A shiver of delight ran through Tony and she smiled as she raised her eyes to meet Caleb's.

'You're beautiful!'

Surprised, Caleb chuckled, 'Men aren't beautiful elfling.'

Tony exhaled slowly. 'Perfect then!' She scooted across to the other side of the bed and held out her hand to Caleb. 'Will you lie down on your stomach please? To start with,' she added as a look of disappointment had flitted across his features.

May I Touch You?

Lowering himself onto the bed, Caleb had to master his impulse to tear off Tony's nightgown and lay her down beneath him. He rested his cheek against his hands and wondered, *did Tony mean it when she said she wants to touch me?* She shifted closer, throwing her curtain of hair over her shoulder out of the way, as she leant down to briefly kiss Caleb's mouth and gently caressed her fingers against his neck. Sitting up again, Tony lightly traced her hands across Caleb's shoulders and down his arms. Her fingers trailed and followed the line of muscles along his back and across his hips.

Caleb swallowed hard when a moan escaped from his throat as Tony's exploring hands briefly cupped his buttocks before continuing down both his muscular thighs. For a brief moment Tony traced her forefinger against the star shaped birthmark on Caleb's hip. *Beneath me, I can feel my penis hardening and I'm worried that the sight of my full arousal might frighten Tony when I am finally allowed to turn over.* Seeing the frown descend upon Caleb's brow, Tony's hands stilled.

'Am I making you uncomfortable?' Tony fought to keep desperation out of her voice.

Caleb managed a twisted smile. 'Actually the opposite, the more you touch me, the more aroused I become and... I don't want to scare you with it.'

Tony leant forward to press a tender kiss against Caleb's shoulder. 'Do I really excite you? Will you show me?' Her child like enthusiasm and Innocence surprised Caleb into laughing. His laugh turned into a moan as Tony caressed her hand down his side and then under him to curl her fingers around his growing erection. Tony's eyes widened in surprise as she slowly stroked along his hardening length.

'That's amazing!' She whispered. 'It's hard and yet it's soft. Will... will you turn over for me?' She released him and sat back as Caleb rolled over. Once he had settled, Tony leant forward and placed feather light kisses against Caleb's lips, his jaw and throat as her fingers danced across his muscular chest. *I am fascinated by the softness of the hair over his chest and the way his nipples harden beneath my touch.*

Her teasing kisses followed the trail of her fingers down Caleb's chest to his stomach. As her hands caressed down his thighs, Tony finally studied Caleb's erection. As a frown began to slowly descend upon her brow, Caleb felt his chest constrict painfully around his heart.

'If this is all too much for you...'

Raising her eyes to meet his, Tony shook her head. 'I'm just a little puzzled, I know part 'A' is supposed to go into part 'B' but that is just so large and I don't see how it is possible.' Although Caleb was relieved that Tony wasn't disgusted at the sight of his erection, he wasn't sure how to answer her question.

Her Loving Touch

Mary chuckled from where she stood beside the bed, closest to Caleb. 'You stretch, my Lady, and adapt to his size.'

'I see!' Tony didn't sound completely convinced as she lightly trailed her forefinger down Caleb's erection. A shiver of longing for something more substantial ran through Caleb but he didn't' want to push Tony to do too much too soon.

Seeing his struggle, Mary instructed her mistress. 'Wrap your hand around him, my Lady, and stroke long and hard.'

As Tony obeyed, Caleb bit down on his bottom lip to contain his moan of desire and bunched the sheet beneath him between his hands as he tried to hold off ejaculating too soon. When Mary instructed Tony to use her other hand to tease Caleb's balls, his body jerked in pleasure and a dewy droplet appeared at the head of his penis.

Before Caleb could open his mouth and attempt to explain, Tony had lowered her head and shyly ran her tongue over the tip of his erection. Caleb choked back a strangled cry as Tony moistened her lips and took his penis deep into her mouth. For a moment he forgot how to breathe.

'Tony you don't have to do this...' Caleb could not get any further with that sentence as Tony ran her tongue along his length and he was incapable of further speech.

Removing her lips from his penis, Tony studied Caleb's face as she continued to stroke him with her hand. 'Does it please you?'

Caleb uttered a fractured laugh at the Innocence of her question. 'Oh God! Yes!' He swallowed hard. 'But I don't want you to do anything that you dislike.'

Watching Caleb struggle to maintain control over his body as I pleasure him, gives me a feeling of power. I am in control, I dictate his enjoyment and in the end he will give in completely. 'I don't know what I dislike if I have never tried it. I like... the way you respond when I touch you. Show me... how to bring you to completion.' Although Caleb's lips parted to instruct her, he was incapable of getting the words out. Mary supplied the instructions needed.

'Stroke his Lordship harder and faster, my Lady, or take him back into your mouth. You'll know he has reached the point of no return when his balls tighten under your teasing fingers.'

As Tony lowered her lips once more upon his penis, her curtain of hair fell in a pool upon Caleb's thighs. His sharp intake of breath and the jerk of Caleb's body as she slid him in and out of her warm, moist mouth increased her feeling of power. When Tony felt his balls tighten, she raised her head to watch as her hand stroked him faster. A satisfied smile settle upon her face as Caleb finally gave in and Mary laid her hand over his mouth as he cried out in release.

Further Experiments

Tony continued to stroke him until his body slumped back into the mattress and then as Caleb struggled to catch his breath, she lay down in his arms. Her hand played lightly across Caleb's chest until he had recovered enough to speak again.

'Are you all right?' Tony's concern touched him. A fractured laugh escaped from Caleb.

'Beyond all right, my elfling! Do you think that experiment answers all your fears?' Running his fingers through her hair, Caleb rolled onto his side so that he could kiss Tony.

'Not yet,' Tony slipped out of his arms but at his surprised look, she kissed him briefly before she pulled her nightgown off. Caleb's eyebrows rose in surprise as she wasn't wearing any underwear. *I can't believe that I can feel a knot of excitement building in my stomach once again. So soon.*

'Tony, what exactly do you have in mind?' Caleb's fingers were itching to caress her supple body. She slipped back into his arms and laid her head against his undamaged shoulder.

'Not everything… just the feeling of your naked body against mine… perhaps your lips and hands touching me… if it's not too much for you to cope with?'

Caleb chuckled. 'It would have been too much of a temptation before you… touched me. If we get too carried away Mary can always throw the pitcher of water over us.' He glanced up and smiled at Mary. 'How are you coping?'

She had moved around to sit on the edge of the bed beside Tony. 'I'm fine, thank you, my Lord. If Lady Tony is satisfied by this next experiment, as you call it, then you can approach the Earl if you still wish to marry her.'

Glancing back at Tony, there was no hiding the love on Caleb's face as he tenderly traced a trembling finger along her jaw. 'I don't need an experiment to know that Tony is the only woman I ever want to spend the rest of my life with. I was prepared to wait until she felt the same way too.'

'Oh!' Tony's eyes widened in surprise. 'I so want you to make me yours!'

Smiling Mary patted Tony's bare calf. 'Not tonight, you're not, my Lady! After you and Lord Delacourt are wed.'

Tony giggled, 'Yes Ma'am!'

Trailing her fingers across Caleb's chest, Tony gave a low hum of pleasure. 'I do like this. It's so soft.' She caressed the hair on his chest in awe causing Caleb to chuckle.

'I could say exactly the same thing.' He traced his forefinger lightly across Tony's breasts. When she uttered a gasp of pleasure, Caleb lowered his head to twirl his tongue around her nipples. As Tony moaned, he raised his head and drew her closer into his arms.

'I've wanted to do that ever since I placed Aidan's thumb into his mouth instead of your breast.' Caleb pressed a tender kiss against her lips. Tony raised her hand to cup his face.

'So have I!' She admitted, and taking his hands into her own, Tony placed them against her breasts. 'I like it… very, very much!' She placed a feather light kiss against Caleb's cheek and then his jaw.

'Mary...' Caleb caressed his hands against Tony's breasts until she purred.

'Yes, my Lord?'

Caleb claimed Tony's lips for a moment. 'You'd better have that jug of water ready!'

Mary chuckled, 'Yes my Lord.'

Pleasuring Tony

The urge to take full possession of all that Tony offers is strong but due to my release at her hands I'm able to maintain control over that burning need. This is her time, about her needs and pleasures and I want to focus on her complete satisfaction. Slowly, tenderly his hands caressed down her body and as Tony arched into his touch, Caleb's lips followed his fingers across her sensitised flesh. While Tony enjoyed the feel of his hair covered chest against her breasts, Caleb laid claim to her mouth as his hands caressed lightly down her back until he cupped her backside. As he lifted her hips up, Caleb slid one of his thighs between hers.

Mary stirred, prepared to act if necessary but settled back to watching when she realised that Caleb had no intention of sliding both his hips between Tony's. As he rained tantalising, teasing kisses against Tony's throat and breasts, his hands were urging her hips to move rhythmically so that his thigh massaged against her pubic bone.

A sheen of fine perspiration beaded over their naked bodies as Tony picked up Caleb's rhythm and actively sought her first orgasm. Caleb's hands covered and moulded her breasts as his mouth smothered the cry of pleasure that escaped from Tony as she clung to Caleb in her release.

His kiss became less consuming and more tender as Caleb allowed Tony a moment to catch her breath and relish her bliss. When she began to kiss him back and move her hands sensuously against his chest, Caleb released her mouth to lavish his attention upon her breasts. Tony uttered a mew of pleasure as his wicked tongue flicked and teased her nipples before Caleb would then suckle upon her breasts.

He caressed a hand across her stomach before dipping between her thighs. As his fingers eased through her moist curls, Tony's hips rose up to meet his intimate caress but when he used his forefinger to circle her clitoris, Mary raised a protest.

'Be careful, my Lord, that you do not puncture her maidenhead.' The Maid spoke softly against Caleb's ear so that Tony, distracted by Caleb's caresses, didn't hear her.

Chuckling, Caleb acknowledged her warning. 'Yes ma'am!' *Although I'm amused by the Maid's warning, I am actually thankful for it as it would be very, very easy to become carried away at this point.* Regaining his mastery over his control Caleb remembered that this was for Tony's pleasure and not his own.

Tony's entire body quivered as Caleb continued to stoke her fire, his lips teasing her breasts while his fingers slid through her moist passage. Raising his head, Caleb's eyes hungrily devoured the absolute pleasure expressed on Tony's face. As he stilled his caressing hands, Tony uttered a protest, her eyes flying open as her lips parted to plead for the completion that was so closer now.

'Caleb… please… touch me!'

At the blaze of desire in Tony's eyes and the trembling of her fingers as she reached up to touch his face, Caleb swallowed hard to suppress his own primal need to claim full possession of Tony's body and take them both to fulfilment. *I'm erect again, it would be so easy to just let go of my control, to take what no other man would ever be allowed to possess.*

Caleb dragged in a sharp, shuddering breath to steady his resolve and with his eyes locked upon Tony's, he eased his forefinger slowly into her intimate passage. She was moist but so incredibly tight. Her eyes widened, her lips parted in a gasp and her body instinctively rose up to meet his penetration.

Tony uttered a whimper of a protest as Caleb withdrew his finger but sighed in relief when he thrust an additional finger inside of her vagina. This time he came hard up against Tony's virginity and Caleb realised *how easily I could destroy it and with it any shred of reputation to which Tony still clung.*

A cry of anguish was torn from Tony's throat as Caleb completely withdrew his thrusting fingers but he was already moving down the bed. Mary had risen to her feet ready to smother Tony's cries when she orgasmed again. As Caleb parted Tony's thighs, Mary opened her lips to protest until she realised that it was his shoulders and not his hips that Caleb eased between Tony's trembling limbs.

Tony was a little embarrassed as Caleb breathed in deeply her scent of arousal but didn't have the strength to protest as he parted the lips of her sex and his tongue lapped against her clitoris. Wantonly, her body bucked up to seek out more of his wicked, teasing mouth. Caleb slid one hand up her body to fondle her breasts as he thrust his tongue deep into her vagina. Mary placed her hand over Tony's mouth as she exploded in pleasure and he continued to use his tongue against her convulsing flesh until she collapsed boneless and breathless into the mattress.

Heart, Body and Soul

Wiping his mouth with the back of his hand, Caleb moved up the bed to take Tony into his arms. He was really fighting to maintain control now. *Tony is moist enough now that my penetration will be easier. Her hymen will only be a momentary check before she takes my penis, all of me, deep inside of her. I pray that I would have enough strength to hold still inside of Tony, allowing her time to get used to my size, my girth, deep inside of her.*

My weight on top of her before I begin to thrust. Deep, slow, powerful strokes which will mark her forever as my woman. To feel Tony's body lift up to meet each of my possessions. To teach her the dance that we alone will move to music that no one else can hear. To hear her cry out my name as her internal muscles spasm and I spill my life creating seed deep inside her!

His control now fracturing around him, Caleb eased his thigh between Tony's as he lowered his head to take possession of her mouth. She moved sensuously against him as her hands rose, trembling, to thread through his hair. *She is mine for the taking; heart, body and soul.*

For the briefest moment Caleb thought Tony was crying as he felt moisture against his cheek but somewhere deep down he registered the truth, that Mary was flicking water on his face. With a great deal of difficulty, Caleb released Tony's lips and dragged in a deep breath, fighting to control his primal instincts.

His chest heaved in an effort to get enough oxygen down to his tortured lungs and to find the strength he needed to draw back from Tony as her fingers dug into his scalp, trying to get him to kiss her once more.

This time Mary splashed a little more water into both their faces and the shock caused Tony to release Caleb to dash the water out of her eyes. It took all of Caleb's will power to remove his hands from Tony's luscious body and to roll onto his back. Also gasping for breath and control, Tony managed to sit up and look at her Maid in puzzlement.

At that moment she couldn't remember that Mary had orders to not let them get carried away by their desires, *all I know is that I have never felt as complete as when I was in Caleb's arms.* Mary smiled in apology as she laid the glass of water back down on the bedside table.

'Sorry but you were about to go too far,' she explained. 'As enjoyable as it would've been, we did set boundaries that we need to adhere to.'

Not able to trust his voice to come out steady, all Caleb could do was nod, laying his arm against his eyes as he tried to concentrate upon regulating his racing heart. Tony didn't resist as Mary threw her nightgown over her head and forced her arms into the sleeves.

With this minimal protection cladding her once more, Tony leant over Caleb and briefly pressed her lips against his as she laid a trembling hand over his chest while he dragged in deep, calming breathes. He was still fully erect and couldn't stop the moan rising from his throat when Tony lightly caressed his penis.

'Tony... I'm so sorry... I thought... I was strong enough to resist... but you... are just so perfect.' Raising his arm from his eyes, Caleb propped himself up on his elbow.

'You were unbelievable Caleb! Wherever you led I was prepared to follow.' With less shyness than she had originally felt, Tony continued to stroke him. 'So what do we do about this?' She added.

A twisted smile answered her. 'A flick to the tip of the penis will take care of the erection.'

Tony screwed up her nose. 'Is it as pleasing a result as this?' She continued to caress her hand along his pulsating length.

A fractured laugh escaped from Caleb. 'Hell no!' Anything else he may have added was lost in a jumble of incoherent words as Tony took him deep into her mouth and suckled hard. Mary only just managed to reach across the bed in time to smother his shout as Caleb's seed shot down Tony's throat.

May I Speak To Your Father?

Permitting Tony to lie down in Caleb's arms, Mary waited until he had managed to catch his breath before firmly drawing her mistress to her feet. With incredible difficulty Caleb sat up and swung his legs over the edge of the bed. He wordlessly accepted his underwear and trousers when Mary handed them to him and even managed to put them on. *There is no way I am going to be able to get to my feet, not immediately any way.* Tony knelt down in front of him and tenderly ran a hand through his tousled hair.

'Are you all right?' Her concern always touched him anew and Caleb managed to nod.

'May I... speak to your father, Tony? Were your experiments... successful?'

Amused Tony cupped his face between her hands. 'Do you have any doubts that they were satisfactory?'

'I already knew, without any doubts, that you were the love of my life, but I want you to be happy.'

Smiling, Tony kissed him. 'We will be Caleb! Discuss with Papa how we can navigate around this scandal so that we can start this new life together as soon as possible.'

'I suppose it would raise too many questions if we were married tomorrow.' Caleb managed a shaky laugh.

Assisting Tony to her feet, Mary agreed. 'Some things are just worth waiting for, my Lord.'

Burying his head in his hands, Caleb groaned. 'Having tasted paradise, Mary, it only makes me hunger for more!'

The Maid chuckled, firmly directing Tony's unsteady footsteps towards the door. 'For now you have to obey the rules set down by society. Oh, and Lord Delacourt, I'll be sleeping on a trundle bed in Lady Tony's bedroom. Just in case you get any ideas in the middle of the night.' Mary unlocked and opened the door.

Laughing Caleb raised his hand in a fencing gesture to register the hit. 'Understood Mary. Good night ladies.'

'Good night Caleb.' Tony was already halfway out the door.

Mary smirked. 'Sweet dreams my Lord,' she added, softly closing the door behind her.

Unprepared Conversation

Running his hands through his hair a couple of time, Caleb finally managed to drag himself to his feet and staggered towards the window to open it again. Leaning against the sill, he allowed the night air to cool his overheated flesh as he breathed in deeply to fill his lungs and calm the ache inside him.

How easy it had been for my primordial needs to override every etiquette that I have learned as a gentleman. The fact that Tony would have welcomed me into the core if her being didn't mean it was right. It just meant that I should never have lost control to allow us to come to that point.

Frowning, desperately trying to prevent his thoughts from recalling every glorious second that had just taken place, he pressed his forehead against the window. Thus distracted, he didn't hear the knock on his bedroom door, or the door opening.

It wasn't until a hand was gently laid upon his arm, that Caleb realised that he was no longer alone. Half expecting it to be Geoff, Caleb was undisturbed by his half naked state. His eyebrows rose in surprise as he turned to find not his cousin beside him but his host.

Embarrassed, Caleb ran an unsteady hand through his tousled hair as he reached for a dressing gown hanging over the back of a chair. 'My apologies, my Lord, I didn't hear you knock.' Caleb's face became a mask but he frantically wondered, *perhaps we hadn't been as quiet as we had hoped.* The Earl smiled as he took one of the arm chairs beside the empty fire place and Caleb slipped into his dressing gown.

'Understandable my boy. She is bewitching isn't she?'

Blinking twice, Caleb opened his mouth to ask, 'Who?' but he received a look from the Earl and tried to bring his brain back into working order. Caleb sat down in the chair opposite the Earl. 'Sorry, I thought I'd have a few more clothes on when I had this conversation with you, Lord Stirling.'

A smile danced across the Earl's face. 'And time to recover from Tony's experiment?'

This time it was more difficult for Caleb to keep the horror from his face; he had absolutely no idea how to answer so it was just as well the Earl didn't truly expect one. He laughed at Caleb's struggle to speak.

'I wasn't deliberately snooping. So was a decision made?'

'Well… I have permission to ask you for Tony's hand in marriage.'

The Earl steepled his fingers together. 'What will you do if I refuse?' There was no hint of a threat in his words, it was merely an enquiry.

Sighing, Caleb stroked his chin. 'Well then, it'll have to be a dash to Gretna Green as I'm not going to let any man take away my soul mate.'

'No need for a flight across the Scottish border, my boy, I give you my blessing. If you, make my Tony happy then I'm happy.' Pausing for a moment to think about it seriously, the Earl added, 'I'm actually the least of your worries. I've been fascinated by the bond developing between you and Aidan. The news that you'll be taking away his sister may seriously dent that friendship.'

Shaking his head, Caleb chuckled. 'I've been working on that already, my Lord. When Duncan Gray had a local map out today, I showed Aidan how close my estate is to Stirling Manor. He'll be only a short ride or drive away from Tony and he may also stay for short visits or during the school holidays once he heads off to Eton and Cambridge.'

The Earl studied him carefully. 'You have been doing your ground work haven't you? Even so there will be objections to your union. The timing too is unfortunate. I'd hate the scandal of the kidnapping to taint such a happy event but there's no escaping from it. I don't suppose you're prepared to wait six to twelve months before you are married to prove that you're not marrying Tony for fear that she may be in the family way?'

Groaning Caleb buried his head in his hands. 'Lord Stirling I can barely stand to wait six to twelve hours let alone months before I'm allowed to marry Tony! If you dragged the good Reverend Gray out of his bed tonight, I'd raise no objection.'

Leaning forward the Earl patted Caleb's knee. 'Now that would give the gossip hungry Ton something to talk about.' Chuckling he hauled himself to his feet. 'Good night, my boy. I'll try to arrange it so that you can propose to Tony in private but you might have to contend with an audience.'

Casting a furtive glance towards the rumbled bed, Caleb sighed as images of making love to Tony flashed before his eyes, he stated, 'Actually it's probably safer if we're not completely alone, I don't know if I'm strong enough to resist the temptation of the most beautiful woman I have ever met! I thought that there was nothing on this earth that could make me forget what it means to be a gentleman.'

This time it was the Earl's turn to sigh. 'I knew a love like that once. Enjoy every single minute of it Caleb and I pray that it lasts longer for you than it did for Grace and I.' The Earl didn't wait for Caleb to reply as he left the room.

For a moment Caleb just sat there staring at the wall as he thought about the heartache if he were to lose Tony too soon. *I had never really before now considered how hard it must have been for the Earl, or my own mother to go on living after losing their soul mate.*

Rising out of his chair, Caleb closed the window once again before changing for bed. Slipping between the sheets, he should have felt like rejoicing, *so why do I feel like a black cloud hangs heavy over me?*

You Can Ask Me Anything

Turning down the bed in Tony's room, Mary softly hummed as she insisted her mistress to change her nightgown to one that was thicker and put on underwear. Although she obeyed, Tony was bemused as to why she needed to change until Mary showed her the damp spot and asked her to use the discarded garment to wipe away the moisture trickling down Tony's thighs before she slipped into clean clothes. At Tony's look of concern, Mary smiled.

'It's all right, my Lady, those juices will make it easier when you and his Lordship finally consummate your marriage.' When Tony had climbed into her bed, Mary drew up the bedcovers round her before sitting down on the bed and took one of Tony's hands between her own.

'You know you can ask me anything, Lady Tony, about this next chapter in your life. It would normally be your mother who discussed the facts of life with you before your marriage but if you feel you can't talk to Lady Charlotte then I'm here for you.'

Tony was moved by Mary's concern. 'Does it always hurt, or is it just the first time?'

'The first time there is the tearing of the hymen which lasts less than a few seconds but also you will be so tight and using muscles you've never used in that way before so you can be tender for a day or two afterwards. As you become accustomed to his size and girth as well as learning to match his rhythm, it becomes less painful.' An impish grin appeared on the Maid's face. 'And much more enjoyable.'

Some of the tension left Tony as she laid back against her pillows. 'How... how close did we came to... doing something we couldn't take back?'

Rising to her feet, Mary straightened the quilt. 'You were both ready for the commitment which is why I'll be sleeping in your room while Lord Delacourt stays here. I'll just check on Lord Aidan on my way downstairs to rinse out your nightie. I'll change and then come back to you.'

'Thank you Mary, for everything. If Aidan can't sleep, he can come to me.'

Mary chuckled as she headed out the door. 'For your protection or his?'

Tony smiled impishly. 'A little of both.'

Impatiently Waiting

Quietly entering Aidan's bedroom, Mary wasn't surprised that a candle still burned and William was slumped into one of the arm chairs. She had arranged for the Footman to remain with Aidan while Tony was in Lord Delacourt's room. William looked up from the book he had been reading and immediately rose to his feet and crossed the room to join Mary.

'Does Lord Aidan sleep?' Mary whispered as she kissed William's cheek.

'No he does not!' came a sullen reply from the bed as Aidan sat up. 'Can Bunny and I go join Tony now?'

Mary smiled at the boy. 'Of course my Lord.' As Aidan threw off his bedding and scampered to his feet, Mary added, 'Socks.'

Thrusting Bunny's ear into his mouth, Aidan tore through a drawer until he pulled out fluffy bed socks. Mary and William followed Aidan out of the room and paused at Tony's door to watch the boy climb into his sister's bed. He slipped on his socks and threw himself under the covers.

Satisfy Me

Softly closing the door, Mary took hold of William's hand and led him down the corridor. 'Do you have any other duties you need to deal with tonight Will?' Mary whispered as they headed downstairs to the deserted servant's service area. She was walking rather hurriedly, Tony's nightgown scrunched up in one hand.

'Free as a bird. Do you need to do some washing?' William smothered a yawn.

'Yes, but first I want you to satisfy my needs!' Mary stated calmly and William stumbled slightly in surprise.

'What if we're seen?' Even as the words left his lips, the thought of being caught just made William even more excited. It was late so the service areas were empty as Mary led him to the laundry room.

'I don't care! I have to return to Lady Tony's room tonight so it has to be now!' She cast a saucy glance up at her swain. 'If you're not up to the task, Will…' He scooped Mary up into his arms and carried her the rest of the way as they both laughed.

Throwing Tony's nightgown into a sink, Mary tore off her own bloomers before dropping to her knees to undo William's trousers. He had begun to take off his jacket but looking up as she drew out his penis, Mary said, 'There's no time to take our clothes off, Will.'

The Footman was incapable of answering as she took him deep into her mouth. As she sucked and licked him into an erection, Mary undid the buttons at the top of her dress so that she could draw her breasts free. When she put her hand into his trousers to caress his balls, he uttered a growl of pleasure and carefully drew his penis out of her mouth.

Wrapping his hands around Mary's waist, he lifted her up onto the table and pushing up her skirt, thrust deep inside her. Mary wrapped her legs around his hips and brought his mouth down to her breasts as William withdrew and thrust even deeper.

Previously their love making had been civilised, gentle, quiet exploration. Now it was hard, fast and primitive as Mary threw her head back, gasping for air. While William gritted his teeth in concentration, he sought to satisfy Mary's desires which had arisen from watching Caleb and Tony's experiments. Reaching down to fondle her own breasts, Mary twirled her nipples between her fingers and William covered her mouth with his own to muffle their cries as they climaxed in pleasure.

As they struggled to catch their breath, William laid his head against Mary's breasts and tenderly stroked her thighs. Raising his face, they shared a gentle kiss before he assisted her down off the table. They rearranged their clothes but before William left the laundry room, Mary tenderly caressed his cheek before turning her attention to washing Tony's nightgown.

THURSDAY
The Earl's Private Word

Having barely left her room the next morning, Tony was surprised to get such an early request to present herself to her father's study. She had carefully chosen her dress so that she appeared in the best light and had even permitted Mary to style her hair into a cascade of curls down her back and a few attractive curls framing her face instead of her usual plait. *Even though I am prepared for what will eventuate sometime this day, I still feel a knot of apprehension building in the pit of my stomach. What if Caleb has changed his mind? What if Papa has said "no"?*

Aidan clung to his sister's hand as they headed downstairs to the study, and Tony wondered, *how will Aidan handle the prospect of losing me?* Pausing outside the study door, she took a deep breath as her trembling fingers reached for the door handle. Glancing up at Tony, Aidan squeezed her other hand reassuringly.

'Everything is going to be fine.' His quiet assurance calmed the doubt in her and managing a nervous smile she stepped into the room with an assumed air of confidence.

The Earl stood at the French windows, staring out across his estate and he was alone. This surprised Tony and made her wonder, *Has Caleb managed to speak to Papa yet?* Turning at their entrance, Earl Stirling smiled.

'Ah my dear girl, I wanted to have a private word before Lord Delacourt speaks to you.' He indicated to his daughter to take a seat before sitting down not behind his desk but in the chair beside her. Aidan climbed up onto his sister's lap as their father took her hand between his own. For a brief moment of panic, Tony wondered, *is Papa going to forbid the marriage?*

'I want you to tell me the truth, baby girl, are you prepared to accept Caleb's proposal just due to the scandal? I don't want you to sacrifice your happiness if this is not truly what you want.'

'Do you dislike Caleb, Papa?' Tony was puzzled by his concern.

'No, I think he is a good man but is he the right man for you?'

'Oh Papa, he's perfect!' A small sob escaped from Tony as she returned the pressure of her father's fingers. 'I love him!'

The Earl finally smiled and the tension left his body. 'That's all I need to know.' Rising to his feet, he held out his hand to Aidan but Tony shook her head.

'It's all right, Papa, Aidan can stay with me.'

'It's rather unusual Tony.' The Earl's eyebrows rose in surprise.

That caused her to laugh. 'That seems to describe me perfectly!'

Why Is Everyone So Serious?

Accepting this statement, the Earl left his children alone in the study together.

'Why is Papa so serious Tony?' Aidan picked up a quill from the desk and used the feather to tickle himself under the chin.

'Getting married is a serious business, Little Bear. Papa doesn't want me to feel pressured to accept an offer just to avert the scandal that we're currently in the midst of.'

'Why is there a scandal?' Aidan frowned as he looked up at his sister. 'Because of the abduction or because of the barn?'

'A little of both.' Tony sighed deeply. 'It's all my fault for dressing like a man. Trying to be something I'm not and never could ever be.'

'Would we've had as much fun if you had been in dresses all the time?'

Pausing to consider the question, Tony didn't immediately answer. 'I do find them rather restrictive but I think once I got used to it we would've got into just as much mischief as we did in trousers. My main concern is that it's impossible to wear my sword in a dress. It compromises my need to protect you.'

'Who will protect me when you leave?'

Tony chuckled, 'You're surrounded by protection so long as someone knows where you are. Also when Phillippe Du Bois returns from Paris he'll begin teaching you fencing and Ang Lee will train you in defence.' She dropped a kiss onto the top of his curly blonde head. He scowled at such a girly gesture but didn't protest as Tony's arms tightened around him.

Caleb's Declaration

At the sight of such a touching scene, Caleb paused on the threshold of the study as he realised, *I am about to ask Aidan to give up the one person he loves most in the world and for a moment I find it hard to accept. That would mean I would have to give up any chance of future happiness and that causes my chest to squeeze remorselessly against my heart at the thought of a life without Tony.* As the siblings looked up at his approach, Caleb forced those emotions down and tried to smile.

For a brief moment, though, Tony had seen the anguish in Caleb's eyes and lowering her gaze to rest upon Aidan, she thought she understood what Caleb felt. *I will miss my daily interactions with my brother but to refuse a life with Caleb is causing my heart to pound a painful beat against my temples.* Caleb sat down in the chair recently vacated by the Earl.

'Are you going to ask Tony to marry you?' Aidan blurted out.

'Yes I am,' Caleb replied calmly, 'and I understand that is a problem for you Aidan.'

The boy frowned. 'Yes… and no.' His response surprised both adults. 'I'll be very happy to have you as a big brother but I will miss seeing Tony every day. The last couple of days have made me realise that I see Tony not as a sister, or even a brother but more as a mother. That has to stop. It's not right… or that's what Grandmother Henry said.' Even though the little boy was resolved to accept this change he was unable to stop a tear running down his cheek. Sniffing inelegantly, Aidan added, 'I don't suppose it's possible that you could live here with us?'

Caleb gently brushed the boy's tear away with his thumb. 'I'm sorry Aidan, I have my own home and estate to look after. We'll be able to visit each other on a regular basis.'

'It won't be the same though!' Aidan sniffed again.

'No Little Bear,' Tony kissed his cheek. 'But we're getting ahead of ourselves as Caleb hasn't actually asked me to marry him yet and I haven't accepted.'

Both gentlemen looked at her in surprise and in Caleb's case, a little horror. 'But you are going to, aren't you?' The quickness of Caleb's question revealed his own doubts. Tony smiled as she caressed her hand against Caleb's.

Taking a deep breath to calm his fears, Caleb lowered himself to one knee and drew out of his trouser pocket a small jeweller's box. Lady Isabella had brought it to the Manor with her. Opening it and presenting it to Tony, he said, 'Lady Antonia Stirling, will you do me the honour of your hand in marriage?'

Tony didn't even look at the ring but kept her eyes locked upon Caleb's. 'This is all so sudden! I'm sure I'm going to need some time to think about this.' At her portrayal of maidenly indecision, a broad grin spread across Caleb's face as his thoughts inadvertently returned to the previous evening lying naked in each other's arms.

'Perhaps, my elfling, needs further experiments?' One mobile eyebrow rose to mock her. As Tony's thoughts followed a similar train to his, she inhaled sharply as colour flooded her cheeks. *I can almost feel Caleb caressing me again.*

'Touché my Lord!'

'Well?' Aidan glanced up puzzled at his sister. 'Are you going to marry Lord Caleb or not?'

Caleb chuckled at the boy's impatience but decided to take matters into his own hands and easing the ring out of the box, he slid it onto her left ring finger. She glanced down at the diamonds twinkling back at her.

'Yes I am,' Tony said quietly and laid her hand over Caleb's as he leant forward to kiss her.

I Need To Tell Someone Privately

I must keep a tight hold over my control as I can't afford to give into my primal self like last night. The ready response of Tony's lips beneath his, though, made it a struggle to withstand her allure. Aidan gently pushing against his shoulder recalled Caleb to their current location and he rose to his feet.

'I suppose we should let our families know of our decision.' Caleb held out his hand to assist Tony to her feet. She settled Aidan on the floor first before rising.

'Gather everyone on the morning room but I need to tell one person privately. He deserves that much.'

'Duncan Gray?' asked Caleb.

Smiling Tony agreed. 'Do you feel safe enough with Caleb for a few minutes?' She asked Aidan.

'Of course!' The boy immediately reached up to take Caleb's hand. 'He's going to be my big brother!'

Caleb was moved by the boy's enthusiasm and allowed himself to be dragged out of the room. Tony followed them out but headed upstairs instead to the school room.

Knocking quietly on the door and calling out his name before she entered, Tony found Duncan hard at work at his desk. He was frowning, deep in thought and didn't immediately notice her presence. Glancing over his shoulder to look at the original document he was working from, Tony was able to decipher enough to know that this wasn't school work, nor was it personal.

It screamed out to her "Top Secret" and she tapped Duncan on the shoulder to gain his attention. The fact that he jumped, startled, suggested how deep his concentration had been. Self-consciously the Tutor turned over the original document and covered his work with the blotter. He took off his glasses to clean them as if to cover up his actions.

'If the government has already got you working on secret portfolios for them, it might be a good idea to lock the door.' Tony suggested, not at all offended by his actions.

'Sorry, I wasn't expecting to see anyone just yet. Aidan has hardly shown any interest in school work the past couple of days.'

Laughing, Tony added, 'Well today's probably going to be the same. I have some news I want to share with you before I tell everyone.'

Casting a scrutinising glance over Tony, Duncan noted the glow that surrounded her, the content smile that lingered on her lips and finally the diamond ring in her finger. 'So Lord Delacourt has asked you to marry him.' Rising to his feet, Duncan took both her hands into his.

'You're not surprised?' she asked.

'I've been expecting the announcement for days now.' Duncan smiled.

'You're not upset?'

Shaking his head, Duncan kissed her cheek. 'No, I've been watching his Lordship closely and had come to the conclusion that he can give you the life you deserve. I'm happy for you Tony. My only concern is…'

She sighed, 'This scandal? How to insist that Caleb's offer has nothing to do with the abduction?'

Releasing her hands, Duncan gathered up all his papers and locked them away in the top drawer of his desk. 'Exactly but if there's no rush to actually get married then society should have moved on to the next scandal by the time you wed.' He linked his arm through Tony's and led her out of the school room.

'How long do we have to wait? I was hoping it could be in the next couple of weeks.'

Laughing, Duncan apologised, 'Sorry but most women spend six to twelve months planning their big day.' He paused to glance down at her, thoughtfully. 'There isn't a need for a speedy wedding is there Tony? You haven't been...' He hesitated to raise such a delicate subject.

'Compromised? No, I just...' Tony's colour rose as they headed down the main staircase. 'I've had a taste of... heaven and I hunger for more.' She used the same words Caleb had said last night.

Duncan's breath caught in a sharp intake of air. 'So you have found the passion you've been looking for after all!'

Her eyes sparkled as she raised them to meet Duncan's. 'Most definitely!'

Patrick's Warning

As Patrick Stirling strolled around the corner of the main hall towards them, Tony slid her arm out of Duncan's.

'Go on ahead, I want to have a quick word with Patrick.'

Duncan hesitated. 'Is it safe to be alone with him?'

'I won't be going anywhere with him but he might prefer to not be with a room full of people when I tell him my news.' Tony patted his hand.

'All right.' Duncan went on towards the morning room with misgivings in his heart.

'Well sweet coz, why has a family conclave been called?' Patrick took possession of both of Tony's hands and he cast a sweeping glance down her attire. 'You're looking absolutely delicious this morning. Female attire suits you.'

Sighing Tony admitted, 'I miss my sword.'

Patrick's eyes danced wickedly. 'Ah yes, I often wondered if your wearing a sword had more to do with lacking a certain male appendage than your need for protection,' he drawled.

'I had never really considered it that way. I suppose I really was deluded about who I really am.'

Before Tony could allow her thoughts to dwell upon her failings, Patrick had noticed the ring on her finger. Raising her hand to study the sparkle of the diamonds, he drawled, 'What a pretty trinket, my sweet coz. Has Papa been endowing you with sparkling baubles?' Although his tone was light, there was a note of desperate need for no other reason being correct. Tony took a deep breath before she admitted the truth.

'Patrick, Lord Delacourt has asked me to marry him and I have said yes.' Tony paused to allow her words time to sink in as her cousin raised his eyes to rest upon her face. His fingers tightened slightly around hers and his chest heaved as Patrick dragged in a deep breath.

'I see!' His tone was as smooth as silk as he fought to keep his emotions under control. 'Don't you think it would have been wiser to wait and be certain that his Lordship had impregnated you before you rushed into wedlock?'

Colour rushed up Tony's cheeks as his words stung. 'Patrick! How many times do I have to tell you that Caleb did not compromise me? I accepted because I want to marry him, not because I have to. I'm sorry that I can't return the feelings that you have for me or that you think I dislike you just because I prefer that Papa is succeeded by a son rather than a nephew. I didn't instigate Papa's second marriage to spite you but to ease my own guilt that Mama's only surviving child was a daughter.' Tears welled up in Tony's eyes as she admitted her greatest fears 'If I had been a boy, it wouldn't have been necessary for Mama to suffer all those miscarriages and still births, and just maybe... she'd still be alive today.'

As a tear fell down her cheek, Patrick brushed it aside with his thumb. 'You shouldn't blame yourself Tony, you don't decide what sex you're born. As for your mother's health, that was compromised by an infection. Tell me honestly, sweet coz, and I'll never ask again... do you love Delacourt?'

Tony was a little taken aback by her cousin's sudden tenderness as she nodded. 'Yes I do, very, very much!'

Brushing away another tear, Patrick kissed Tony's cheek. 'Then I wish you joy, my beautiful cousin. Don't... don't let your guard down just yet, Tony, some people... aren't what they seem to be.'

Frowning, she looked up at Patrick as he released her and took a step back. 'Do you know something about Caleb that I should be warned about?'

'No, not him exactly, just... just be careful who you trust. I'm sure you'll understand if I don't come into the drawing room with you.' He was already distancing himself from her.

'Of course Patrick, that's why I wanted to tell you in private. To spare you the pain.'

Patrick bowed elegantly. 'Always thinking of others, sweet coz.' He turned and walked away and didn't look back. As she stepped into the morning room, Patrick's cryptic warning was momentarily pushed to one side as Tony joined Caleb in receiving congratulations from their family.

I Thought This Was My Wedding?

The gentlemen quickly melted away as the ladies got down to the serious business of planning a wedding. Books, magazines, notes seemed to appear out of nowhere. Most of the discussion went on around Tony; her attempt to suggest a wedding in under four weeks was scoffed and Charlotte put forward the suggestion of Spring, next year as it would be three months after giving birth and she should have regained her figure by then. *I don't see why I have to wait almost a whole year just to please my step-mother.*

The reception would naturally be at Stirling Manor but the ladies weren't certain that the local church was going to be big enough. *The guest names being thrown around, I barely recognise half of them. When my relatives start on my clothes and what constitutes suitable presents, I am beginning to feel invisible as anything I say is ignored or rejected as unsuitable for the daughter of an Earl.*

As her future was being organised for her, Tony picked up one of the magazines that the ladies were referencing and began to flick through it. Her head had begun to ache at the momentous task and she almost wept with joy as Aidan slipped un-noticed into the room and taking his sister's hand, led her out to freedom. The women didn't even notice Tony's departure as they continued to argue the merits of Irish lace compared to French lace.

Waiting outside the room was an anxious Earl Stirling accompanied by Caleb. Tony fell gratefully into her father's arms.

'Thank you Papa! Have you made arrangements for Caleb and I to elope and escape this nightmare?'

The Earl chuckled as he hugged his daughter. 'Not exactly, baby girl, but I do have an errand for the two of you. I've made arrangements with Mrs Preston and our cook, Mrs Hill for a celebration supper for all the villagers and local gentry tonight and I want you to personally issue the invitation to Reverend and Mrs Gray. The fresh air will do you good.'

Tony kissed her father's cheek. 'Are you sure you can't come with us to the Vicarage now and convince Reverend Gray to marry us immediately? Can't we escape this circus?'

The Earl's eyebrows rose. 'Now what sort of message would that send to the Ton? We're trying to suppress the scandal, not add to it!'

'Unfortunately, Tony, I have to agree with your father.' Chuckling, Caleb linked his arm through Tony's. 'As much as I want to be married to you right this very minute, we have to act in an appropriate manner as befits our stations in life.'

Casting a look of suspicion up at him, Tony said, 'That sounds like someone has been coaching you to toe the party line. You didn't feel that way last night!'

Glancing guiltily at the Earl, Caleb coughed in embarrassment. 'That's your fault Tony, you make me forget every principle that was installed in me! All that matters is being with you; the rest of the world ceases to exist. Unfortunately the rest of the world does exist and it is judging us six days to Sunday so we have to not give them anything to criticise.'

Tony sighed. 'All right, but I'm not waiting a whole year before we can be wed!'

Giving her shoulder a fatherly pat, the Earl said, 'I'll champion your one month wish but you may have to settle for three months. Now off to the Vicarage before it's noticed that you're no longer in the room.' Stirling urged them out of the house before leading Aidan upstairs to find his Tutor.

Tony's Lament

Considering the shortness of notice, it was a surprise that nearly everyone in the village as well as from the estate attended the gathering at the Manor that evening. A formal engagement after the official notice went into the London newspapers would be held for the cream of society. *This party is just for the local people of Stirling and to me, is more important, as these are the people who mean more to me than unknown Lords and Ladies,* reflected Tony. *I am overwhelmed not by expensive presents but how much love, devotion and respect I have apparently created amongst the residents of the district. Even if I did roam around the countryside in male attire.*

Although I'm not going too far away, they have expressed sadness at the void that will occur with my absence from their daily lives. It makes me a little sad, that by taking such an active role in the village I have perhaps robbed Charlotte of the opportunity to make her position as Lady Stirling her own. By being more productive in local affairs, perhaps Charlotte would feel less inclined to pine for the excitement of London or Bath?

When Tony explained her concern to the Dowager, Lady Margarette, she immediately dismissed the notion.

'If Agnes Henry had spent more time teaching her daughters how to be useful members of society instead of turning them into mindless beautiful dolls, then you wouldn't have needed to fill the void Charlotte has created in the community. You were still a child when she married your father and Charlotte had plenty of time to make the role her own!'

That is a little hard on my docile step-mother but I'm not even going to try and argue with Grandmama. 'I suppose it doesn't help that I grew up with these people.' Her tactful suggestion earned her a shrewd look from the Dowager.

'That's true as is the fact that your mother was adored by all and you are so like her. When you leave the Manor a great deal of responsibility will fall upon Charlotte's shoulders; for one thing she'll have to take care of her own children! I'd better have a word with Charlotte and get her ready for the transition.'

Noticing the Dowager's lips thinning, Tony shook her head. 'No Grandmama, you'd only scare her to death. I'll sit Charlotte down with Mrs Preston and Mrs Gray and we'll slowly walk her through her new responsibilities.'

Although Lady Margarette's lips were still pursed, her eyes twinkled. 'Impertinent child! Scare her to death indeed! She'd probably use her pregnancy as an excuse to get out of doing anything that looks remotely like hard work!'

Tony chuckled, 'You're definitely not going to talk to Charlotte! Any harsh word from you and we'd end up with Charlotte taking to her bed for the remainder of her confinement… in tears! That's all we need!'

'Cheeky minx!' The Dowager paused to consider Tony's words and had to acknowledge there was some truth behind her teasing tone. 'I'll leave it up to you to deal diplomatically with your step-mother. I suppose we should've been a little stricter with Charlotte when she first married Julius.'

Tony shook her head. 'It wouldn't have worked Grandmama, Charlotte would've been trading one dominatrix in her mother for another in her mother-in-law. Maybe now she'll be strong enough to cope with the responsibility.'

Glancing around the crowded room, the Dowager noticed Mrs Heather Gray, the Reverend's wife was approaching with a local five year old girl.

'You might consider including Lizzy for these discussions. She could benefit from some real life lessons rather than focusing on her appearance.'

Tony grinned. 'And you wonder why I feel you maybe too aggressive to instruct the sisters?'

Chuckling Lady Margarette pressed a kiss against her granddaughter's forehead. 'I'll leave the joy of teaching to you.'

Bridget's Sacrifice

As Heather Gray joined them, Tony's smile included the Reverend's wife. 'Oh no, Grandmama, I'll be relying on the expertise of those more skilled than I.'

Heather's eyebrows rose in mild interest. 'What are you volunteering me for now, my Lady?'

'Helping Charlotte to make the role of Lady of the Manor her own once I've left,' answered Tony, acknowledging the presence of Bridget, the five year old girl, who was waiting patiently to speak to Tony.

'Of course Lady Tony, but it just won't be the same without you.'

Bridget tugged upon Tony's sleeve. 'You'll still be here for the Autumn Festival won't you Lady Tony?'

Casting a searching glance between the older ladies, Tony hesitated. 'Well that's still being debated as to when I will be wed.'

'Don't you have any say in when you can marry Lord Delacourt?' Bridget frowned in concentration.

Biting down on her bottom lip, Tony tried to not smirk. 'Apparently not.' She crouched down so that she was eye to eye with Bridget and noticed that the girl's doll wore an identical dress to Bridget. 'My goodness, Henrietta is looking very pretty today. Is that a new dress?' added Tony.

The little girl seemed to be steeling herself for a big revelation. 'Aye because I want you to have Henrietta for when you have your own baby.'

Tony's heart nearly broke to see how brave Bridget was trying to be. 'Oh I can't take Henrietta from you, she's your best friend!'

Bridget's bottom lip trembled slightly. 'I want to give you something to show how grateful I am for all you've done for my family.'

'You and Henrietta can make another doll when I have a little boy or girl but I won't take Henrietta away from you.'

Bridget was relieved but still a little worried. 'I can't... I don't have enough material... at the moment.'

Caressing the child's cheek, Tony smiled. 'I want you to come downstairs to see Mrs Preston. I'm sure we can find some material for you.'

Bridget's face lit up. 'And stuffing?' Standing up straight, Tony held her hand out to the child.

'Of course.'

As Tony glanced around for Caleb or her father, Heather slipped her arm through Tony's. 'I'll come for a walk with you as I want to talk to your cook about those delicious macaroons she makes,' explained the Vicar's wife.

One of Tony's eyebrows rose in amusement. 'Protective custody Mrs Gray?' She teased, and catching Caleb's eye, gestured to him.

'Not really my dear,' Heather smiled. 'Don't tell Matthew or Duncan but standing or sitting for long periods still hurts my lower back so a gentle stroll now means I don't have to rush home just yet.'

'I tell no tales,' promised Tony, patting Heather's hand and as Caleb approached them, she explained where they were going.

'Do you want an escort?' His offer was touching but Tony shook her head.

'We're not leaving the house and will be surrounded by servants. I just wanted to keep you updated to my whereabouts.'

'All right then.' Caleb's worried look eased into a smile. 'Don't be too long as I think your father wants to make a toast soon.' He briefly kissed Tony's cheek before he joined his cousin who was hailing him.

Below Stairs

The stroll down to the servants' domain was uneventful for which Tony was grateful as Heather Gray was really too fragile to offer any real protection. Both the Housekeeper, Mrs Preston, and the Cook, Mrs Hill, were found in the kitchen. As Tony entered the room, the Maids dropped a hasty curtsy before returning to their work. A look of concern formed on Mrs Preston's face.

'Is there anything wrong, my Lady? Are you dissatisfied with some aspect of the party?'

Smiling, Tony shook her head. 'Not in the least Mrs Preston. Everything is perfect! With such short notice you, Mrs Hill, and all your staff have done a marvellous job. I hope we haven't put you to too much trouble?'

Mrs Hill dusted the flour absently from her hands. 'Not at all your Ladyship. Tis always a pleasure to be of service to you.'

The Cook picked up one of the not-so-perfect biscuits and offered it to the blushing child.

'Thank you Mrs Hill.' Bridget bobbed a brief curtsy and almost dropped her biscuit.

Removing Henrietta, the doll, from Bridget, Tony handed her to the Housekeeper. 'Henrietta has come to visit us,' Tony explained and Mrs Preston looked rather closely at the doll's new dress.

'My goodness Bridget did you sew and design this outfit for Henrietta?'

'Aye Ma'am.' The child's words were a little muffled by biscuit.

'What do you think?' Tony asked quietly of Mrs Preston, 'I was thinking of talking to Amelia Scott about an apprenticeship for Bridget.'

Joining them, Mrs Hill lifted up Henrietta's dress to examine the hem and Bridget's stitches. 'Are you thinking of sending her to school first? She'll need numeracy and literacy if she wants to be more than just a seamstress.'

Bridget brushed crumbs off the front of her dress. 'Will Henrietta be able to go to school with me?'

'Yes of course,' replied Tony.

'Will you still arrange material for me, Lady Tony?'

'Of course.'

Mrs Preston handed the doll back to Bridget. 'If you're interested in making dolls to sell, Bridget, I think I could put in an order for at least two.'

Pinching one of the not-perfect biscuits, Heather Gray added, 'if you get into production, I could help you sell the dolls on market day.'

Bridget's eyes opened wide in surprise. 'A stall of my own at the market? Just like Papa's fruit and veg?'

Heather nodded. 'Perhaps at first your Papa will let you have a corner of his stall until you've enough produce for your own table.'

'Bridget needs some material and stuffing.' Tony kept them on track as Bridget was overwhelmed by all the attention.

'Of course,' said Mrs Preston. 'I'll see what we can lay our hands on.'

Tony's presence in the kitchen was causing an obstruction in one of the doors and Mrs Hill said politely, 'Will there be anything else my Lady?'

'Actually,' Heather began, 'I wanted to speak you Mrs Hill about the recipe for your macaroons. I have never tasted any as delicious or as light as yours.'

Mrs Hill blushed in delight. 'Thank you Mrs Gray… but…' The recipe for her prize winning macaroons was a secret.

Seeing her dilemma, Tony saw a possible solution. 'What about a trade Mrs Hill? Your macaroon recipe for Mrs Gray's Angel cake?' That caused the Vicar's wife to pause this time and Tony quickly added, 'on the understanding that neither of you can use the other's recipe in any cooking competition.' This was the reason both the women had hesitated in giving away their secrets.

'That would be acceptable,' agreed Heather.

Mrs Hill was still a little hesitant, 'Actually, I'd rather trade for Mrs Gray's recipe for her apple strudel. I've never seen any other done as well.'

'All right then, it's a deal!' The two women shook hands and placing her hand on Bridget's shoulder, Tony urged her towards the door.

'Papa will be waiting for our return in the ball room.' Tony said, linking her arm once more through Heather's.

'Of course Lady Tony,' agreed the Vicar's wife. 'It'll be time for Bridget to go home to bed.'

The small child was valiantly trying to smoother a yawn as she took Tony's other hand and they headed back upstairs. 'I'm not at all tired!' Bridget's yawn belied her words and brought a smile to the lips of the two women.

Raise Your Glasses

Although the Earl managed to conceal his concern as Heather returned Tony safely once more, Caleb looked openly relieved as he took his fiancée's hand and raised it to his lips. He led Tony to where Preston was pouring out glasses of champagne and the Earl accepted one from the Butler. Looking up to meet the concern in his daughter's eyes, Earl Stirling smiled like a naughty school boy.

'This is my first glass of wine, Tony, honest! I want to toast my only daughter's happiness with proper etiquette.'

Caressing her hand against her father's arm, Tony managed to smile. 'Of course Papa, just this once then.' She released his arm to take the glass Caleb handed her. She raised a questioning glance up at her beloved.

'Yours is only lemonade, Tony.' Caleb quietly reassured, and Tony's heart swelled in her love for this wonderful, understanding man.

'Thank you.' Tony turned her focus back to her father as he tapped his glass to gain everyone's attention.

'Ladies and gentlemen, family, friends and neighbours! I want to thank you all for attending at such short notice the engagement of my daughter Antonia to the luckiest man in the world, Lord Caleb Delacourt. I may be biased, I'm only her father.'

There was general laughter at the Earl's joke and Tony sighed. 'Oh he's not in the least biased!' Tony whispered into Caleb's ear and he chuckled.

'Let the Earl have this moment, it can't be easy to lose you to another man.'

Although Tony smiled, it didn't reach her eyes and a chill swept over her as she thought not of her father but her cousin Patrick. *He has been very withdrawn since I told him of my engagement and I had half expected to see hatred in his eyes when he looked at me. Instead I see concern, even fear on Patrick's face.* The Earl's voice brought Tony back to the present surroundings.

'So I ask you to all raise your glasses as we toast the happiness of Antonia and Caleb!'

Obediently the assembly raised their glasses and repeated, 'To Lady Tony and Lord Caleb!' They drank to the couple's future and a cheer broke out chasing away Tony's previous doubts.

Bed Time For Aidan

With the formal toast over, it was now time for the children to be heading home so Tony wasn't surprised to see Duncan carrying Aidan towards them. The boy's head lay on his Tutor's shoulder and he was obviously very tired. As the Earl, his Countess and the Dowager thanked, in the entrance hall, the visitors that had to leave, Tony held out her hands to take her brother.

'Ready for bed, Little Bear?' There was a tenderness in her voice that made Caleb realise how hard it would be for both siblings when Tony came to leave the Manor. Aidan willingly transferred to his sister's arms as he yawned.

'Will you stay with me Tony? Do you have to come back downstairs?'

Caleb's eyebrows rose in surprise. 'And leave me to deal with all these people on my own?'

The little boy studied him for a moment before answering, 'Come with us,' offered Aidan.

231

Duncan laughed as he shook his head. 'That would give society something to talk about!' he drawled.

Frowning Aidan turned his gaze upon his Tutor. 'But I'd be there to protect Tony's reputation.'

Caressing her hand against Aidan's hair, Tony smiled. 'Of course you would, but I can't retire until all our guests have left, Little Bear.'

'Oh I see.' Aidan yawned again. 'Goodnight Duncan. Caleb, I'm glad you're going to be my big brother.' The boy's words robbed Caleb of speech as Tony carried her brother up to her bedroom.

So Quiet Upstairs

After all the noise, lights and activity downstairs, the upper floors seem eerily silent and foreboding. The absence of Aidan's usual chatter, exhausted by all the excitement, only adds to the sense of menace. By the time we reached my bedroom, I had begun to wish that Caleb or Duncan had accompanied us.

Chastising herself for being fanciful, Tony entered her room which already had the bed turned down and several candles lit. A gentle smile lingered on her lips at Mary's thoughtfulness and that she'd probably be along at any minute with a mug of hot chocolate for the young Lord.

Barely had Tony sat Aidan down on the bed to help him change into his nightwear, when a hand encircled Tony's waist from behind as another hand covered her mouth to muffle her scream. A harsh laugh against her ear caused Tony to fight against her captor. The hand around her waist held a pistol and as Tony continued to struggle, he pointed it menacingly towards Aidan.

'Be still, me fine buck or the boy gets the first bullet!'

Tony stiffened at the familiar voice and immediately obeyed, knowing that Nigel Sutherland would have no qualms about killing a five year old boy. Removing his hand from her mouth, Nigel turned her around and pushed her down onto the bed beside her brother.

'How did you escape custody?' Tony's breathing quickened in indignation as Nigel leered at her and backed towards the door to lock it.

'It would seem that I'm not y'r only enemy, me fine buck!' Nigel scrubbed a hand over his chin. 'Me God, y'r even more beautiful as a woman!' He picked up Tony's left hand to look at her diamond ring. 'So all the noise downstairs was some sort of engagement party. I'd have thought it'd be too soon to know for certain that Lord Delacourt had planted his seed inside ya!'

Tony's hand came up to slap Nigel's face and took him by surprise, especially as his pistol was still pointing at Aidan. He didn't retaliate but grinned instead.

'What sort of seed?' The Innocence of Aidan's question caused Nigel to laugh. Tony raised beseeching eyes to Nigel to not answer that question. That only amused him more but he wasn't in the mood to placate her.

'Impregnate y'r sister with a pretty little baby just like ya!' Tony sighed but was grateful that Nigel hadn't been more graphically crude.

'I'm not a baby!' protested Aidan. 'I'm five!' He frowned as he processed the rest of Nigel's statement. 'Caleb didn't do anything naughty in the barn, Doctor Masters said so!'

Nigel laughed, 'And Doctors can't lie? Enough, get y'r coat and we're getting out of here.'

Why Are You Doing This?

'We don't have to drag Aidan out into the cold this time. Why don't we lock him in his bedroom and I'll come with you? But if you take my jewellery box you'd probably get more for its contents than any ransom.' Tony tried to reason with him.

Nigel shook his head. 'It has to be both of ya. I'm following a plan this time. Grab y'r coats. We've a long way to go tonight.'

Watching the way Nigel's muscle is working along his jaw, I can foresee an image of our future and it will end in blood split, feared Tony. 'Is this about money? The pearls I'm wearing are worth more than a ransom Papa could raise at short notice.'

'I'm not going to discuss this with ya.' Nigel struggled to keep his temper under her direct attack.

Standing up, Tony grabbed the sleeve of his jacket. 'Are you doing this for money or revenge? If you're going to kill us anyway do it now rather than drag us out into the night. Or is it your intent to humiliate us until we beg you to put a bullet into our brains?'

A whimper escaped from Aidan as he reached out for Tony's hand. 'I don't want to die!' As tears welled in the boy's eyes, Nigel pulled his arm away from Tony.

'There's nothing in the plan about killing anyone. Get y'r coat now!'

Tony's Warning

As Tony opened her wardrobe, there was a knock at the door. She glanced questioningly up at Nigel as they heard Mary trying to open the door before calling out. 'My Lady? I have Lord Aidan's hot chocolate.'

'How do you want me to handle this?' whispered Tony.

'Send her away.' Nigel held his pistol against Aidan's head.

Nodding, Tony's hand shook as she unlocked the door and opened it a fraction. 'Sorry McKenzie, I was just changing Aidan and didn't want cool air entering to give him a chill. The party has over excited Aidan a little so I'm going to stay with him until he drops off to sleep. You may as well go to bed McKenzie, I won't need you again tonight.' Tony took the tray from a surprised Mary and closed the door once more. Nigel locked the door as Tony automatically poured out the hot chocolate for Aidan before she went back to her wardrobe.

Sipping his drink, Aidan silently watched the two adults acting as if this was a normal situation. He complied with Tony as she took off his jacket and dressed him a jumper and then an outside warmer jacket. Tony let her brother finish his chocolate as she drew on a jacket and then her own overcoat.

Taking a deep breath to steady her nerves, Tony turned to face Nigel. 'There's still time to change your mind and get a head start on the man hunt that will result from escaping custody. We'll only slow you down if you have to flee England.'

Grabbing a fur knee rug off the back of one of the chairs, Nigel threw it around Aidan before picking the boy up. Tony didn't need Nigel to press his weapon against Aidan's temple to get her to unlock and open the door before following him out of her bedroom.

I wouldn't do anything that would jeopardise my brother's safety. Unarmed and outweighed, I feel even more vulnerable in female attire and I can only hope to lull Nigel into a false sense of security to lower his guard enough so that we can escape.

Mary Disobeys The Rules

Pausing, staring at the bedroom door, Mary tried to rationalise what had just happened. Slowly turning, Mary headed down the passageway with a normal tread. When she reached the corner, Mary picked up her skirts and began to run. Her mind racing, she tried to think what her next move should be.

Traversing through the entrance hall where the Earl was seeing guests out of the Manor, Mary paused, debating going to the Earl with her suspicion but instead she turned her footsteps to the ballroom. There were protocols to be observed with her next actions but there wasn't time to honour these. *If I'm right then Lady Tony and Lord Aidan are in danger.*

Taking a deep breath, Mary stepped determinedly towards the Butler, Preston. He stiffened in indignation and bore down on Mary with an icy stare but she refused to be deterred.

'I'm sorry Mr Preston, I know this is highly irregular but I must… I must speak with Lord Delacourt. I think… I think Lady Tony is in danger.' Mary's explanation immediately melted the iceberg as Preston grabbed hold of Mary's elbow and propelled her further into the room.

Caleb was at first surprised to see the two servants bearing down upon him. Searching Mary's face and seeing her worried expression, Caleb's surprise turned to concern. Absently he excused himself to the people he had been talking to and he quickly closed the space between them.

'What is it Mary? Is Tony all right?' Caleb's concern moved Mary and she actually hoped that her suspicions were wrong.

'Lady Tony wouldn't let me into the room when I brought up Lord Aidan's hot chocolate and she called me McKenzie. Her Ladyship has always called me by my first name and not my surname.'

Caleb paused for less than a heartbeat before he was striding for the door. 'Preston, order my phaeton to be brought round, if I can't stop them leaving the house then I'll need to be on the road after them immediately!'

'Of course, my Lord.' Preston gestured to William to run down to the stables as Caleb raced out of the room and up the stairs. *My heart is ready to explode that the fear of losing Tony could possibly come true.*

I Won't Lose Her Now!

Stopping only briefly at his own room to grab his pistols, Caleb burst into Tony's bedroom but it was already empty. He checked Aidan's bedroom just in case, but his mind was already racing ahead to the pursuit.

Slipping back into his own room, Caleb changed into his boots and his overcoat before collecting a few odds and ends that he might need. Caleb slung his gun holsters onto his hips as well as Tony's scabbard and her sword. Before leaving the bedroom, Caleb threw a rug over his arm, for Aidan and the journey back home again. *I will not be coming back without them!*

Running down the stairs to where Mary and Preston were waiting for him, Caleb could feel the adrenalin coursing through his veins. *This time, if I get my hands on Nigel Sutherland, I won't just render him unconscious!* Preston led Caleb, not to the front doors, but a side entrance.

'I thought it would delay your departure if you had to explain what has happened, Lord Delacourt.'

'Good idea.' Caleb nodded in appreciation of the Butler's efficiency. 'Inform the Earl that if I haven't returned with his children by daybreak then do whatever the kidnappers ask.' Caleb drew on his driving gloves and accepted his hat from Mary.

'Should I alert Mr Delacourt to the situation, my Lord?' asked Preston. 'Shouldn't you take him with you?'

Caleb shook his head. 'I should be right on their tail this time. They're only minutes and not hours ahead of me.' The Butler followed Caleb out to where is phaeton had just been driven up by the Groom, Noah. Before he leapt up into the vehicle to take the reins, Caleb was surprised as Preston pressed a silk purse into his hand.

'What's this for?'

Preston coughed as he tried to be delicate. 'Its money from the Earl's safe. You don't know what trouble you may run into and a little extra cash may come in handy.'

'Thank you Preston, I hope to bring them home in a couple of hours.' Caleb threw himself up into his vehicle and took the reins from the Groom. The servants stood back as the horses sprang forward and once again Caleb set off to rescue Tony and Aidan.

Tony Assesses Her Options

As the carriage raced along the roads south, Aidan lay stretched out along the seat, completely covered by the fur rug and his head resting on Tony's lap. Calmly stroking Aidan's hair, she used her time to consider and discard their options. *This time I'm not hampered by a sprained ankle or cumbersome crutches but still I have to get away from Nigel and find suitable transport to get Aidan home. I can't rely on Mary understanding my secret message or that Caleb would learn of our abduction before it is too late!*

Nigel hasn't spoken to me, and even though he hasn't attempted to assault me, he won't even look at me from his corner of the coach; I still have the sinking feeling that this abduction is not going to end at all well.

If this is just another abduction with ransom as the key goal, Tony mused, *will Nigel take us back to the On the Rocks Inn? It is too dark to make out any passing land marks and anyway the curtains and blinds are down to obscure any view.*

Birling Gap

So it wasn't until they finally came to a halt that Tony could obtain any clues to their current location. There was an Inn but it wasn't the On the Rocks. This was a place she had never been before. Nigel lifted Aidan out of the carriage before he allowed Tony to descend.

They were in the middle of the small coastal village of Birling Gap that consisted of a dozen houses, the Inn, a small chapel and a jetty where a ship was moored. It was a coastal hamlet situated on the Seven Sisters, not far from Beachy Head.

This wasn't a deserted dock as some of the crew carried produce off the ship while other crew members loaded new boxes and barrels. No one paid any attention to their arrival except a man who looked like Blackbeard the pirate. He was Captain Mark Sheppard.

'You Sutherland?' the Captain asked around his pipe.

'Aye.' Nigel shifted Aidan in his arms as the boy stirred.

'No one said anything about you bringing your family.'

'I'm not related to this monster!' Tony bridled up in indignation. 'I am his hostage and not his wife!' As if to substantiate her words, a sudden breeze picked up off the sea and caused Tony's overcoat to flutter open to reveal her silk dress beneath it. The crew wolf whistled in appreciation and were growled at by their Captain.

'Shut your yaps you dogs. This isn't some cheap harlot but a Lady.'

'Ya have no idea!' drawled Nigel and Tony cast him a speaking glance.

'Can we please move this along gentlemen, I need to get my brother somewhere warm!' The obvious well educated tones of her voice made the Captain swear. He strode forward to get a closer look at Tony in the moonlight.

'You kidnapped the Earl's children again? I thought you just wanted to escape prosecution for the first abduction?'

'This time it'll be different.' Scowling, Nigel wasn't happy about being grilled. 'It's been organised down to the last detail! Can I take them down to a cabin now?'

The Captain stroked his beard. 'It'll be at least another half an hour before we sail. It'll be warmer in the pub in front of the fire. There's no heating on the ship.'

Nigel's Plan

Grabbing hold of Tony's arm, Nigel dragged her into the Anchor Inn and thrust her into a chair in front of the fire before laying Aidan in her lap. The boy stirred and raised his head from his sister's shoulder.

'Tony?'

'Yes Little Bear?' His sister glanced around the room at the strangers drinking around them as she stroked his hair.

'I want to go home now. I don't want to leave England. I want to go home now!' His voice broke on a sob and Tony rocked him in her arms.

'I know Little Bear, so do I! When Caleb gets here, we'll be going home!' She promised with confidence.

'Oh I'm expecting y'r hero any minute now.' Throwing himself into the chair opposite, Nigel snorted. No one was even remotely worried about the pistol he openly laid in his lap. 'He's very much a part of the plan I've been given.'

'Plan you were given?' Tony sat up a little straighter as she locked her eyes with Nigel's. 'So someone else broke you out of custody? Someone else is orchestrating this abduction? To what end? Have you been told what will be the end game? Do you really think this can be a win-win situation when someone else is calling the shots?'

Nigel snarled at the inquisition. 'I've done everything that the first letter has told me to do!'

'First letter? What does the second letter say?' Tony felt that they were close to learning if they would survive this time.

'Me instructions were to not open the second letter till we reach the French coast.' A muscle twitched along Nigel's jaw.

Her mouth fell open as Tony stared at him in disbelief. 'Aren't you even curious about what insane request will come next? What if you're told to put a bullet into your own brain?'

Nigel shook his head. 'No, they promised me I get to keep the ransom and their payment.'

'Who are you working for? Who are they? Who hates us enough that they would want to hurt us like this?'

'Patrick?' Aidan's voice made Tony jump as she hadn't thought he had been paying attention.

'Yes, but…' Tony thoughts went back to when she had told Patrick about her engagement. *He had looked worried for me and not angry. Could it be that he had already put his plan for Nigel to escape into action and couldn't stop it going ahead? Did he really hate me that much?*

Time For Drinks

As Tony dashed away a tear, Aidan said, 'I'm thirsty.'

Nigel uttered a bark of a laugh. 'So am I.' Turning slightly in his seat, he gestured to the Innkeeper, 'Charlie, hot chocolate for the boy, a bottle of red for me and a pot of tea for the Lady.'

'You're becoming almost hospitable Mr Sutherland.' Tony's eyebrows rose in surprise.

Briefly Nigel glanced back at Tony. 'Actually Charlie forget the bottle of red wine, just give me that half bottle of rum.'

This time it was the Innkeeper who looked surprised. 'Are you sure Nigel? Don't you think you should keep your faculties sharp in this venture?'

'It's not for me, but for the hero!' A diabolical grin crossed Nigel's features.

Shrugging, the Innkeeper went back into the kitchen to get his wife to make the hot drinks. Tony opened her mouth to ask what Nigel meant but with one look at his expression of inappropriate mirth, she decided to keep the question unasked.

When the drinks arrived, Aidan shifted to sit on the floor at Tony's feet in front of the fireplace and smiled up at the pretty, plump maiden who handed him his hot chocolate. Nigel didn't say another word as he stared moodily into the flames while Tony sipped her tea.

Nigel's foot twitched in his impatience. He barely touched the bottle of rum that Charlie placed on the table beside him. Pulling a handkerchief out of his pocket, Nigel took a swig of the rum and then spat it out into the handkerchief. *Such behaviour defies logic to me but I'm not prepared to ask for explanations. The longer we wait, the more agitated Nigel is becoming and the more I'm worried that maybe, this time, Aidan and I are on our own.*

I've Come To Take You Home

With his drink finished, Aidan curled up under his rug, warm now inside and out. He had no doubts about either Tony or Caleb being able to protect him and had no qualms about falling asleep on an Inn floor.

When the front door burst open and Caleb entered with both pistols drawn, Tony wasn't the only one to sigh in relief, to her surprise Nigel did as well. *For me plans to succeed, I need to capture Lord Delacourt as well but the vengeful fiancé is not going to be an easy conquest.* Quickly scanning his surroundings and assessing the risk factor around them, Caleb took a step closer to his fiancée.

'My darling elfling, if you wanted to travel abroad you only had to tell me! I hope I haven't kept you waiting too long.' Caleb drawled. Uttering a sob of relief, Tony sprang to her feet and scooping Aidan up into her arms, she ran across the room to join Caleb. Being careful not to get between Caleb's pistols and Nigel, Tony reached up to kiss her beloved on the cheek.

"I am so glad to see you. I didn't think I could do this alone.'

Keeping his eyes upon Nigel, Caleb answered, 'You would've managed, and Lord Tony would've re-emerged to take care of his little brother.'

To everyone's surprise, Nigel was smiling as he laid his pistol down on the table beside him. 'I would've been disappointed if ya hadn't accepted our invitation Lord Delacourt. This party is going to be so much more fun now that y'r here.' Nigel stuffed the corner of the rum soaked handkerchief into the neck of the bottle of rum.

'The party is over Sutherland, I'm taking my intended bride and brother home now.' Caleb moved forward to place his body protectively in front of Tony and Aidan.

The Flaming Attack

Rising to his feet, Nigel leant over to touch the end of the handkerchief to the flames and hurled the alight bottle of rum at Caleb's feet. In the resulting explosion of fire, Caleb shielded Tony and Aidan behind him as he raised his hands to protect his face. Nigel laughed when Caleb was blasted backwards from the force of the explosion and he was knocked unconscious.

Tony screamed once in horror, placing Aidan into the chair she had just vacated as she knelt down beside Caleb and the Innkeeper ran across with water to douse the fire. When Charlie came back with another jug of water, Tony accepted it from him and slowly poured the water over Caleb's face and hair to douse the burns.

'Send for a Doctor!' Tony ordered as she tenderly moistened Caleb's scorched flesh.

'I've already sent off my lad, miss,' replied Charlie, bringing Tony more water as she glanced over her shoulder to check on her brother.

'What the devil is wrong with you?' Tony demanded of Nigel as he picked up Caleb's dropped pistols. There was a gasp of surprise from the patrons by her unladylike language.

'Oh please! This monster just tried to blow up my fiancé and I'm mad as hell!' Tony retorted, stroking Caleb's hair back from his face.

Doctor's Assessment

An uneasy silence settle upon the Inn so that when Doctor George Stevenson hurried into the public bar, he was taken back by the funeral like atmosphere. Bending down beside Tony to check Caleb's condition, Doctor Stevenson reassured them all. 'He's still alive, the fall meant he hit his head.' The patrons went back to their drinks as Tony moved slightly to give the Doctor more room to attend to Caleb.

'What about his burns, Doctor?' asked Tony, her voice trembling slightly in her concern for her beloved. The Doctor was busy emptying his medical bag.

'What did you use to wash his burns?'

'Only water, I didn't know what else to use.'

The Doctor nodded. 'No, you did the right thing Miss.'

'Lady Antonia Stirling and this is my fiancé Lord Caleb Delacourt.' Tony clarified.

Doctor Stevenson cast a glance across at Nigel. 'You kidnapped them again? What is wrong with you Nigel?' He really didn't want an answer as he began immediately applying an ointment gently over Caleb's closed eyes and forehead. Caleb's raised hands, covered by his driving gloves, had shielded his lower face from the blast.

'There could be some scarring, the bandages will have to remain on for at least a week before his Lordship attempts to use his eyes. Every day, though, the bandages will need to be replaced, the area cleaned and fresh ointment applied. By the end of the week you should know if he is temporarily or permanently blind.'

Irrational tears fell from Tony's eyes. 'I won't be here to take care of Caleb, I assume Sutherland is still going to drag me off to France to await his ransom.'

'All three of ya are coming with me, that's the plan.' Nigel placed Caleb's pistols into his overcoat pockets.

Stunned, Tony looked up in disbelief at the big man. 'But he needs medical attention!'

'The Doc can provide ya with whatever ya need to look after the hero.' Nigel grunted.

Placing small pads of moist gauze over Caleb's eyes, the Doctor paused in covering the patient's eyes and forehead with a larger pad. 'You can't guarantee being able to keep his Lordship's wounds sterile!'

Nigel shrugged. 'It'll keep her Ladyship busy and stop her trying to stick a dagger into me heart.'

'Don't tempt me!' Tony shot back at him, holding up Caleb's head as Doctor Stevenson began to secure the pads in place with a bandage.

'This is madness Nigel,' the Doctor said as he packed up his medical bag once more. 'Leave the three of them here and just get yourself safely out of England.'

Resuming his seat. Nigel shook his head. 'Prepare a medical kit for her Ladyship Doc and don't do anything cute like adding a dagger or a scalpel so that she can use it as a weapon.'

'I'll have to go home as I don't have enough supplies with me.' Seeing the mulish set to Nigel's jaw, Doctor Stevenson sighed as he rose to his feet.

Nigel nodded. 'As long as y'r back before we set sail, doc.' He picked up his pistol from the table beside him, pleased at how smoothly his plan was working out.

He's Coming With Us

As the Doctor left the Anchor Inn, Tony remained kneeling on the floor with Caleb's head cradled in her lap. She kept her face expressionless but was secretly worried by the length of time that Caleb remained unconscious. She could feel the large lump at the base of his skull where his head had hit the floor.

Tony removed her overcoat and draped it over Caleb. *For the briefest moment when I thought that Caleb had been killed I wished that I could die too but my instinct to protect Aidan overrode any grief. In my relief that Caleb is alive I am almost prepared to forgive Nigel for his actions. Almost. But not completely.*

So when Nigel rose to his feet to adjust the rug around Aidan, Tony snapped at him. 'Don't touch him! I swear if you hurt my brother I'll rip your arm off and hit you over the head with it!'

That imagery caused Nigel to grin as he sat back down again. 'Ya seem to forget that I'm the one with the gun.'

'That won't stop me if Aidan is in danger!'

Nigel laughed. 'Settle down tigress, don't tempt me to declaw ya.' He ran a hand along his jaw as his eyes swept down Tony's figure. 'Mind ya, it'd be fun to try and finish what we started back at the On the Rocks Inn. This time the hero won't be able to intervene!'

Stiffening in disgust Tony said quietly, 'Try it and I'll introduce you to a whole new world of pain! No man but Caleb is allowed to touch me.'

'What makes him so special?' Sitting forward in his chair, Nigel became very interested.

Tony glanced down at her unconscious fiancé and her expression immediately softened. 'Just a glance from him makes my heart quicken. I feel safe when I know that he is near. My body tingles when he touches me. I can't imagine a future without him.'

Exhaling slowly, Nigel took a moment to digest this information. 'Oh wow! I really wish I hadn't asked the question now.'

Tony's lips thinned in displeasure as she glared at her abductor but decided to keep her tongue between her teeth. Captain Mark Sheppard entered the pub just as Tony was contemplating pushing Nigel's face into the fireplace.

'We're going to need a couple of able bodied men to carry the hero.' Nigel gestured to Caleb's inert body on the floor. The Captain looked down at Tony cradling Caleb's head and was momentarily robbed of speech. His pipe had gone out and he had to relight it before he could address Nigel.

'Seriously? You're abducting the hero as well? What on earth were you thinking?'

Nigel shook his head. 'It's all to plan, Captain. Just get me the muscle to help me move his Lordship. I have everything under control.'

The Captain, unconvinced, chomped down upon the stem of his pipe as his eyebrows rose. 'You're the boss.' He sauntered out of the Inn and returned a couple of minutes later with two burly lads and a stretcher.

Departing England

As the Captain reached out to assist Tony to her feet, she raised questioning eyes to the pirate's face. He smiled kindly down at her. 'This isn't the first body we've had to move due to the effects of rum. Though normally it's inside them rather than wearing it.'

As the lads gently picked Caleb up and laid him out on the stretcher, Tony's overcoat slipped off him and she noticed that there was a damp stain of liquor soaking Caleb's clothes. The lads paused long enough for Tony to replace her overcoat back over Caleb before they carried him outside.

The fact that Caleb's bandages didn't even raise a curious glance from any of the three men, makes me wonder if this cocktail fireball is a common occurrence amongst this class of people?

Picking Aidan up, wrapping his rug tighter around him, Tony obediently followed Nigel out of the Inn. *I hope the Doctor manages to return before we leave the dock as I don't know what I will use for bandages, let alone the ointment the Doctor wants me to apply to Caleb's burns on a daily basis!*

'Take them down to one of the cabins,' ordered the Captain and Tony reluctantly handed Aidan to Pierre, the first mate, to carry the boy out of the chilling night air. Captain Sheppard remained beside Tony while they waited on the dock as Doctor Stevenson came hurrying down the street towards them.

Captain Sheppard

As the breeze picked up, a shiver ran through Tony and she glanced speculatively up at the bearded Captain. 'I suppose there's no point asking you for help?' She asked.

The Captain puffed for a moment on his pipe. 'I'm afraid Nigel Sutherland is my client.'

'I see, so if we managed to escape from Nigel, will you be available to bring us home again?'

A couple more puffs. 'Once we have landed on the French coast, if you can pay your passage and if you can escape from Sutherland, then I'll bring you home.'

'That sounds like you doubt we could get away from Nigel.' Both of Tony's eyebrows had risen.

A couple more puffs. 'You've a five year old boy and an unconscious, possibly blind hero; yes I seriously doubt your ability to escape.'

'Thank you Captain, I feel so much more confident about the future now!' Tony drawled and turned her attention to the Doctor.

Doctor's Instructions

'Sorry if I kept you waiting.' The Doctor paused to catch his breath. 'I realised that Lord Delacourt will be in considerable pain when he does wake up so I've prepared a little something extra to help with that.' Handing a medical bag to Tony, Doctor Stevenson looked up at the Captain. 'Do I have time to slip aboard and give his Lordship an injection?'

Another couple of puffs on the pipe. 'Of course Doc, after you, my Lady.' Captain Sheppard followed them on board his ship and down to the crew's cabin. Pierre had laid Aidan down on one of the bottom bunk of a set of two double bunks in the crew's cabin. Caleb's unconscious body was placed upon the bottom bunk opposite Aidan. Nigel was getting edgy.

'Can we leave now?' demanded Nigel of the Captain.

'As soon as the Doctor is satisfied that his patient is ready to travel.' Puffing on his pipe, Captain Sheppard sauntered out of the cabin as the Doctor knelt down to inject Caleb with a dose of morphine. Rising again, Doctor Stevenson ignored Nigel's attempt to push him out of the room and turned to address Tony.

'Keep his wounds clean, change the dressings daily and try to get him to a Doctor by the end of seven days before he attempts to use his eyes again.'

'What are his chances?' Tony dragged in a deep breath to steady her nerves.

He shrugged. 'He's young, fit and healthy. This situation is a complication that you could do without but that seems to be in the hands of others. Good luck my Lady.' Nigel was becoming more insistent about the Doctor leaving.

'Thank you Doctor Stevenson, can you let my father know that we're all right for now? To expect a ransom demand soon?' Tony asked as Nigel pushed the Doctor out of the cabin door.

'I wish I could do more for you, Lady Antonia.' The Doctor just managed to get the words out before Nigel shut them both out of the room and turned the key in the lock.

No Time For Tears

A sob escaped from Tony before she could contain it and angry with herself, she dashed away a tear that trickled down her cheek. *It would be very easy to collapse to my knees and bury my face into Caleb's chest and sob my heart out. That isn't going to solve our current problems.* So taking several deep slow breaths, Tony pulled herself together. Bending down to adjust the fur rug over her brother, she paused to caress her hand against Aidan's hair.

Straightening up again, she picked up the bag of medical supplies the Doctor had given her and using the meagre light from the lantern above her, she looked through the bag. For a briefest moment she felt relief as her fingers touched something metallic. The relief was short lived as she withdrew a pair of round nose scissors. They were sharp enough for cutting bandages or gauze but much too blunt to use as a weapon.

Dropping it back into the bag, Tony was feeling a little disappointed until she heard it go clunk and not thud into the bottom of the bag. As of metal hitting metal. Casting a furtive glance at the door to ensure that no one had snuck back into the room from behind her, Tony slipped her hand between the two thin layers of cardboard that supported the base of the bag.

Biting down on her lip to contain her squeal of joy, her fingers drew out a thin stiletto blade. It was small, sharp and deadly. *A perfect weapon for a woman. It will mean having to get close and personal unlike my sword. I feel naked without my male attire and especially my sword.* Slipping the blade into her cleavage, Tony checked to ensure that it could not be seen before placing the medical bag at the end of Aidan's bunk.

With the limited light from the overhead lantern, she did a hasty but thorough search through the cabin for anything that could be used as a weapon. *Either Nigel had swept the room clean or nothing in the way of weapons is kept in the crew's cabin as I found very little to use to defend my boys. A box of matches. A letter opener. Empty wine bottles. Nothing that could really be called a weapon.*

Caleb's Darkness

Caleb's scream of terror caused Tony to fly across the room and drop to her knees to grasp his shoulders and try to shake him out of his nightmare.

'You need to wake up, Caleb. Aidan and I are safe, we're not harmed. You shielded us from Nigel's' flaming cocktail but…

you were burnt.' Caleb raised his hands to claw at his bandages but Tony captured his hands between her own and held them against her breasts. 'You have to leave the bandages on. We can't afford to let any infection get in to hamper your recovery. I know the darkness is frightening but we will survive this!' Tony wrapped her arms around Caleb and brought his cheek against her chest and rocked him.

'Oh God, Tony! Why didn't you leave me behind? I'm useless to you!' Caleb's trembling arms encircled around her and held her tight.

'Your being on this ship isn't my doing. It's all a part of Nigel's master plan. He was told to abduct all of us and take us to France. I'm worried about your medical care if we're on the run but to be honest, I'm not sorry that you're here. I'm scared Caleb and I don't think I could think clearly if it was just me and Aidan.' Tony felt her tears once more bubbling to the surface as she put a voice to her fears. Taking deep breathes to calm his own emotions, Caleb reached up to caress his hand through Tony's hair.

'It's all right elfling, we'll get through this. Together.' Exhaling slowly, Caleb continued to improve his control over his own terrors. *The darkness is overwhelming and frightening but just possibly only temporary. Our current predicament is more pressing and needs our immediate attention.* 'Is Aidan all right? Is he here with us?' Caleb needed to hear or feel his presence.

'I'm fine… a little queasy.' Aidan's voice was heard from across the room.

'Sea sick?' *I can feel the movement of the ship now that my heart is no longer pounding in my ears,* mused Caleb. Tony picked up an empty basin and placed it on the floor close to Aidan's bunk.

'He's perfectly fine on still water.' She explained, finding a boiled lolly in her jacket pocket and gave it to her brother to suck on as he laid his head down again. 'Go back to sleep Little Bear, it'll all be over soon.'

What Are Our Escape Options?

Tony moved back to Caleb's side as he sat up and swung his legs over the side of the bunk. 'Do I smell as bad as I think I do?' He ran his hands over his body to check what weapons Nigel had taken from him. His gun holsters were empty, Caleb had expected that, reaching round, he felt Tony's scabbard on his hip. With a sigh, he discovered that too was empty.

'Just a little of rum and singed cloth. You're not soaked through are you? I can give you my jacket or overcoat but I don't have anything else for you to change into just yet.' Tony glanced around the cabin and screwed up her nose. 'The clothes left lying about by the crew would not be… an improvement.'

Caleb undid his overcoat and jacket to feel over his shirt. 'My overcoat seemed to take the brunt of the alcohol. I'll survive.' He reached inside an inner pocket of his jacket and drew out the silk purse full of money and offered it to Tony. 'That's part of the ransom money from your father. I stuffed another wad of cash in my boot.' Reaching down he slid his fingers into his boot to drag the additional money out. 'Find a safe place for the money, Tony, then we need to consider what we can use as weapons.'

Tucking the purses into the medical bag, Tony suddenly retrieved one again and stripping off her pearl necklace, earrings and engagement ring, she slid them into the purse. 'Give me your signet ring, Caleb and I'll hide it away with the money.' She reached out to take his hand and gasped. *I'm surprised that even here and now, Caleb's touch can make my skin tingle in pleasure.* With his ring placed in the bag with her jewels, Tony tightened up the strings and secured it in the medical bag.

She placed her hand in the one Caleb held out to her as she knelt down in front of him. Using her free hand, she drew the stiletto dagger out of her cleavage and placed it into Caleb's hand. 'Apart from this, a box of matches and some questionable

252

laundry, there's nothing in the cabin to use as a weapon.' Tony said, allowing her hand to fall onto his knee so that Caleb could test the sharpness of the blade with his other hand.

'Where did you find this?'

Absently Tony's fingers trailed across his knee. 'Doctor Stevenson hid it in the bottom of the medical bag he gave me.'

'Where were you stashing it?' Caleb felt the rising desires by her caress and Tony didn't suppress this as she unbuttoned her jacket before slipping his hand slowly into her cleavage. A sigh slipped from Caleb's lips as he carefully lay down the blade so that he could draw Tony closer to seek out her lips beneath his own.

As his mouth caressed sensuously against hers, Caleb's hand explored her flesh beneath her bodice. Teasing, tantalising strokes which caused Tony to sigh in pleasure.

'I so desperately want to get you naked and beneath me!' Caleb murmured against her mouth as he tweaked and rolled her nipples between his thumb and forefinger. Placing her hands on his knees, Tony eased his legs apart so that she could slide closer and press against his body.

'As much as I want to feel your fabulous, muscular, naked body pressed against mine…' Tony paused as Caleb slid her jacket and dress off her shoulder and lowered his head to trail tender kisses along her jaw and down her collar bone. 'Shouldn't we be concentrating on how we're going to get out of this mess?'

Cupping, moulding her breasts beneath his gentle hands, Caleb didn't immediately answer as his lips trailed slowly down her chest until he suckled upon her nipple. Tony uttered a cry of delight and momentarily gave into the wicked pleasure before she finally tugged on his hair to force him to raise his head.

'Oh Caleb please, we can't do this here and now.' She purred as he continued to caress her flesh.

'For my sake?' Caleb teased, nibbling on her earlobe.

Tony ran her hands up his thighs, 'No, Aidan's. The reason he is supposed to remain in his bedroom because one night he had gone to his mother's room. He interrupted Papa and Charlotte making love. That's when he started coming to me instead. I don't want to damage him any more than he already is.'

With a sigh, Caleb released her. 'We can't do anything until we actually dock in France.'

Tony righted her clothes and did up her jacket before caressing her hand through Caleb's hair. 'I had an idea. There's a gap beneath the door, I could slip a sheet of paper underneath, use the blade to poke the key out of the lock and draw it under the door on the paper.'

'What then?' Caleb ran a hand through his damp hair.

'If we got out without being seen, we could hide in the life raft until we dock. Then slip off the ship while they're still looking for us.' Tony rose to her feet, stretched and then sat down on the bunk beside Caleb as he scrubbed a hand over his chin.

'I see a couple of problems with that. Chiefly the length of time Aidan would be in a chilly life boat. There's also the lack of weapons. I want to get my pistols and your sword back from Sutherland. The odds are greater that we'll be seen before we dock whereas afterwards the crew will be too busy unloading the cargo and not all hanging out above deck.'

Caleb Wants A Decision

'So what do we have to do until we reach the French coast?' Sighing, Tony laid her head upon his shoulder.

Slipping his arm around her waist, Caleb chuckled as he placed a tender kiss against her hair. 'Well the idea I had you have already vetoed!' He teased and knew without a doubt that she would be blushing.

'Caleb! I meant what can we prepare so that we're ready to act when Sutherland walks through that door?'

He laughed. 'We need to conserve our energy until we have to act. I want you to take a moment to consider your answer to my next question.' The seriousness of his tone worried Tony and a shiver of fear ran through her.

'All right. What is it?'

Dragging in a deep breath, Caleb let it out slowly before he finally spoke, 'I need to know now if I'm to let Sutherland live this time?'

'Caleb!'

He slid his fingers across her knee to find her hand. 'Think about it Tony. Last time I pulled him off you was to prevent you having to live with the guilt of killing a man. If he had violated you, I think I would've snapped his neck but he hadn't and I'm now regretting that decision. If I had killed him then, we probably wouldn't have had to hide in the barn, nor would we be in this current situation.'

Tony wrapped both her hands around his. 'Hindsight is a flawed and biased tool, Caleb. Nigel isn't behind this abduction this time, someone else wants to humiliate us... someone else... I think wants us all dead!' Her voice trembled and Caleb squeezed her fingers.

'Well we know Sutherland would want to humiliate us but to go as far as murdering us that's a little extreme.'

'He has instructions to open when we reach France.' Shaking her head, Tony sighed. 'I need to know what Nigel is supposed to do next.'

'When we take back our weapons, you can search him for these instructions but what about my question?' Caleb dropped a kiss on the top of Tony's head.

'Only as a last resort. We're not killers Caleb and if you want to hurt him for burning you I'll understand but kill Nigel only if we're in danger. My paramount concern is keeping Aidan safe.'

A tremor ran through Tony as Caleb tightened his grip around her waist.

'My paramount concern is to keep you both safe… any way I have to!'

Inhaling slowly, Tony tried to control her trembling. 'All right agreed. So what do we do now?'

Releasing her, Caleb shifted on the bunk so that he didn't bump his head as he lay down. 'We conserve our energy until we need to act.' He patted the bunk and Tony willingly lay down in his arms.

'Is it wrong that I feel scared?' Her words came out as little more than a whisper.

'No it's perfectly natural but we're going to be fine. Trust me Tony I won't let anyone hurt you or Aidan.' It would have sounded ridiculous with Caleb's eyes bandaged closed, that very important sense now lost and without any real weapons. Tony found it reassuring, not ridiculous as she buried her nose into Caleb's shoulder. She tried to not breathe in the rum fumes as she forced her body to relax.

Nigel's Horror

With an incredible show of will power, Nigel Sutherland had deliberately kept away from his hostages. *While Lord Delacourt was unconscious, it would've been the perfect chance for me to get me revenge on her Ladyship and finish what we'd started at the On the Rocks Inn. Me instructions, though, had been fairly clear that Lady Tony was not to be touched. That is why I am so confident that the second envelope does not contain orders to kill the hostages. If me employer's end game is to murder them, why would he be worried about Lady Tony's virginity?*

To avoid temptation, Nigel held off from going down to the cabin until the ship had finally docked in France. Unlocking the door and flinging it open just in case someone was waiting behind the door to jump him; Nigel was frozen in shock.

By the limited light for the lantern swinging overhead, Nigel was only just able to make out Tony sitting astride someone on the bottom bunk. Her overcoat and jacket lay discarded on the floor but what had captured Nigel's attention was that although the skirt of her dress fanned out around her; the top of her dress and chemise had been pushed down off her shoulders and her breasts were exposed.

Ignoring his arrival, Tony appeared lost in the moment as she rose and fell slowly upon the figure beneath her. 'Oh Caleb! You're magnificent!' Tony's cry caused Nigel to roar like a wounded bull which gave Caleb, who was standing in the shadows, his location. Taking Nigel by surprise, Caleb's arm enclosed around Nigel's neck from behind and he choked off the abductor's air ways.

Distraction accomplished, Tony slid off the pile of pillows she had been astride and she hastily pulled up her chemise and dress to cover her breasts. She kept out of the way as the two men struggled together but realising that he was losing, Nigel lowered one hand to his overcoat pocket.

Feeling Nigel's altered position, Caleb instinctively knew that he must be reaching for pistol. 'Tony! Watch out!' Caleb called out, putting more pressure on Nigel's wind pipe to force him to black out.

Slipping the stiletto blade out from the rug that covered Aidan, Tony grabbed hold of Nigel's arm to keep it in his pocket as she pressed the sharp knife against Nigel's' stomach.

'Pull out your pistol and I will gut you! Do you understand me?' Tony threatened into Nigel's face as he was becoming blue around the lips.

'Ya don't have it in ya to kill me!' Nigel croaked.

Tony thrust the blade a little further into Nigel's flesh. 'Don't bet on it Sutherland!' She released his arm to put her hand into Nigel's pocket to withdraw his pistol. Swinging the weapon, Tony smacked Nigel across the head and he went down like a stone.

Caleb let him go so that he didn't fall with Nigel. Tony dropped to her knees to search Nigel's pockets and pressed into Caleb's hands his own pistols and her sword. Tony took Nigel's pistols and placed them on the floor beside her before searching for his instructions. Finding the envelope, Tony tore it open and quickly scanned it as Caleb felt his way across the cabin to wake Aidan.

Nigel's Second Instructions

'Are you ready to go Tony?' Caleb picked up Aidan as Tony pulled on her jacket and overcoat. She put Nigel's pistols into her pockets but kept her blade in her hand.

'I've just read Nigel's' second letter.' Her voice came out as barely a whisper as she did up the buttons of her jacket.

'Is it what you feared? Is it signed?' His tone was light and unworried as he secured the fur rug around Aidan as he stirred awake.

'No signature… I was right.' Swallowing hard on the bile that rose in her throat. Tony rose to her feet and picked up a pencil from the table before writing a brief message at the bottom of Nigel's instructions. Her chest heaving in anger as she stuffed the paper back into Nigel's' pocket.

Without saying another word, Tony grabbed the medical bag before she took Caleb's hand and led her boys out of the cabin. She paused for only a moment to lock the door and pocket the key before heading up on deck.

Disembarking

The crew were too busy unloading their cargo to hinder the hostages escape. When they ran into the ship's first mate, Pierre,

Tony instinctively raised her blade and drew Caleb and Aidan protectively behind her. Holding up his hands in a submissive gesture Pierre shook his head.

'You have nothing to fear from me, Mademoiselle. The Captain has a message for you. If you escape he suggests you head for sanctuary.'

'I see.' Although Tony lowered her knife, she did not lower her guard.

'Did... did you kill him?' Pierre asked.

A harsh laugh came from Caleb. 'She wouldn't let me!'

'Bon!' Pierre nodded. 'You're not natural killers Monsieur. I suggest you use the ramp rather than the rope ladder. It'll be easier to navigate for his Lordship.'

'Thank you, I don't know what the Captain plans to do with Nigel now.' Reaching into her jacket pocket, Tony withdrew the key to the cabin and pressed it into Pierre's hand.

Smiling, Pierre shook his head. 'Don't worry about him Mademoiselle, he is no longer your problem. I hope we see you again soon.' He bowed to Tony and went back to co-ordinating the unloading of their cargo.

As difficult as it would be to negotiate the rope ladder, the ramp, with no hand rail and only the aid of the moonlight, was after all just planks of wood. Tony momentarily slipped her blade into her cleavage and took Caleb's hand to guide him.

Once they both had their feet firmly on the dock, Tony breathed a sigh of relief and took the blade out again before she led Caleb and Aidan onto the shadows of the sleeping French village of Hon Fleur.

Trilogy Preview

Stirling Masquerade

Having been abducted for a second time, Lady Antonia (Tony) Stirling, her brother Lord Aidan and the now blind Lord Caleb Delacourt must fight to escape not just their abductor but also the hostile environment of a post Waterloo defeated France. With an immediate flight cut off they must travel to Paris in search for assistance to get safely home. Assuming a disguise, the trio find not only unexpected allies, but also that their enemies are closing in around them. The single dream of reaching English soil once more is superseded by the essential need to stay alive.

Stirling Conspiracy

Finally making it home from their ordeal in France, Lady Antonia (Tony) Stirling, her brother Lord Aidan and Lord Caleb Delacourt still cannot relax their defences. Now, though, they have a wedding to look forward to as they contemplate their future life together. It is up to Abraham Bell, A Bow Street Runner to work out who, from his list of suspects, want to achieve their goals so badly that they are prepared to kill to get it. Can Bell solve the mystery before the killer or killers finally succeed?

ABOUT THE AUTHOR

Anne-Marie Price was born and raised in Perth, Western Australia. She lives with her parents Margaret and Laurence and has two cats, Mickey and Jackson.

She has been a member of the Society of Women Writers WA since 2009 and has been their secretary since 2011.

Anne-Marie has had articles and flash fiction stories published in the SWW In Print Magazine as well as The Readers World Magazine.

In 1997, she obtained a Degree– Library And Information Studies, in 1998 a Diploma of Comprehensive Writing and in 2009 a Cert IV Training and Assessment to assist her ability to teach others the craft of writing.

Writing is in the blood of the Price family with Anne-Marie being the fourth generation of writers. Anne-Marie has been writing fiction since the age of ten and still uses pen and paper as a preference for a first draft.

Also By This Author

Hostage Of Diplomacy
2015
Contemporary Romance

The Search For The King James Bible
2015
Supernatural Romance

Stirling Trilogy
2016
Historical Romance

261

www.ingramcontent.com/pod-product-compliance
Lightning Source LLC
Chambersburg PA
CBHW061603170626
46811CB00001B/299